Tales of Hardooth 8

WHAT NEW OCCURENCES DO WE FACE?

Dara J. Carr

Tales of Hardooth 8

WHAT NEW OCCURENCES DO WE FACE?

Dara J. Carr

FOUNDATION PUBLISHER

Foundation Publisher
foundationpublisher.com
info@foundationpublisher.com
ISBN: 978-0-999-6147-7-8
Library of Congress Control Number: 2020923751
Foundation Publisher and its columned logo are trademarks belonging to Foundation Publisher.

PRINTED IN THE UNITED STATES OF AMERICA

This story is fictional. No actual person or event is depicted. Any similarity with any person, living or dead, or any event, is entirely coincidental and unintentional…and seeing as how we're talking about mutated people from other planets, it ain't too practical either!

TXu 2-010-841

OTHER BOOKS BY

DARA J. CARR

The Semi-Dragon Tale

Revenge Cometh Forth

Here Are My Shorts (a collection of short stories)

Volunteer...Spy?

The Original Owlam

What New Things We Can Learn?

The Lies We Tell to Survive

Countless Enemies and Discoveries

Enemies From Beyond

More Troubles, More Enemies

Reflections and Beginnings

WHAT NEW OCCURENCES DO WE FACE?

1

One murder is tragic. Two murders…a coincidence? Three murders is a pattern formed by a serial killer. Four murders is confirmation of a serial killer…who so far has only struck against Owlamites…of which they are aware.

Farn of the Sixth was found murdered Tulivren 18, 1801. Zoya of the Third was found murdered on Tulivren 29, 1801. Nesh of the Fifth was found murdered Thorinale 14, 1801. Shalam of the Second was found murdered Inamyon 11, 1801.

Soolchakan can no longer stand the thought of burning the bodies like trash so he has them entombed in caskets in the vaults on Zhagool. Now there were four bodies on Zhagool and no one could figure out what had happened. All four bodies had been cut open. The brain, the liver, the heart and in two cases the kidneys had been removed. All of the skin on the back from the waist up to the scalp had been removed. Why? Who was doing this horrible thing?

Then Eerok of the Fourth was found dead on Consoray

9, 1801. He was murdered and gutted in the same manner…then entombed on Zhagool.

Sowee of the Third was the next one killed on Consoray 28, 1801…on Satroco Isle. This was where the remaining Teltermak were living since being run out of North Chilamte. Soolchakan had the Owlamites taking a good look at the Teltermak…just in case they were involved in this grisly affair.

All of a sudden six Owlamites were dead, all killed in the same manner and no one could figure out what had happened or who did it. 1801 ended with all of the Owlamites being very confused…and very scared.

1802 started with some good news. On Statichy 18, 1802, Azar and Meffin of the Third announced the birth of their son Banabar (*Appreciate*).

Shortly after that Majim and Araba of the Sixth announced the birth of their daughter Yeema (*Pretty*).

After that there was no more good news on the planet. The monitors were consistently coming up with nothing moving other than comets or meteorites.

On Strebale 8, 1802, Sona of the Second was found dead. She too was murdered and gutted in the same manner.

On Lergan 12, 1802, Balak of the Third was found murdered and gutted.

On Marrem 20, 1802, Zintom of the Third was found murdered and gutted.

On Citendali 16, 1802, Lorib of the Third was found murdered and gutted.

On Inamyon 2 1802, Maga of the Fourth was found murdered and gutted.

In a two year period, eleven Owlamites had been murdered in the same brutal manner and since none of the survivors were experienced in forensics or crime investigation, plus the fact they had no idea who to suspect, they were no closer in finding out who was doing this.

In 1803, Aya of the Second and Azar of the Third were found murdered bringing the total of dead to 13.

In 1804, nine more Owlamites were murdered bringing the total to 22. Of the nine Owlamites who died in 1804, Chyning of the First was found dead and gutted on Whegire 21, 1804. Now there were only two from the first generation of Owlamites, that they knew of. Others who died in 1804 were Monaha of the Second, Sodona of the Second, Alam of the Fifth, Mila of the Third, Anda of the Third, Za-Ing of the Eighth, Amma of the Third and Naban of the Third.

On Roistume 16, 1804, Soolchakan made a *Voice of Power* decree that no one should be alone under any circumstances. All those who died were alone. Even with the decree, the bodies were piling up...and each one, for some inexplicable reason, was somehow alone when it happened. He repeated the decree, however, for some very odd reason, it did not seem to work. For the first time that Soolchakan was aware of, Owlamites were not obeying the *Voice of Power*...why?

They tried to be vigilant, however, the bodies still kept on piling up. There was no pattern by day of the week, generation, month, gender or any other possible category. The only similarity that they could find was that all of them were murdered and gutted in the same manner.

In 1805, Nasahan of the Third and Yumok of the Sixth were murdered.

In 1806, 13 more were murdered while 1807 saw only one die. In 1808 four died. In 1809 three died. In 1810 thirteen more were killed. Still there was no explanation of how they were going out by themselves…in spite of the decree.

In 1811 five more died. In 1812 four more died. In 1813 no one died. Because of that, the remaining Owlamites were hoping that the slaughter was over. No such luck, in 1814 four more were killed. In 1815 one died. In 1816 nine more died… including Kiyalee of the First, on Lergan 23, 1816. Now there was only one member of the first generation that remained. In 1817 no one died. In 1818 five more died. In 1819 three more were killed.

Ever since the birth of Yeema in 1802 there had been no more additions…just subtractions.

Soolchakan, along with all the rest of the Owlamites were getting very irritated over this conundrum. He went to the one who was showing the greatest amount of intelligence of all the Owlamites – Bikaropin. "You said that you were trying to figure out some pattern of these murders? What have you got?"

Bikaropin threw his arms out in frustration. "Nothing! I've tried to see if there is a pattern…somewhere…but…NOTHING!

In 1806 and 1810, each of those years we lost 13...in 1813 and 1817...no one was killed. 1807 and 1815 we only lost one each year." He shook his head. "Eleven were killed on Initikoy, sixteen on both Gosskoy and Tadkoy, ten on Hartkoy, twelve on Miviskoy and Astekoy and thirteen on Leegkoy." He bit his lip. "Two of the three members of the first generation are gone. The entire second generation has been wiped out...all fifteen of them. Among the third generation, 38 of the 40 were killed. We started with 31 members of the fourth generation and 15 of them were killed. The fifth generation had 20...now 7. Generation six had ten...now six. Generation seven had 6...now 4. Generation eight had 3...now 2. It all depends on...who they...whoever *they* is...or are...can dupe, into going somewhere alone and...they strike."

Soolchakan scoffed. "I don't let anyone go anywhere alone...not even to the toilet. We have got to figure out... something. We're back down to 38 Owlamites...and no clue who is doing this...or how."

Bikaropin looked a little desperate. "We still have the other very odd mystery. We never...or should I say *you* never allowed us to teach any of the children how to hop to different dimensions or Jump to...anywhere...until they were at least 40 years old. Yet somehow...Byrib Jumped out of here at the age of 25 and got killed, Yotam Jumped out of here at the age of 19 and...Banabar...that boy Jumped out of here at the age of 6 and became...a casualty. His mother Meffin...still hasn't gotten over that one. I've heard some of the others say that age has something to do with it...but...both Kiyalee and Chyning were over 10,000 years old when..." He trailed off and bit his lip.

"I know," said Soolchakan bitterly. He shook his head. Damel and Layis were both just in their 50's. Bornam and Fywinn were adolescents in their 60's. Even Ponipa was only 76." He sighed deeply. "For our own defense...I am going to have to resort to something...really crazy. Since there are only 38 of us left...we all stay together as a group."

Bikaropin frowned. "How are we going to do that? We still have to watch the outer space monitors and...there isn't enough room in there...for 38 chairs." He looked up in thought. "We might be able to fit...10 chairs in there."

Soolchakan clenched his teeth. "Then we'll put 10 chairs in there and...the other 28 will sit there in the auditorium...staring at each other...until we get an answer."

"An answer to what?"

"To whatever the *chokwad* is going on! If we don't find out soon...we're going to be in even more trouble than when...there were only four of us. I've been the *Power* for 1,834 years...and I don't plan on stopping any time soon...or being the last *Voice of Power*."

The setup was done. The 10 who were sent to the monitor room were sent in two at a time. The first two would be in there for half a mithpell. Then the next two would come in at the half mithpell point. The next two came in after another half mithpell. This would continue until there were 10. The first two would then rotate out for a different two, making sure that the people in there were rotated and that no one spent too much time in there. The rest would sit (bored to tears) in the auditorium…until they all went en masse to a kitchen for some kind of sustenance.

This setup went on for sixteen days with no results. Every single one of the Owlamites was getting very impatient, and again, bored to tears, with this arrangement, however, Soolchakan had ordered it and, no matter how boring, they were all still desperate enough to do anything to survive.

On the seventeenth day, the group that was sitting in the auditorium started noticing that Tatab of the Sixth was acting very peculiar. While all the others were looking at each other, bored, she was shaking her head and could not focus on anything. She also did not seem to be able to hear any of the others talking to her, mentally or orally.

Soolchakan focused on Tatab. He sent a quick mental message to Bikaropin asking her age. He responded that she was 80 years old. Soolchakan nodded thinking about how she was in the latter stages of adolescence. He sent a mental message to the other 36 Owlamites to concentrate on her and what was going through her confused mind. He had to pay special attention to Mahanee in this endeavor. She was still grieving over the fact that six of her ten children were dead along with her beloved husband Zormun.

Before starting this group boredom, Soolchakan had armed himself with a pulse pistol. He had also ordered that Hisang, Poolkiy, Korpem, Bak and Bikaropin all be armed as well. As they watched Tatab start perspiring profusely, all six pistols were activated…as a precaution.

While reading Tatab's confused mind, they all found that she was receiving some kind of landmark…whether she wanted it or not. The imagery started up, in her head, for a Jump. They all followed her lead. Soolchakan ordered all of them into Spy as a precaution. She Jumped…and they all went with her.

They ended up on some tropical island. Tatab just stood there with a dull-eyed look on her face, her mouth hanging open and looking as if she was about to just fall down. She was standing about one teckist away from a rather strange looking, and very noisy, machine.

Here was this very sophisticated machine on a beach, on a very humid island, somewhere near the equator, with ten grinning Teltermak Elf standing there looking very proud of themselves.

"Once again, we have one of them," shouted one of the Teltermaks trying to be heard over the loud machine.

Over the several millennium their accent and dialect had changed, however, because of some occasional spying on them, all Owlamites understood what he was saying.

"I know," shouted another. "It seems that each time…we have to use more power and it is still taking longer."

"Whatever it takes to be successful, we'll spend all the energy we have to, in order to get one of these things," said the first one.

The others just grinned.

One of them picked up a rather large knife and started walking towards Tatab. She did not react to him at all. She seemed to be in some kind of trance.

Soolchakan did not wait. He brought his pulse pistol up, hopped the business end into Home dimension and fired. The one with the knife suddenly had a rather large hole all the way through his upper torso, a very shocked look on his face and blood spraying out of his back.

The other five Owlamites brought their pistols up and, rather quickly, there were ten Teltermak corpses laying there, bleeding in the sand, with somewhat shocked looks on their dead faces.

Bikaropin and Maramee went to the machine and started taking a good long look at the loud contraption. Pomani was there as well and found some kind of instructional manual for the thing. The three of them crowded around the manual. Bikaropin found what he wanted, walked to the keyboard for the machine, punched in a few characters and the machine powered down and shut off.

"Blessed silence," sighed Mymin.

Tatab stood there wobbling and shaking her head as she cleared the cobwebs. She looked at her surroundings in complete confusion. "Unh…where am I?" Then she got a somewhat angry look on her face. "How did I get…here?"

"This machine had something to do with it," said Bikaropin. "It seems to have some very unusual qualities, in getting some… frequencies…at which our brains function. I don't know how, but it can control us."

"We need to get this thing back to the gorge…in order to

understand it better," said Pomani.

Soolchakan glared at Pomani. "Gorge, MY BUTT! Get this thing on one of the ships in dimension 45. THAT is where we'll study it. All of us will go there and try to find out what this thing is and...how it can control our brain functions."

Joz pointed towards the trees. "I think...they have some kind of...boat or...a shuttlecraft of some type hidden over there."

Soolchakan brought his pistol up at the ready. "Spread out! Let's look this island over and...see if there are any more Teltermaks or...and any other technology here that we need to confiscate or steal away from them."

The others started looking very cautiously through the trees for...anything that was not part of the natural flora and fauna. They found that it was a very small island and that the strange mind machine and the shuttlecraft were the only pieces of unnatural or manufactured things that were there. Somehow the Teltermak had been able to keep some of their technology, up to and including, building a flying shuttle.

Soolchakan tried to think of what to do next. He hated having to rely on Bikaropin all of the time, however, he knew that the great-grandson was a lot smarter than anyone else in the current Owlam community. "Bak, Araba, Or and Inorim...take that craft of theirs and see if you can figure it out. See if you can...fly it somewhere and...figure out if it has some kind of programmed flight path back to...wherever home base is located." He sniffed. "For safety sake...fly it in Spy. The rest of us, get that noisy monstrosity into 45, on a Chok ship and we'll...study it there."

Maramee pointed at some kind of tool chest that was beside the machine. "What do we do with that?"

Soolchakan wanted to slap her. 'Stupid question,' he thought! "We take *everything* to 45 with us. We leave nothing behind...other than those vulgar Teltermak dead bodies." He glared at the bodies. "Hop their clothing somewhere...else. Leave them here with nothing, absolutely nothing. Let them rot! Let the carrion eaters feast on them."

34 of the Owlamites gathered all of the equipment and Jumped to one of the Chokchakchok ships in #45. Soolchakan chose that one because those giant ships always had plenty of room for anything to be stored on them.

After flying the Teltermak shuttlecraft around Hardooth for four days, the quartet joined the rest in dimension #45.

Bak, being the eldest, reported in to Soolchakan. "That ship, when you place it on automatic, it will fly you, by the most direct route possible, to Satroco Isle. We haven't been there in a few years, because we've been preoccupied with..." His voice trailed off and he looked down sadly. He cleared his throat and looked up. "It seems that the Teltermak have those potion factories up and running again. They have thousands of full bottles in cold storage."

Soolchakan nodded. "Were you able to determine... anything else about it?"

Bak clenched his teeth. "Yes! We found that, in the

backlogs of the ship that it was at the scene of each death of an Owlamite over the past 18 years." His body shuddered. "Those... *cannibals*...seem to have picked the internal organs that they like the best. They take them and put them in a refrigerator on the ship and take them back to Satroco for..." He turned away looking as if he was about to throw up.

Soolchakan nodded. "All right, they've gone back into the potion manufacturing business and they're still...uncivilized cannibals." He stood up. "It's time that we get rid of that bunch. I don't know how many of them there are but...we are now on a quest to destroy the Teltermaks...before they completely wipe us out." He hung his head. "First though, we have to figure out what that...wretched mind-manipulating contrivance is...and how it can control us. If those monsters have another one of, or several of those things, taking control of this one won't help very much. We have to get all of them...as soon as possible before all of us end up as the main course in one of their hideous banquets."

Hisang and Sazha went on a spying trip to Satroco Isle. They came back reporting that the Teltermak were rather miffed over the fact that the "Team" had not returned from a certain unnamed island with a new supply of Owlam guts. They were not sure which island the Team was on because the members of the Team were the ones who chose randomly where they would go to perform their dirty deed. It was also reported that the shuttlecraft was a prototype and the Teltermak did not have any backup craft.

The mind-manipulator was something different. The Teltermak had been fooling around with different frequencies and had been able to use this machine to control several different races of Elf. For some reason, again, they were primarily interested in the Owlamites. The instruction manual did not have the reason listed as to why, however, it did have it listed in bold print that they were to do everything that they could to get any of the Owlams alive...for further processing...yet they murdered them.

Soolchakan had never thought that the word "processing" could ever sound so sinister. They wanted the Owlamites to "process" for food and they like their meat *fresh*. At the same time they were back to making potions. Either they were not putting so much emphasis on the *Tuzine* any more or they were putting more on the potions. He decided that it was time to empty their potion warehouses again while killing as many of the blood-lusting monsters as they could. Wiping the entire race out actually sounded inviting, considering the fact that to the Teltermak, Soolchakan and his children were nothing but food.

Bikaropin made a discovery regarding the mind-manipulator. He could use some of the Chok technology to find any other machines like this one and wipe the memory banks clean. The drawback to this was, if they have a backup hard drive then wiping the current hard drive did little damage to the other machines. He dug further into the Chok computer and found that it could wipe the memory banks of the others clean and identify the exact location of the other machines. He found that there were fourteen other machines. He used the Chok computer to erase the hard drives of the other fourteen, identified the exact location, informed Soolchakan of this information and waited for further instructions.

Soolchakan listened to all of the information from Hisang and Bikaropin. "We've got their silly shuttlecraft. We know the location of the other machines. What we need to do is get to those other machines as quickly as possible, swipe them, and kill any Teltermak that are in that location. They'd be the ones who are adept at using this infernal contraption."

Mahanee did not like the thought of killing every last one of them. "Do we have to kill…the children?"

Soolchakan walked up to her and got right in her face. "You have had to bury six of your ten children because of them. How many more of your children do you want to bury before you realize that *their* children will grow up to kill *more* of your children. Either you kill *all* of them, or you, and your children, just surrender to them, as food." He stopped and let the thought sink into her head. "Now, make your choice. Make it quickly. We don't have time to fool around with those monsters. Is it *your* children or theirs who die?"

A tear ran down her left cheek. "We kill them. All of them," she said sadly. She turned away to try to hide more tears. Hisang, Maramee, Poolkiy and Ometik were still alive. Zorkeen, Banama, Sunok, Alam, Fomin and Nesh were all buried in caskets in a vault on Zhagool. "We kill *all* of them," she sobbed.

Over the next 64 years, the Owlamites hunted down and killed over 2,000,000 Teltermaks in some fifty locations. The nasty monsters had spread out to several different places in the world in spite of any attempt at keeping them on Satroco.

It had taken only nine days to obtain and Jump all of the mind-manipulation machines to a Chok ship in dimension #45. Each machine had a team of technicians that were there to repair and alter the program to make it more efficient. Ridding the world of all of those technicians was very high priority. After finding the machines and destroying any trace of the machines for the Teltermak, the machines were completely dismantled in dimension #45. To assure that they were completely disabled, they looked over all of the parts of the disassembled contraptions. When they found certain parts that were very unique, just to these machines, those parts were completely destroyed.

Another thing that the Owlamites did was steal every potion bottle that was in cold storage on Satroco Isle. There were some 800,000 bottles. They moved the bottles to a derelict ship in dimension #45. The Teltermak were keeping the things cold so... put them in a ship that does not have any heat on and they should stay nice and cold...if not frozen.

They used telecommunication devices to find most of the Teltermak. Each time they swiped one of the mind machines, there were numerous angry calls made by high ranking Teltermaks, attempting to find out what the problem was. The theft of the potions caused a tremendous upheaval and that turned out to be the greatest assistance in finding many of the places the Teltermak had moved to and were trying to take over and control.

2

The nineteenth century saw no more births among the Owlamites. In the year 1900 ATUT, the population was still only 38. During the twentieth century there were no new births either...or the twenty-first century...or the twenty-second century. Soolchakan figured that none of the women were interested in having children now because of the fact that so many of them had seen many of their children entombed on Zhagool. Bonarain had been the only death that the young ones knew of...until now. Those deaths were probably causing them more grief than he could imagine. He felt that he should just let them be the ones to come to terms with it and start procreation in their time.

The twenty-third century ATUT started basically the same. There seemed to be no end to the moratorium on procreation. The surviving 38 Owlamites lived their lives doing anything they pleased...other than watching the monitors for alien invasions... or looking for any surviving Teltermaks (which were dispatched quickly).

Zerbolud 1, 2221, Soolchakan was adding another page in his boring memoirs, which now consisted of over 45 rather large volumes, of his personal observations. He was wondering how to write something that he had annotated over 10,000 times before. He wanted to put it in words that did not make it sound like so much tautology. He was staring at the blank screen…when the klaxon went off. There was a new intruder from outer space entering their star system.

Araba was on watch in the monitor room at the time. She was adjusting the system to focus on the fleet of ships of the intruder. As usual, the intruders saw the mineral wealth of the planet Bri and were orbiting the planet taking a full inventory of what they were finding.

Soolchakan grimaced. Each time before, he had gone out there with his Team. Once before he had gone out there after Bonarain disappeared. Now, Kiyalee and Chyning were no longer here as well. He was now the one who went to the Bridge and start the translations of the aliens. Bikaropin was now the one who went to the engine room to compare the engines of the new intruders with what was known already. Meffin was now the sneak thief who could find and purloin all kinds of goodies from the unsuspecting victims. Meffin was not as proficient as Chyning, however, she could still steal your teeth from you without you realizing that they were gone.

They did not have to worry about anyone staying behind to watch any children. Yeema was the youngest Owlamite and she was over 400 years old.

All 38 Owlamites donned their spacesuits, climbed into their single seat fighters and Jumped to Bri. They found a fleet of

80 cylindrical ships all orbiting and scanning the large planet.

Once again, the flagship of the fleet was sitting off to the side, doing nothing but "supervising" while all of the other 79 ships did all of the work. Soolchakan, Bikaropin and Meffin headed for that one with their assignments. Soolchakan found out later that Namaheen and Pamaki went in with Meffin to do some wholesale and mass theft.

The engine room was nothing new. The light speed engine was the same kind that had been found in all of the others. If you cannot come up with something new and improved, you just have to stick with what does work. The laws of physics are what they are. Hard to do any changes.

There was not very much on board that was worth pilfering. The three women did decide to take something, just to say that they had done something or had a trophy of some kind.

Mahanee joined Soolchakan in the Bridge. He was almost done with the new language. Listening in was getting boring when all you hear is arrogance. The only ones that he could mess with had been that one bunch the Korpynch. He had played with their superstitions. In order to do that, your victim has to be superstitious. This bunch, who called themselves Kivist, did not seem to have any handicaps of that nature.

This bunch looked a lot like the Heyyah. The primary difference was the fact that they had a large bulging upper torso and four arms. Their complexion was a little darker like some Heyyah and they had a wide variety of hair colors.

Mahanee started listening in. **"Are we going to have to**

kill them?"

Soolchakan rolled his eyes. **"No, because of their altruistic attitude we're going to go for unconditional surrender,"** he sent sarcastically. He listened in for a while longer hoping for any kind of crack in their armor and/or attitude. Nothing. He hung his head. 'Where do all of these monsters come from,' he thought? 'Why do you always have to come here?' He sent out a message to all. **"This bunch won't listen to reason and we can't scare them. We're going to have to defeat them."**

Bikaropin sent a message back. **"Have you tried to reason with them?"**

'Never entered my mind,' thought Soolchakan. He shrugged. 'Why not try it?'

Before he could make any attempt, Shashy broke in. **"We need to try, at the very least. It doesn't make any sense to start by shooting."**

Ha-Ami had to break in as well. **"This…shoot first and ask questions later just isn't good policy."**

Soolchakan grunted. **"If you'll all just SHUT UP, I might have a chance to try…something!"** He hopped the business end of his public address system into Home. "This is Soolchakan! Drey Sssorg of the Owlam! Why are you here in my star system? What are your intentions? If you are here to conquer, be advised that no one has ever been successful in taking this system. Many have tried and because of the Owlam…all have failed."

The Bridge crew did not seem very shaken by the message that came out of nowhere. Many of them turned to what appeared to be the Commander with what looked like haughty sneers on their faces.

The Commander leaned back in his chair. "I am Fovokom, Tramquist of this Advance Kivist Attack Fleet. I don't know what a 'dry slob' is but it means nothing to me anyway. If you want to live, you'll stop annoying me and surrender. Keep annoying me and I'll have the greatest enjoyment of torturing you myself... just for fun." He turned to one of the crew. "Second Nossok, Shijonimp, cut off that transmission. I don't want to listen to or barter with future slaves."

A crew member, who was fiddling with all kinds of dials and switches, responded without looking back. "Tramquist, Sir...I don't know where that transmission came from. All I know is...it did not come in through our receivers."

Fovokom stood up. He turned to another crew member. "Tharment, Bibfosh...go show that officer how to do his job."

Bibfosh walked over to the communication console. He pushed Shijonimp away and started fiddling with dials and buttons for himself.

Soolchakan just shook his head. "I do not use archaic systems like yours to communicate." 'Here we go again,' he thought. "I use our Multifastidigeous Thonlock Communicator in order to send my signals. Your system cannot receive it because it is too simplistic to accept our messages from the Thonlock."

Fovokom snarled, showing his brown teeth. "Find a way

to cut that thing off! I'm tired of listening to it! We have things to do and what we say to each other is none of their business."

Both Shijonimp and Bibfosh were messing with the dials, buttons and switches now. A third officer came over and joined in as well.

Soolchakan tried to keep the laughter out of his voice. "As I said, your system is too archaic and simplistic to receive our transmissions. We send them out on a wavelength, and systemic grid, that you are incapable of shutting off, or of even understanding. Now, listen to me! Leave now…or we will be forced to destroy you."

Fovokom held his fists up in the air. "Nothing is superior to the Kivist Empire! We *will* shut you off and make sure that you don't bother us again. You don't know our power or what we can do with our system."

Meffin showed up on the Bridge. "**If you're interested in talking to these *Fovoks*, this ship is currently armed with what they call torpedoes. 50 high grade, 80 middle grade and 150 low yield. They also have some pretty nasty pulse guns, that they call Hoozoo grade power cannons.**"

Soolchakan repeated all of this information to Fovokom. He also informed Fovokom that "*fovok*" was a dirty word in the Owlam vocabulary. The information was rather explicit as to what *fovok* actually meant.

Mahanee sent a few little tidbits of information to Soolchakan as to what some of the Bridge crew were doing.

Soolchakan sighed. "Before you ordered Shijonimp to shut your communications system down, he was relaying some lovey-dovey message to somebody named Arkapira."

The color drained from the face of Shijonimp as he violently shook his head back and forth. He waved all four of his hands as well, trying to deny the accusation.

Soolchakan had to really fight hard to keep from laughing. "If you check the logs (snort), you'll find that he was getting rather (chuckle) graphic about what he was going to do with her once he (cough) was off duty (choke) tonight."

Shijonimp closed his eyes and clenched his jaws showing his brown teeth.

Soolchakan cleared his throat several times in order to regain his composure. "You have a...I believe the rank is called... Vindelo... and a person of that rank named Twavomp. For quite some time now, he's been shirking his duties while he has been using his screen to watch pornographic cinema. Again, if you don't believe me, check the logs."

Twavomp stood up looking as if he was either going to fill his pants or lose his lunch - or both.

Soolchakan continued. "There is a Third Nossok, Ababisha who is drawing pictures of the (ahem) exalted *fovok* – Fovokom as a...I believe the creature is some kind of rodent...called cheebee."

Ababisha stood up shaking his head and hands in an attempt at denying the charges.

Soolchakan sniffed. "Shall I continue...or do you believe

me now when I say that your system is archaic and we can monitor it without you being able to stop us? Or maybe I should tell the crew about the messages that you are sending to someone named Piytbee. Should I tell them about how she has obtained her rank… while in *your* bed?"

Fovokom fell back into his Command chair with his eyes and mouth wide open in shock. "Someone figure out a way to shut that *smish* off," he muttered helplessly.

Several of the Bridge crew were now doing all kinds of things with their keyboards.

One of them turned to the Commander and snapped to attention. Tramquist, Fovokom, we've been attempting to triangulate on this transmission and…it appears to be originating… from…right here, inside the Bridge."

Fovokom buried his face in hands…all four of them. He then looked up. "Call the fleet away from this…mineral planet. Start the assault on the inhabited planet immediately. We need to find this…arrogant…*dry slob* and…force him into total submission." He took a deep breath. "Execute the command… NOW!"

Soolchakan growled under his breath. "**Start blowing up their ships. Maybe if we take some of them out… they'll change their minds. Start killing their ships… now**."

Bak called in. "**They just blew the tips of my pulse cannons off. I hopped the tips into Home and…the response was immediate**."

"**Mine got blown away as well**," sent Waybar. "**Their defense system is...too fast.**"

One of the Kivist ships suddenly blew up. Masam called out. "**I threw a bottle, inside the light speed engine fuel area, as they were firing up. Apparently, you have to hit them with something innocuous in order to avoid their defense systems. Their computer can somehow react to a weapon because it's a piece of hostile equipment. A bottle isn't.**"

Another ship blew up. "**The innocent stuff works,**" sent Faroog. "**All I had was a chunk of sheared metal.**"

"**I agree,**" sent Nofani. "**I tried a hand-held bomb and...it was destroyed immediately after I threw it.**"

Soolchakan shrugged. "**Okay...everybody start throwing junk in their light speed engines. If that is the only thing that works, then let's do it.**"

Two more ships blew up. Porim and Ayino confirmed that non-hostile junk was not attacked by their defense systems. Unknown hostile weapons were somehow detected by their computer system rather quickly and the defensive reaction was just as fast. Five more ships blew up.

Soolchakan watched the reports that were coming in to the Command ship. "Hey, Fovokom! How many more of your ships do we have to exterminate before you get the message...and leave? Do I have to destroy your entire fleet...as well as you in order to get the message across?"

Mahanee sent to Soolchakan. **"They sent some transmission back to their home planet regarding what's going on here. They've already received confirmation that some home office has already received the message and that they're sending...reinforcements from... something called...Vevetcho."**

'This may be a long war,' thought Soolchakan. '38 of us against...millions of them.'

Before (what was left of the fleet) got to the orbit of Makatindi, they had lost 26 more ships.

Soolchakan again called out to Fovokom. "How much more of your fleet do we have to destroy before you get the message? Turn back now and we'll let you live."

Fovokom looked up at nothing in particular. "SHUT UP, YOU DRY SLOB! We will kill most of you and take the rest of you as slaves. Now quit disturbing me while I take over you and your star system!" He growled. He looked around the Bridge. "Continue on! We cannot go back in defeat! We must destroy anyone who is arrogant enough to try to stand against us!"

Soolchakan closed his eyes and shook his head. **"We save the flagship for last. Once we've destroyed the rest of the fleet...the flagship goes into dimension 45... and the entire crew goes out into space. I've already got the Command pass codes. We can get all we want from them."**

By the time they reached the orbit of Dilhazass and Weeloow the fleet had been whittled down by 29 more ships.

"Fovokom, have you had enough yet?"

Fovokom was starting to look scared. "SHUT UP, SLAVE! I am really going to enjoy torturing you…and your family!" He looked around with clenched teeth. "Just as soon as I figure out how to find *you*…specifically. I will find you and I will enjoy torturing you."

Soolchakan looked off to the side disgusted. "**Keep killing the *chokwads*.**"

Before they reached the orbit of the running twins, the flagship was the only one left. Soolchakan, Bikaropin and Mahanee were the ones who touched different places in the ship and hopped it to dimension #45. Now Fovokom was finally startled enough to be speechless. Soolchakan sighed as he looked around the Bridge at the reaction of all of the crew.

Efor called in. "**Do we start eliminating the crew now?**"

"**Of course,**" sent Soolchakan. "**I've already got all of the command codes to get into their computer system. We don't need any of them. Start with the Bridge crew.**" He looked at Fovokom. "Goodbye…*fovok*." He was not sure who grabbed Fovokom. He just watched as the Fleet Commander and all the rest of the Bridge crew disappeared rapidly…one by one. "**Before any of you try to hop into the dimension with this ship…I suggest that you get rid of all of your…hostile weapons. I wouldn't want anything bad to happen to any of you because their defense system hasn't been shut off yet.**"

Bikaropin called to him. "**What if the thing looks at us as hostile? We're not normal to this ship. What then**?"

Soolchakan felt a little pang of disgust. "**Let me try something.**" He stepped out of his fighter. He hopped into Ghost. At least fifteen different pulse rays were fired at him. "**We have to figure out how to shut the defense system off before we can do anything in this ship.**"

Bikaropin nodded. "**Give me the command codes... and I'll try it.**"

Soolchakan sent the codes to Bikaropin, Inorim and Namin. He had confidence that between the three of them they could find something.

The main duty of the Owlamites was to keep close watch on the outer space monitors. They felt that the Kivist would not stop to survey Bri the next time. They were going to have to be ready to get rid of another fleet...at a moment's notice.

Four days later, Bikaropin called in. They had found and disabled the inner defense system of the ship and they were now looking for anything that could assist in landmarking a place on the home planet of the Kivist. He was also looking at some of the other information in the computers. He found that the home planet had the same irritating defense system. If an unidentified spaceship were to get within range, it would be fired on by over 10,000 defensive satellites that were surrounding the planet, no exceptions.

Soolchakan looked at the information with some anxiety. "More and more I'm hating these people. They like to attack, kill and enslave. All of that with an incredibly powerful defense system which tells me that they're very paranoid as well. He chuckled. 'Of course, any conqueror would be in total fear of being conquered themselves.'

Bikaropin continued to look for some weakness in the planetary defense system of the Kivist while the rest of the Owlamites continued watching the skies for the next invasion force.

They searched for quite a while, however, they could not find any path they could take to get around that incredible defense system. According to what they found the system was not just satellites floating around in outer space, it was also some kind of stationary satellite inside the atmosphere, along with fixed fortifications on the ground as well. Any weapon that was not recognized by the defense system would be instantly destroyed.

Meanwhile, they discovered a large fleet of Kivist ships coming toward their star system.

"Here we go again," said Soolchakan. "Another group of *bimyocks* that are too stupid to know when to quit." He looked down at the small monitors to see if they had a count on the ships. Not yet. They were currently too far away. "Maybe we can hop some of them...into dimension 2...or just destroy them. That should confuse the *h'oolyach* out of them for a while."

The 38 Owlamites went out to meet the incoming Kivist.

Once within range, they counted 244 ships. They also read the minds of the ship commanders and found out that this was an all-out attack. There were only 16 ships that had been left behind. They were in port for repair or they had not been finished yet. Otherwise they would be here.

They were over nineteen million teckfar from the orbit of Denhahbon when they started blowing up enemy ships. None of the survivors slowed down at all. They just kept coming at flank speed.

Soolchakan once again tried to communicate with them. They refused to listen. They just kept charging on ahead.

Bikaropin called out to Soolchakan. **"They don't want to listen. They have an order in their computers that commands them to fight on to the last. It also states that once they've built a 1,000 ship task force, they will attack with that and avenge anyone who dies in this campaign."**

Soolchakan clenched his teeth. **"Bikaropin, find something that we can landmark their planet. Also, find something...that we can attack them with...that they can't or won't defend against. Find something...or this'll go on forever. Years ago, I tried placing all of their guns in Ghost, but...it doesn't seem to be working with this bunch. They have too many defensive systems!"**

By the time the enemy fleet did reach the orbit of Denhahbon, 51 more ships had been destroyed. The Owlamites were beginning to become appalled at the amount of debris that was floating around in the space of their star system. The only consolation was that before any of it could reach Hardooth, there were several gas giants, with powerful gravitational pull that could capture most of the debris - hopefully.

Soolchakan ordered that one round of attacks should be a case of hopping the enemy ships into another dimension. That way, there would be a little less debris and a few more ships that they could purloin from an enemy. There was still the order from a previous *Voice of Power* where they were supposed to slam an enemy ship into the backside of Niygool. Now was a perfect opportunity to line a ship up for that order.

The next round of ships destroyed was another test. Instead of blowing them up, they were Jumped to the nearest gas giant (in this case it was Weeloow). The ship was placed just outside of the upper atmosphere of the gas giant. Going at flank speed, the ship had no time to react to this movement and was inside the gravitational pull of Weeloow before they could even react. They had no time or capability of turning around and escaping the gravity of the gas giant and were therefore doomed to be crushed by the atmospheric pressure of the giant and their remains were forever lost inside the gas.

That plan worked so well that Soolchakan ordered another 38 ships to be crashed into Rogoth.

The enemy had just passed the orbital area of Denhahbon. There were only 49 remaining in their ill-fated attack. 38 of these were blown up rather quickly. The last 11 were then hopped into dimension #2 where they were joined by five other ships that had ended up in that dimension.

Now the Owlamites had 49 of the enemy ships in other dimensions where they were able to extract all of the personnel from these ships and then add them to the collection parked in dimension #45.

The Owlamites spent the next three years going through the computer logs of all of the Kivist marauders in an attempt at finding some landmark on the home planet where they could get around that defensive system. They were finding all kinds of annotations about "The Great Tower". This was some special building on their planet that housed all of the primary offices of the government on the planet. All coordination went through this building. Now all that had to be done was find a picture of this great tower.

Araba and Namaheen found, what they thought was, a picture of the tower, almost at the same time. Two different pictures. They called Soolchakan to come look at it. He in turn called Bikaropin. Soolchakan and Bikaropin noticed that the main entrance to the two buildings was totally different.

Bikaropin shrugged. "Okay, what do we do now? They're obviously different so they both can't be the same building."

Soolchakan smiled. "Right now, that just might not matter. If they're both on the same planet, we still have something to work with."

Bikaropin smiled. "So…we both….Jump to one…then the other. We find out if either one is on the Kivist home planet and…"

"We have our landmark and our target," said Soolchakan emphatically!

They chose the building that Araba found. The two of them studied it. They hopped to Spy and then on the command from Soolchakan they Jumped. They found themselves in front of an incredibly tall structure made of gray concrete. It was some 70 stories in height. Each floor was not a normal height as other buildings go. Each floor was at least two and a half times taller than most, which made a skyscraper that was an enormous spire.

Bikaropin chuckled. "Now we go inside and find out if we are on the main planet of the Kivist."

Soolchakan had turned around to take a panoramic view of the area. He tapped Bikaropin on the shoulder and motioned him to turn around. Now both of them were facing away from the structure…and facing the *other* structure that had been pictured in the photograph found by Namaheen. This one was a white brick structure that was the same height as the other building. They were standing in a very large, and crowded, main plaza between the two buildings.

Bikaropin looked back and forth at the two towers. "Which one do we start with?"

"Go back and get some help," said Soolchakan. "The more people we have here, the faster we'll find out any and all information we need." He nodded. "Bring everybody. Half of us in the white structure, half in the gray. Find some…conference room where they do all of their planning…like the plan that they have to build 1,000 ships and send them to Hardooth."

In a very short time, all 38 Owlamites were in the center of the square separating the two towers. Soolchakan made the decision as to who would go to which building. They moved to the buildings, started reading minds, taking notes and looking for any intelligence data that they could find.

The two buildings were the government, however, they were a different part of it. The white structure was of a theocratic nature while the gray one was of a politically autocratic nature. It was religion and the secular butting heads against one another. Both attempting to be the top governing one. The only thing that kept them from warring against each other was the fact that they were both ambitious in the taking of as many star systems as they could and bringing them under the influence of the empire before any civil war.

Right now, the Kivist Empire only had control of eleven conquered star systems. The defeat at the hands of the Owlamites had knocked them down to, currently, having only a minor toe-hold on those occupied systems. One good nudge and the subjugated systems would be able to revolt against their captors… and probably win.

"We need to hurt them…badly," said Bikaropin. "The main problem is their defensive system. I can't…find any way around it."

Shashy huffed. "Well what do you need? We have all kinds of weapons that we can throw at them…and yet you say that none of them will work?"

He sighed. "Whatever we throw at them, this defensive

system thinks like, and as fast as, a computer. It is so fast…by the time we Jump something here…even though it is set to blow up in only three or four miths, the defensive system has already spotted it and is destroying it."

Mahanee shook her head. "So we need to drop something that is so…innocent, so inoffensive that…that their system won't recognize it as a threat…and won't attack it." She shook her head. "But, it still has to be big enough to cause damage."

"Exactly," said Bikaropin. "Something that is not usually used as a weapon but…in our case we *are* using it…as a weapon."

Soolchakan stood there grinning. "Drop something. Something that is innocent. Something that is not a weapon. Something that has never been used as a weapon."

Bikaropin looked at him suspiciously. "Yes…exactly." He frowned. "What did you have in mind?"

"How about…a bell?" Soolchakan now had a very evil grin on his face.

Bikaropin nodded cautiously. "Yes, a bell would, or should, be innocent enough. The problem is, it'd have to be an incredibly large bell…in order to do sufficient damage…to just about anything."

Soolchakan's grin was now even more devious as he chuckled and his eyes were dancing with eagerness. He chose the four eldest along with Bikaropin. "Mahanee, Hisang, Maramee and Poolkiy…we're going to go look at a bell. The rest of you… go get ready in your fighters. When we…drop the bell…all of us will be here to witness…the mess made by…the *bell*."

Bikaropin was shaking his head. "This bell would have to be…*enormous*…in order to do anything worthwhile." He huffed as he shook his head with complete skepticism.

"Form a ring," said Soolchakan still grinning. "I'm going to show you something…that you probably won't believe…until you see it."

The ones he had named joined in a circle. Soolchakan Jumped the six of them to the great desert on that planet in dimension #198. He was the only one really facing the bell when the Jump was accomplished. The others followed his gaze and were all now gawking at the sight of the giant bell.

Soolchakan chuckled. "Behold! The Great Bell of the Whimich people. They're now extinct. We put their bell here… because we had no other place to put it. We thought that it'd scare them if we stole their primary religious icon. All it did was irritate them and they actually started building another." He looked at Bikaropin. "If we drop that thing from high in the sky…say just inside the atmosphere of the Kivist planet, will that make a big enough mess…that'll get their attention?"

Bikaropin could do nothing but stare at it with his mouth hanging open. Soolchakan slapped him on the back of his head to bring him out of his trance.

"Well boy, will that work?"

Bikaropin nodded weakly. "It doesn't matter…what height you drop that thing from…it'll make a mess…a big mess.

The only question...how deep will the hole be?" He shook his head. "It'll crush...*anything* it lands on."

Mahanee looked at Soolchakan. "So now we have our weapon. How do we get it there?"

"Simple," said Bikaropin. "We hop this thing...into a different dimension...say Spy. We Jump it to the Kivist planet... just outside of their atmosphere. Then, we hop it to Home...and Jump it a few teckpell inside their atmosphere...and let gravity do the rest."

Poolkiy pointed at the other pieces that were there. "What about them? Do we do the same thing with them?"

Soolchakan nodded. "The framework that holds the bell up, the hammer and the framework that holds the hammer up. Yes, we can use all of them...if we have to. I hope that the bell, by itself, will be enough to convince them that we are not going to go down without making a tremendous mess on their planet."

Hisang chuckled. "So we drop that bell on their main government buildings."

"No," said Bikaropin. "We choose a secondary target. We let them know that that is just the first one. A second one will be dropped on those main government buildings...if they don't capitulate...or at least change their minds about attacking us."

Maramee sighed. "So...when do we do it?"

"As soon as possible," said Soolchakan. He took one more look at the big bell and chuckled. "I can't remember how long that thing has been sitting here." He scoffed. "Judging from the size of some of the dunes that are going up one side of that thing, it has been quite some time."

Soolchakan received the word from all of the rest of his clan that they were currently orbiting the moon around the Kivist home planet. They were waiting there to make sure they did not accidentally join with someone else when the bell was Jumped to an orbit around the planet.

The team of six took hold of the giant bell and hopped it into Spy. They got in their fighters and parked them around the bell. They then Jumped the bell to an orbit of the Kivist planet.

Soolchakan looked down and saw the capital city. "**NO! I don't want the thing dropped on the capital city. We have to hit somewhere else. It is the people who make the decisions in the capital city who need to see the example of what we can do. *Then,* we should be able to get them to listen.**"

Bikaropin sent back to him. "**There's a city on the west coast of this same continent. That city is a major industrial center. They manufacture half of the parts that go into building the Kivist spacecraft.**"

Soolchakan sniffed. "**That's a good target. I need some ears in the capitol buildings. When we hit that other city, I want to know exactly what they're thinking and if we need to make a second example.**"

Mahanee called to him. "**Do we want to drop this**

thing...upside-down?"

Soolchakan shrugged. **"That's as good as any position."**

Bikaropin thought about it for a moment. **"We need to get the bell to the other position by Jumping it there. If we wait until the planet orbit gets the bell into the best position, we'll run out of oxygen before we're ready to drop."**

Soolchakan grunted in disgust. **"Fine! Show us where it is and then we'll Jump the thing over there."**

Maramee was a little concerned. **"What do we do with the bell in the mean time?"**

"Leave it here," sent Bikaropin. **"We won't be gone that long."** He scoffed. **"It ain't goin' anywhere."**

Bikaropin sent the landmark of the industrial city. The six of them Jumped to that location, got a good look and then Jumped back to the bell.

Soolchakan was getting a little impatient. **"Is everybody ready to make this Jump?"** After receiving five affirmative answers, he called out again. **"All the rest of you, go to the two capitol buildings and get me some feedback on the destruction of a city...by an innocuous attack."**

The great bell was Jumped to a position over the other city.

Soolchakan had a sudden concern. **"How far are we from the capital city?"**

Bikaropin came back. **"This city is about 600 Teckfar from the capital...why?"**

"Because I didn't want them taken out as well. I don't know what's going to happen when this thing hits, but it could make a very large hole and possibly even cause a quake." Another concern hit him. **"Who is the oldest male currently hovering over the capital city?"**

"This is Korpem...why?"

"After the bell hits, make sure that you tell them that we did it. I want you to do it because they heard a male voice before and I want them to hear a male voice now. So as soon as they hear about any disaster, make sure that we get the credit."

Korpem snickered. **"Can do."**

Soolchakan collected his thoughts. 'I hate this,' he said to himself. 'All of these people who have to die, in order for us to stop them from conquering our planet. How many more have to die... before we're left alone?' **"Is everybody ready?"** After getting all affirmative responses, he closed his eyes. **"Hop the bell to Home and...Jump the bell inside the atmosphere... and...DROP!"**

He did not need to give that last order. As soon as the bell was inside the atmosphere - gravity *absolutely* took over. The giant bell started falling even before he gave the order. The six Owlamites positioned their craft so they could watch the entire episode unfold.

Bikaropin called out. "**Just in case, I think that the six of us should hop to Observation...just to be safe**."

"**Good idea**," sent Soolchakan. "**Do it**."

They watched as the bell got smaller and smaller as it fell away from them. From the height they were located when they dropped the bell, it seemed to take forever to finally arrive at ground level. When it hit, they saw a shock wave go out in a huge circle away from the center point of impact. At a certain point the wave stopped and they were looking at an enormous crater surrounding a large mess of destruction.

Soolchakan sent the message to the other Owlamites that impact had taken place.

Korpem started telling the tale in the gray building. Bak started telling the tale in the white building.

Mymin called back to Soolchakan. "**I don't know if it was your intention but, they felt a quake...here in the capital city a few mith after impact**."

Maramee was looking down in horror. "**Hey...there's a fissure opening up...going northwest from the center point. It's cracking towards the ocean**."

Hisang called out. "**There are two more fissures... going southeast and southwest**."

Poolkiy was a little confused. "**Why are those fissures turning orange**?"

Bikaropin was a little startled. "**That orange...it...it...

that's *magma*! We cracked the ground all the way down through the crust! We just created a...volcano...maybe even a super volcano!"

Soolchakan closed his eyes. "**What are they saying... in the capital**?"

"**They're ignoring us**," sent Korpem. "**They're saying that...the need for revenge against us...is even more important...now**." He grunted in disgust. "**Now they're saying that they need to expand the defensive guardians...to include...anything falling from the sky that...is not normal forms of precipitation. They're going to reprogram the guardians**."

Bikaropin opened his eyes wide in shock. "**They have to shut the whole system down in order to do that! When they take the guardians off-line, we have to hit the computer banks where they're doing the reprogramming. Don't let them bring the things back on-line and we'll be able to take the whole system out... without any worries**."

Soolchakan thought for a moment. "**Do we know where those computer banks are**?"

"**They're on the ninth floor of the gray building**," sent Korpem.

Soolchakan was a little frantic. "**Have they taken the things off-line yet**?"

"**They just did**," sent Korpem.

Soolchakan did not hesitate. "**Take them out...NOW! Take out that entire floor!**" He waited for a response. "**Have you done it?**"

Sazha was the one to respond. "**There were four of us...who all fired at the same time. We took out the entire ninth floor and...the rest of the 61 floors...that were above it...are now toppling onto other buildings nearby, as well as far away and...what a mess.**"

Bikaropin let out a breath of relief. "**That means that they're helpless. The guardians are off-line and they're waiting for an order from the main computer banks to come back up.**"

Hisang broke in on that conversation. "**Remember the fissures that opened up to the southwest and northwest? They cut off a big piece of the continent...and that piece just fell off into the ocean.**"

"**Look at all that dust flying around**," sent Mahanee.

"**That's not dust! That's boiling hot steam**," sent Bikaropin. "**When the ocean water hit the lava, billions of barrels of water and lava, could equal a whole planet-full of very dangerous and noxious steam.**"

Bak broke in. "**We're getting a reaction from the Theocrats. We've knocked out the Autocrats...when we blew their building up. The only one left is the Theocracy people. The higher ups, all the leaders, of the Autocrats were all on the upper floors of that building. Not much left of them after that long...fall.**"

Soolchakan could hardly wait. "**Really! Relay what they're saying!**"

Bak started the oration. "**They're saying that…it must have been against the will of…I don't know…some god that he called…Bone Pus…I think. At least that is what it sounded like he said. Anyway, it was against the will of that god for the Kivist to attack our star system. If it had been the will of Bone Pus for the attack to happen, the Kivist would've been overwhelmingly victorious. This horrible disaster shows that they should never have attacked us. The destruction of the Autocracy shows that they did nothing but make wrong decisions… against the will of Bone Pus. They're going to recall all of the ships that they have…on the other conquered planets and…I don't believe it! They say that they're never going to venture into outer space again…under any hostile conquering condition…unless they can prove that it is the will of Bone Pus. They will use the spacecraft for defensive purposes only.**"

Soolchakan shook his head. 'Look what it took…to convince them,' he thought. "**Bak, can you relay a message for me?**"

"**Absolutely!**"

"**Tell them that we heard their words. If these words are true then we're going back home. We will not attack again…unless their words are lies. If you leave us alone, we will leave you alone.**"

"**They heard it**," sent Bak. "**They're thanking us for not doing any more attacks...and they're asking about assistance in repairing this damage.**"

Soolchakan sniffed. "**Tell them that that is impossible. They left us no choice but to destroy that city in order to show them our capabilities. They're the ones who will have to take care of any repairs...because we will be concerned with our own repairs from damages caused by them. Bak send the message and then, Owlamites... let's go home**," he sent calmly.

Bak called back after a few moments. "**They don't like the fact that we're not going to help them clean the mess up, but they're not going to argue with it. They are going to pray to Bone Pus for guidance...for anything in the future.**"

Soolchakan scoffed. "**They should have done that initially.**"

3

The rest of the twenty-third century was uneventful... except for the fact that the Owlamites went back (secretly) to visit the Kivist planet ten years after the attack. The destruction had been somewhere between catastrophic and permanent. There were parts of the planet that had not and probably could not come back for a very long time. 60% of all of the mammals were now extinct, 45% of the plant life, 75% of the birds, 90% of the reptiles and 55% of the sea life all wiped out because of the ecological disaster that occurred from the steam and ash cloud that blotted out the sun for almost two years. They would be too busy, for a very long time, repairing their planet. Outer space was not very important to them at this time.

The twenty-fourth century saw nothing new as well.

In the year 2400, Bikaropin decided to have a chat with Soolchakan. He was not exactly sure how to start the conversation, other than, as Soolchakan always told everyone: "Open your mouth and communicate!"

Bikaropin cleared his throat several times. "Soolchakan, why...are you...not allowing us...to have any more...children?"

Soolchakan was totally confused by the question. "What

makes you think that I'm not allowing any children to be born?"

"Ever since that Teltermak war...there haven't been any births. The only one who could stop *all* of us from procreating... is you."

Now he was even more baffled. "I have never told any of you to stop having children...completely. I've always left it up to the women." He looked off to the side confused. "At least I think I did. Since they have to bear the greatest burden...and physically bear the child...I figured that I'd leave it up to them as to when they want to put up with a pregnancy and raising an infant."

Now Bikaropin was confused. "But...there are several of the women and men who have discussed children." He cleared his throat again. "They just...don't seem to want to stripe a man... with the mucus. Again, the only one who could prevent *all* of the women from getting pregnant...is you."

Soolchakan frowned as he contemplated. "I never put any forbiddance on anyone. At least...I...don't think I did."

Bikaropin nodded. "Possibly, you did it unconsciously. The thought of all of the ones who...are now entombed on Zhagool. You've buried both Kiyalee and Chyning on Zhagool. You didn't want to have to bury any more...and so you decided, unconsciously, to forbid...any new pregnancies."

Soolchakan shook his head in confusion. "That is horrible! I...don't want to stop anyone from having children." He stood up. "If I put some banishment on any new procreation, I did not mean it. It was an accident. If anyone wants to have children, do so with my blessings. Any banishment of procreation...

stricken from all of the records!" He cleared his throat. He gave Bikaropin a wan smile. "Do you think that'll help?"

"Oh, yes! Absolutely! I think it'll make a huge difference. Thank you." He looked off to the side biting his lower lip.

Soolchakan cocked his head to the side. "Is there something else bothering you?"

Bikaropin took a deep breath. "Actually, yes. I was wondering…when all of those Owlamites were…murdered…how did you…know? How did you know where they were and when each one…was…killed?"

Soolchakan looked at Bikaropin incredulously. "And you're just asking *now* after all of these centuries?"

"It took a long time to conjure up the intestinal fortitude, and a lot of thinking about it, to ask." He smiled weakly.

Soolchakan sighed. He closed his eyes and shook his head. He licked his lips as he was getting ready to answer that question. He looked directly into the eyes of Bikaropin. "When Bonarain vanished…with a daughter that…I don't know if she was born alive or not…I had no way of knowing where she was or what happened to her. After that…I used the *Voice of Power* to attach myself to all of you. At first, it didn't work. After several of my children…were murdered…I honed the skill and fine-tuned it and finally got it so that I could find anyone. If something…very tragic or painful or…a terrifying event happens to any of you, you will involuntarily send me a mental message as to where you are and what is around you. Unfortunately, I wasn't able to find out who was murdering our people because…the Teltermak were so very sneaky about it and had their victims in a trance…or stupor. I haven't figured out a way to get a panoramic view of what is going on with the victim. All I can do, at this time, is get the message that something horrible has happened…where it happened and when…but not how or by whom."

Bikaropin stood there in thought for a few moments. "I don't envy you the tragic messages that you received from them. I'll try to think of a way…that you can get a little more information, if any of these events occur again…hopefully, forbidden by the Great Maker."

Soolchakan nodded. "I agree."

Bikaropin walked away, leaving Soolchakan in a muddle, trying to figure out if he somehow had mentally, inadvertently banished any new pregnancies.

Tadkoy, Strebale 7, 2401, the first child born since 1802. Batar and Ha-Ami gave birth to a son they named Alero (*Flawless*).

There were four more children born in the year 2401 and three more in 2402. In 2403, Efor and Palakim gave birth to the very first set of twins ever born to an Owlamite. Two girls named Eena and Sana were born on Statichy 29, 2403. There was another child born in 2403. Two more children were born in 2404, two more in 2405. Another one born in 2408, another one born in 2412 and another one in 2419. Once again the population was rising. Soolchakan made every effort to be at each birth. He wanted to be one of the first ones to hold each new baby in his arms.

The sounds of children running through the main hallways,

playing, laughing and shouting was heard again, mainly on the first level. Most of the married couples were all moving to apartments on the first level. Soolchakan refused to move from the apartment that he lived in from the beginning - 12-562. He had lived there for too long a time to move out now. He was too set in his ways. Plus, it would be a monumental effort and it would take months to move all of his possessions.

There were several more children born between 2419 and 2520. Then on Inamyon 7, 2536, Or and Shana announced the birth of their son Kazil (*Impervious*). He became the sixty-fifth living Owlamite and the first member of the ninth generation. Soolchakan was very relieved when the eighth generation was showing no signs of inbred mutations and neither did Kazil. Maybe all of the women were still following the teachings of Bonarain, as far as repairing any damage to a fetus before birth, however, they were finding very few things to repair.

On the Winter Solstice of 2581, Bak and Shashy of the Fourth announced the birth of another set of twins. This time it was a boy and a girl. Dosip (*Glorious*) and Dosina (*Elegant*) of the Fifth.

The twenty-sixth century ended with a total of 71 Owlamites. Once again Soolchakan was anxiously hoping for the future. He was still wondering if it had been his mental block that had held any and all of his children from procreating for nearly 600 years. He wondered how many would have been born if it had not been for the blockade. He was also wondering why Bikaropin had not brought the issue up for such a long time. That dead history was all behind them now. What they needed now, as always, was to stay vigilant to any enemies - local planet foes and those from outer space.

The watching of the monitors continued and there were more birth announcements that came in every now and then. Then on Astekoy, Whegire 1, 2659, Waybar and Nofani made an incredible announcement. Nofani has just given birth to the very first set of triplets born to Owlamites. Rasibi (*Herald*), Yamiy (*Announce*) and Kiniya (*Reveal*). Three baby girls joined the fifth generation. Soolchakan did not have enough arms to hold the three newborns. Nor did he have enough ways to contain his tearful joy over this momentous occasion.

With only five days left in the twenty-seventh century, the ninety-fifth living Owlamite was born. They were able to bring in a new century when Ganshim and Ajik of the Seventh gave birth to a baby girl named Jena (*Season*). Once again hoping for the best but preparing for the worst. The next child was not born until the year 2716 ATUT.

On Tadkoy, Marrem 3, 2767, another momentous occasion. Kazil and Itaya of the Ninth announced the birth of the first member of the Tenth generation. They had a son they named Rak (*Unite*). Rak was not just the first member of the Tenth generation, he also became the one hundredth *current* living Owlamite.

Soolchakan uttered several long prayers to the Great Maker. His hopes were that he would never have to bury another Owlamite as long as he lived…the will of the Great Maker be done.

The year 3000 came along. It ended the thirtieth century ATUT. The Owlamite population was now at 155. There had been a lasting peace for the Owlamites…as far as outer space was concerned.

The planet had a different story going on. They found that there were several different locations that the Teltermak had been hiding and repopulating. Once again, they had to search for all of these locations and try to make sure that there were not any more of them. The inability to read the minds of the Teltermak was totally frustrating the opportunity to obtain a complete picture of the intelligence data.

The Teltermak were very good at talking around something and using strange slang terms. Any attempt at finding a dictionary in any of their homes or places of business did not yield any positive results. The only thing that could be done was to continue keeping an eye on them. There was still no clue as to why the Teltermak wanted to capture Owlamites alive (other than their vulgar cuisine) while using, and killing, members of several other races of Elf to commit some of their dastardly deeds.

Soolchakan was livid that some of those nasty people had survived at all. They were like some kind of vermin that infests and eats your house out from under you as well as getting into all of your stored foods.

One good thing about the thirty-first century was that on Citendali 25, 3056, Rak and Jama announced the birth of their son Falchon (*Decree*). Falchon was the first member of the eleventh generation. All examinations of him showed no signs of any inbred infirmities. Bonarain had done such a tremendous job on the second generation, it was showing several centuries and generations later.

On Zerbolud 10, 3064, Quibin and Ta-Ah announced the birth of their new daughter Sisana (*Ideal*). With the birth of Sisana, the population of the Owlamites hit 200 for the first time in several millennium.

Near the end of the thirty-second century ATUT, Mahanee finally conjured up the courage to ask her question. Since her husband Zormun had been killed in the Teltermak War, she had been alone. She wondered if she could find a new mate. Soolchakan was rather surprised and confused. He informed her that she did not have to ask. Just find a man in her generation, not a blood kin brother, and she had the blessing to wed.

Mahanee picked Jee. He was more than 2,700 years junior to her, however, he was a member of the fourth generation. Mahanee always loved to have children around and in 3170 she gave birth to a son named Yunom, in 3188 she gave birth to another son named Choyatim and in 3199 she gave birth to a daughter named Sakimi. Once again it seemed that her intention was that she was going to repopulate the Owlamite nation almost by herself.

The year 3260 brought something new. Previously, there had been ten sets of twins born. On Strebale 14, Xozif and Emaseni of the Ninth announced the birth of twins. This was the eleventh set of twins, however, it was the first time that both were boys. Om of the Tenth (*Affect*) and Oss of the Tenth (*Arouse*). A few months later, Zerbolud 13, 3260, Falchon and Lemee of the Eleventh became the parents of the first member of the twelfth generation. A boy named Quoojad (*Xenolith*). Quoojad had been checked thoroughly for any inbred defects – none were found… thankfully.

The thirty-third century ended with no new nasty surprises…on or off of the planet. There were currently 481 living Owlamites.

Soolchakan was noticing that the survivor ratio that had occurred when the firestorm weapon went off was continuing with the children. The birth rate seemed to be three women to one man (odd). He was not sure if it was some preference by the women or if it was some racial phenomenon. After fourteen sets of twins had been born, only one set was two boys. There were six sets of two girls and seven sets of one each. There were three sets of triplets and of the nine children, six of them were girls. He decided to give it further study…how he was not sure, however, he was going to watch the birth rates.

The thirty-fourth century ended with a total of 606 living Owlamites.

The day was Astekoy, 28 Statichy, 3406. Soolchakan was annotating the birth of another baby girl in the eighth generation. Mok and Larfimi of the Seventh gave birth to their first child – Presha (*Faction*). The count of the living Owlamites was now at 617.

4

Bikaropin interrupted the thoughts of Soolchakan. "Excuse me, Sir, but...we have an emergency."

Soolchakan looked up somewhat surprised and baffled. "I didn't hear any klaxon or alarm. What're you talking about?"

Bikaropin sighed. "It is...not that kind of an emergency. We were out there, in High Country, looking at the dragons. We just found out that there is this rather ambitious Commander in the Dragon Force and he's the big high exalted muckity muck. He's been coming up with these edicts that have consolidated all of the factions of the Dragon Force under his direct command and control."

Soolchakan narrowed his eyes as he was listening. "Is that the biggest part of the problem? If it is, we can just do a little juggling and give back the responsibilities...from whom they were taken."

Bikaropin sighed again. "No, Sir...unfortunately it isn't. He already is the top commander in the Dragon Force. His name is Dozzbin. He's the Commander because he has the largest dragon. He has now named himself as the Commander of the Dragon Hatchery, the Dragonrider Candidate school as well as the

Ringmasters who do all of the medical evaluations and care on the dragons."

Soolchakan nodded. "So he's consolidated all of it under his command. Where is the *big* problem? What emergency is there that requires my attention?"

Bikaropin sat down in one of the chairs. "We got into his secret lair and we read some of the future edicts…that he hasn't released yet. His next step, now that he has fully established his power over all of the dragon things, will be to start getting rid of the High Council and High Courts of High Country. He will then take complete control of the entire country…with him as the top hat in all areas of government – political, economic as well as religious. He will establish a complete military, that is also a theocratic, dictatorship."

Soolchakan narrowed his eyes. "That sounds bad, but not totally disastrous…yet."

Bikaropin nodded. "He will then…begin a new program… where the Dragon Force is *not* for defensive purposes. He wants to start conquering. He'll use the dragons for offensive assault missions on the other countries in South Chilamte…and after that…who knows?"

Soolchakan groaned. "Those dragons are useless as offensive weapons. Part of the reason High Country hasn't been attacked is because all the other races on the planet think that they are *real* dragons. If that *bimyock* starts doing offensive battle with the dragons then…everyone will figure it out and…the Dragon Force is finished…and so goes our security. They can be brought down with…just about any form of large projectile weapon." He shook his head. "Let's just kill him and be done with it."

Bikaropin cleared his throat. "Sir, that might look a little suspicious. I got with Mahanee, Poolkiy, Mymin and Korpem and we think we've come up with a better alternative. We expose him, as a traitor and have the High Country Military, or civilian court, put him on trial, find him guilty, of treason, and execute him."

Soolchakan leaned forward frowning. "I'm listening."

"We've been following his activities…and we can expose him, in a roundabout way, and then…let the High Country court system do the rest."

"I said I'm listening. Let's hear the plan."

"We've been looking at what he was doing in the hatchery. He has sabotaged several of the Candidates in the hatchery, and we know how. There is another one, named Kovarin, that he's been sabotaging and…all we have to do…is make sure that this Kovarin succeeds in a good hatching…with a dragon that is larger than the one that Dozzbin has."

"That just puts that Dozzbin as second in command. That doesn't get him executed for treason and/or sabotage."

"It does if we plant all of the right evidence in just the right place at just the right time."

Soolchakan clenched his teeth angrily. "Are you planning on any fabricating of this *right* evidence?"

Bikaropin held his hands up with a big smile. "Oh no!

Nothing is going to be fabricated! That is the beauty of good and true evidence. No fabrications or it will bring a big question mark on all of the good stuff...if the fabrications are exposed. What we're going to do is put the evidence, which is real, in the right places so that it'll be found by the appropriate people at the appropriate time and then make sure that the *bimyock* gets hit with all the evidence in a manner in which...he has absolutely no defense against it. Then...he gets turned over to the executioner."

"What happens to his dragon...once he's been executed?"

"According to the law, his wife will become the main dragon handler, for that beast. She takes care of the dragon. She just doesn't go on patrols. The dragon, seeing as how he is the largest of those beasts ever hatched, will still continue on as a breeder for the rest of his life."

Soolchakan sighed. "All right. Bring in your fellow conspirators and show me all of the plan."

After listening to the plan, numerous Owlamites were put in several places to make assurances that the plot worked. They did not like the idea of any X factor coming in that could botch the entire scheme.

They knew that the Candidate Kovarin would receive the smallest egg. That had been the way that Dozzbin had always executed his plan in the past for all of his acts of sabotage. When the eggs were laid, Mahanee, Hisang and Maramee started using the methods they had learned from Bonarain, to work on the unhatched reptile inside the egg. Before the eggs were laid, they had to make sure that the smallest egg did, in fact, contain a male embryo. They had been told that the darker the dragon, the more aggressive it will be once it has fully matured. They darkened his skin as much as possible. They worked on slowing the maturing process and putting all of the emphasis on the growth of the reptile. They wanted him big, however, they did not want to get too ridiculous on his size. Seeing as how an egg hatched and made gestation a lot shorter, for an egg laying creature, they had to work quickly in order to get all of the changes in place.

Sazha went to work on one of the women who worked in the hatchery. She put thoughts in the mind of the Heyyah woman Namanti. "You adore this man Kovarin. You will do anything to help him. You like him above and beyond all of the other Candidates." She also obtained some of the thermometers that the Candidates used to keep the eggs at the proper temperature and planted the thought in the mind of Namanti that the thermometers had been obtained from other Candidates for one reason or another.

Korpem followed Dozzbin in order to make sure that the egg chosen for this Kovarin was indeed the egg that the three Owlamite women were manipulating.

Bikaropin continued searching through all of the documents in the private chambers of Dozzbin. The egomaniac was full of grudges from the past where he felt he had been wronged by others. He felt that he was so perfect and that all should listen to him because their opinions were so uninformed. They needed to shut up and listen to the wonderful words of wisdom from Dozzbin. When Bikaropin found anything that looked like something important, he immediately brought it to the attention of

Soolchakan. There were certain things they decided they would make public – at the right time for a trial – and other things that would have to be destroyed so that no one knew just how insanely ambitious, or what an evil genius, Dozzbin was.

Joz found out that there was no way that this Kovarin could possibly care for a hatchling, considering the fouled up instructions that were currently in his possession. Joz found another Candidate who had finished with the process on raising his hatchling to maturity. This other Candidate was mentally manipulated into giving Kovarin a good copy of instructions. Now Kovarin could see what was wrong and what was right and could now take care of an egg and the hatchling properly.

Shashy, Majim and Meffin worked on the personnel called "Ringmasters". These were the medical staff for the dragons. There were three primary Ringmasters and they were worked on constantly in order to keep them involved in the proper upbringing of this new *special* dragon…once hatched.

Kovarin was given the good thermometers by Namanti and was able to adjust his hatching chamber accordingly. He was given the egg the three women had been working on, and would continue working on until it hatched, placed it in the warm sand of the chamber and waited for results. He received the good set of instructions – inadvertently – and was able to adjust to these new instructions.

The day of hatching finally arrived. Mahanee had read the instructions carefully and was ready to relay the information, mentally, to Kovarin in order to assure everything would go smoothly. They did not want him to forget anything.

The Owlamite women were in the hatching chamber waiting for the new arrival to start the process. The tiny dragon pushed a hole through the shell with his right foreleg. The piece of the egg snapped out and the little claw was moving around. Mahanee, Hisang, Maramee, Mymin and Sazha were all standing there waiting for Kovarin to come in and do his duty...but... nothing. According to the instructions, the Candidate was supposed to assist the dragon in breaking out of the shell. The man did not hear the snap. He was still sitting on his bed feeling sorry for himself because the egg had not hatched...yet.

Sazha took a rock and smacked it into another one as hard as she could. This time Kovarin heard the noise. He had himself cocooned in several bedding furs and it became a rather comical situation watching him as he tried to untangle himself from the furs, to get from his room to the hatching room. He ran into the hatching room naked while still chewing on a mouthful of cheese and bread and attempting to kick the last fur, that was wrapped around his right ankle, off. He stood there for a moment staring at the moving leg of the little dark-skinned dragon. He ran back to his bedroom to retrieve the good scroll in order to figure out what to do...properly.

Sazha shook her head. "**I thought I was going to have to make a snapping sound in his head in order to get him in here.**"

Mahanee did send a mental message to Kovarin. "**Ring the bell stupid. You need some meat for the little beast.**"

Kovarin went to the bell and nearly tore it off of the wall ringing it. The Meat Cutters responded very quickly and now he had a fist-sized chunk of meat for the new hatchling. He went through all of the procedures for freeing the head and feeding the beast while the derriere of the lizard was still stuck in the eggshell and giving the ravenous thing sufficient food to make him docile enough for Kovarin to pull it completely out of the shell.

Hisang snickered. "**Congratulations you *bimyock*. You are now a Daddy…to a very hungry little carnivorous reptile**."

The five women stayed and watched as Kovarin did all of the initial things correctly. They almost had to remind him to do a few other things, however, one of the people in charge came to the door and brought some oil that the dragons were supposed to be coated in while they were young and growing.

Mahanee grunted in disgust. "**We may have to stay and assist him for the entire time. He still has a few things to learn…and should be consulting that new scroll instead of falling back on things he read in the bad scroll**."

Maramee shrugged. "**I don't think that all of us have to stay. Maybe we could do it in shifts**."

"**Excellent suggestion**," sent Mahanee. "**You get the first shift**."

Maramee gave Mahanee an obscene gesture as Mahanee grinned and Jumped out of there back to her home in the gorge.

Bikaropin reported to Soolchakan. "Much to the chagrin of this Dozzbin, our friend Kovarin has obtained a live hatchling. Believe it or not, the women made this dragon so dark, they turned him black."

Soolchakan snickered and nodded. "Black! I think they overdid it." He shrugged. "Nothing we can do about that now." He chuckled. "Black, it is." He then added this tidbit of information to his memoirs. He snickered again. There had never been a black dragon. There had been several very dark gray dragons, however, never black. This was going to be interesting.

Over the next few days there were several women who were in the hatching chamber doing everything they could to manipulate the growing dragon. They had to slow the maturation process and accelerate the growing process. It took every bit of willpower they had, however, they needed to keep this new dragon, named Diamond, growing to a point where he was the largest dragon of them all. This was all new territory for these women seeing as how they had only worked on a fetus in the womb before this. The dragon was out of the shell and the manipulations were a lot more difficult.

They definitely had over-emphasized the dark part of the dragon and he was the very first (and only) black dragon. They had been told that the darker the dragon the more aggressive he would be. They wanted this beast to be very aggressive, compared to the other male dragons. They were supposed to have stopped with a very dark brown...or gray...they did not. Diamond is a black dragon.

Dozzbin was very upset over the hatching and did not hide his anger from anyone. He also did not hide the fact that he was very skeptical of this live hatching...until Kovarin supplied the personnel in the hatchery with the hide from the first shedding of skin from the new dragon. Sounds could be fabricated. The meat could be accepted and used elsewhere. A shed skin...no one could manufacture that...except a new dragon who actually did shed the skin.

Dozzbin could not hide his fury and frustration from anybody over the idea that Kovarin had come up with a live hatching, however, he had to accept the fact that there was a living dragon in there. He was baffled as to how because he had done everything he could in order to destroy any possibility of a live hatching. He felt he had to investigate this strange occurrence. The problem was that he was not exactly sure how to do an investigation without raising any suspicions by other personnel in the hatchery. Somehow that dastard had *live* hatched a *cooked* egg and that is just impossible. What could possibly have gone wrong with the plot to shame and get rid of that Candidate?

There came a day when it was determined that Diamond was growing very fast, without totally maturing, and it would be necessary to move him to a larger chamber. The chamber he was in could handle up to a certain size of dragon. His size and the fact that he was not showing any sign of slowing in growing and had no signs of final maturing, made the move essential. The

Ringmasters drugged Diamond. While he was snoozing, he was very carefully moved to the larger chamber.

During the move, all of the upper echelon of the military, including Dozzbin, were there to get their first look at this unique *black* dragon.

After the move, Dozzbin went back to his quarters and flew into a rage. He had wanted to keep Kovarin out of the military. Now there was nothing that he could do about it because everyone had seen this unusual beast that had been hatched in that chamber and the Ringmasters had given account of everything they had done in caring for the beast.

There was the dragon…alive. The Ringmasters had confirmed that it was alive. It was a male and it was growing at a rate that would put Kovarin in the upper echelon of the military. Their system was based on the size of the dragon and not on the leadership capabilities of the Dragonrider. The entire plan that Dozzbin had worked on for years, in order to get rid of Kovarin, as well as others, was coming completely apart.

The day finally came when the Ringmasters declared that Diamond was fully mature and ready to come out. All of the upper echelon had to be there because they knew that Kovarin would be in one of the top three tiers of rank because of the size of his dragon. What the Ringmasters had not told anyone was that Diamond was large enough for *the* top rank. Everyone was expecting Kovarin to be either a Battle Division Commander or a Battle Division Sub Commander. Once the paperwork was given to the High Council members that were there to witness the new arrival finally coming out, they all realized that Kovarin was going to replace Dozzbin as the new Supreme Commander of War Forces.

Thunder was the dragon ridden by Dozzbin. Thunder was a size 51 dragon – up to that time, the only male dragon that had broken the "50" barrier. Diamond came out as a size 55. The one and only, male or female, dragon to ever grow to that size.

When Dozzbin found out that he had been bumped from the top position, he nearly burst a few blood vessels in his head as he screamed in a rage that startled all of the other male dragons in the area. The only way that he could maintain his top ranking position was if Thunder was able to fight a battle for dominance with Diamond and somehow…win.

Diamond bellowed his challenge to all of the male dragons there. He flew up out of the lower part of the canyon and faced the largest of all the male dragons in the country. Thunder was sitting on the highest perch, seeing as how he had won that place in battle with the other males. Diamond once again bellowed his challenge to the one sitting on that highest spot. Thunder bellowed back to accept the challenge. The fight was, surprisingly, very short. Diamond never gave Thunder a chance to get airborne. Diamond slammed his massive body into Thunder as he tried to takeoff and Thunder was pounded to the ground, completely beaten. Thunder was momentarily stunned. When he came to his senses, he slinked off to lick his wounds.

Diamond now bellowed at all of the other males in the area. None of them accepted the challenge because, while they did have a reptile brain, they also did remember that Thunder had beaten all of them and now they had just witnessed Thunder getting slapped down mercilessly by this huge newcomer.

After watching Thunder slink away, Dozzbin turned and went back to his quarters to sulk and fret over what the future held for him…with Kovarin as the Supreme Commander.

The next thing to happen was that Kovarin chose Namanti as his wife. This bit of information was a bit of a shock to many of the elite of High Country, however there was really nothing that they could do about it. Namanti, being rather immature and hardheaded, made the initial accusation against Dozzbin before Kovarin was ready to prepare for and make the announcement himself. It was premature, however, Kovarin was able to build a case (unknown to him that much of the information was being dumped in his lap by certain Owlamites. They were also putting things in other minds to lead them in obtaining information against Dozzbin).

The trial began. Bikaropin was able to obtain the scroll that Dozzbin had used to write his final speech for the trial. He read it and was horrified. He took the speech to Soolchakan the night before the final day of the trial along with Poolkiy, Korpem and Bak.

The younger Owlam men sat fidgeting while waiting for Soolchakan to finish reading the speech.

Soolchakan finished reading and put the scroll down. "This…*h'oolyach*…must never be presented to that court…or any court. I didn't realize...until now just how crafty, manipulative and...devilishly *intelligent* this Dozzbin is." He looked at the scroll and shook his head. "No one should be allowed to hear this stuff. There might actually be someone...in the High Court who...falls for this line of...manure."

Bikaropin nodded. "What do you suggest?"

Soolchakan hung his head. "It may take all of you, but, freeze him." He looked up. "Use every bit of mental manipulation that you can. Don't let him respond to any questions. Don't let him move. Don't let him even realize that he is *in* the courtroom. Keep his mind...dead...until after the final verdict is given." He nodded. "Once he's found guilty, of the capital offense, find one of the personnel who'll be guarding him and make sure that that person is angry and...indignant enough to stop him from saying anything." He glanced at all of the men in the room. "We may have to freeze his tongue later as well. I've been looking at this executioner that they have. He likes to read all of the information on a trial before carrying out an execution. He might be silly enough to listen to Dozzbin and...get that information back to the court."

Korpem snickered. "How about we have this executioner cut the tongue out. It would be a situation where...he decides that the condemned no longer needs a tongue because...he is going to die anyway. He is a confirmed traitor, so who cares what he has to say? Who cares if he dies with or without a tongue?"

Soolchakan nodded. "Good idea."

No one disagreed.

At the trial, it was a bit of an ordeal for the Owlamites. It took several of them, in shifts, in order to keep Dozzbin from doing or saying anything. The man was fighting against them, even though he had no clue as to what was going on. He wanted to read his manifesto as part of his defense. He was trying desperately to move or do anything. He was frozen. He could hear questions being put to him, however, he could not respond, even with facial expressions, unless the Owlamites allowed him to respond. Then it would only be generic objections to what was being said by others. Other than that, he watched the trial as if he were an uninterested observer sitting in the gallery.

Then the trial part was over. He was found guilty on all charges and was given the death penalty – several times over. Finally he was able to move and was attempting to accuse Kovarin of some kind of sorcery when he was brutally beaten into silence by others of the upper echelon of the Dragon Force. He was now going to be taken to the place of execution, without anyone listening to anything he had to say. No one wanted to listen to the words of a condemned traitor.

Dozzbin was familiar with the executioner Quong. Maybe if he could get that man to read the transcript of the trial, he could get him to listen. Upon being turned over to the Chief Executioner, Dozzbin found that his pleading was falling on deaf ears. Quong did not care to hear anything either and (surprise) ordered the tongue of the traitor to be cut out because all of them were very tired of listening to his whining complaints.

The day came for the execution. The condemned was to be dragged through a section of the surf at a very specific location on the western shore. At first, to the Owlamites, this did not seem to be much of a punishment until they observed that the specific location had a lot of huge rocks that the surf was pounding over, through and around. At high tide, you could not see most of the jagged boulders. At low tide, you could see all kinds of nasty looking rocks, great and small.

The dragons were to be used in performing the dragging. A physician was standing by to let the personnel involved know if the condemned was still alive. The physician was to check after every ten drags. This way, no one would know which had been the final fatal drag. It was not until after drag number 70 that the traitor was declared dead by the physician.

Soolchakan examined the gruesome remains himself. It had appeared from the top of the cliff overlooking the area that the man had been bouncing off of high waves. Upon closer examination, the mangled body had obviously been bouncing off of jagged rocks as well. Numerous broken bones, including the entire left side of the skull being caved in, proved that fact.

The Owlamites went back to their home in the gorge. They felt a little more secure now that the traitor was dead and could not betray anyone any more. They also felt a little sick over the spectacle that they had just witnessed.

Ten days after the execution, Soolchakan entered a new

birth into the memoirs. On 9 Zerbolud, 3406, Tamow and Nikoree announced the birth of their new daughter, Quezza (*Fancy*).

Soolchakan was hoping that Nikoree had decided on that name long before any of them had heard about that traitor or that form of execution.

5

On Statichy 11, 3449, Om and Isha of the Tenth announced the birth of twin girls. Hadree (*Linguist*) and Gazee (*Syntax*). Soolchakan was extremely curious as to why they received those names. He still did not press the issue because, again, he had stated that it was up to the mother what names the children would be blessed with...unless it was totally crazy or vulgar. Odd was okay...for the most part...maybe.

That was some of the last good news during the year 3449. Upanahy of the Ninth was murdered shortly after the birth of those twins. Upanahy was killed and gutted in the same manner as the ones who had been killed by the Teltermak some 1700 years earlier. Upanahy was only 83 years old. This began a new round of bodies that were being entombed on Zhagool.

In that same year, Ertom, Nataten, Ral, Zarni, Voyax, Ormnon, Osa, Toompaz, Quee, Veewon and Dosina were also killed. Upanahy and Ral were the only ones who were not fully mature. Ral was only 24 years old.

The next year only one child was born. 11 more Owlamites were found murdered and gutted. Dafinta was 50 years old, Oba was 45. Alero, Maktin and Soldekeran were all three over 1,000 years old. Age did not seem to matter as to who would become the next victim.

Bikaropin was doing everything he could to find any trace of those infernal mind control machines that had been used by the Teltermak the last time this sort of thing happened. He found nothing. He was also completely confused as to where the Teltermak were located. They were once again committing their heinous acts without leaving any clues as to their locations.

The year 3451 brought more tragedy. 15 more Owlamites murdered. Four of them were children.

Certain trips back to Satroco Isle had come up with nothing…at first. Now, Hisang and Poolkiy took another trip back there to check on things. They found the Teltermak potion manufacturing business was back in full operation, however, they could not find the Teltermak headquarters.

Soolchakan hopped to Spy and then Jumped to the plant. He was shaking with rage. His jaws and fists were clenched tightly. "Go," he said in a sinister way. "Bring back…several of the 456 and 459 cannons. This place will cease to exist…TODAY!"

Bikaropin pointed to several others who all vanished. They came back a while later, all carrying one of the cannons.

Soolchakan had calmed down, a little…but not much. "We are going to level this building…once and for all. They've rebuilt and modernized parts of it over the centuries. When we finish, there will be nothing left but rubble…or dust." He turned to his children. "Poolkiy, Korpem, Bak, Or, Bikaropin and Joz… take your shirts off. We're not going to damage our clothing. The women will feed us energy from the cannons...and we'll transfer that energy...through our bodies. When we're finished...I don't want to see any pile of the remains of this building that is over 50 teck high."

The six men and Soolchakan took their shirts off and faced the building. They raised their arms to their sides as the cannons were turned on, ready to use the beam to feed energy to the men. There were several other Owlamites who readied themselves to guard the perimeter with the 456 cannons.

Soolchakan took a deep breath as he ran the imagery through his head. "Are the cannons ready?"

Mahanee, Hisang, Mymin, Sazha, Shashy, Meffin and Ayino all called: "Ready!"

Soolchakan gritted his teeth. "Let's all hop to Home dimension and destroy - NOW!"

The fourteen Owlamites all hopped to Home. The cannons were fired at the men at 50% power. Huge rays shot out from the upper torso and arms of the men and the wall of the potion plant had seven large gaping holes in it. The men each turned back and forth slightly and the holes became larger. As the lower part of the wall was disintegrating, the upper part started crumbling and falling and became smaller debris as well as it fell into the beams coming from the men. All too soon the roof was collapsing down and being demolished by the beams as well.

Several Teltermak soldiers had come out of a building to the left of the plant. Zib, Judog, Daykon and Ganshim fired at the enemy with 456 cannons. The Teltermak were wearing some kind of body armor that would have protected them from normal projectile weapons. Their body armor was worthless against these rebuilt technological power cannons. The Teltermak were being cut in half before they could do anything. A few of the Teltermak saw what was happening and ran for their lives. The faster beams of the cannons cut the retreating Teltermak in half as well.

By now, everything on this side of the potion plant was nothing but dust. Soolchakan started slowly advancing while still maintaining the destructive beams from his body. The other six men followed him. Now (what was left of) the walls on the opposite side of the building were being blasted to dust as well. Any Teltermak personnel who had been inside the building were nothing but red mist, or crushed into nasty looking puddles.

There were no bodies to bury and no potion bottles – empty or full. The processing tables were gone as well. After several thousand years and several refurbishments to the building…there was nothing left to salvage. The concrete was powder and the metals were nothing but slag.

Soolchakan shouted at his children. "CUT THE POWER!"

All of the 456 and 459 cannons were powered down. Just a few moments later, the destructive power beams from the bodies of the seven stopped. The silence was rather eerie. Even in this tropical environment, the bodies of the seven men had steam rising off of their torsos.

Soolchakan looked closely at his right arm. He was a little fascinated (and somewhat mystified) with the steam. He shook his head. "We're going to go home now. We're going to send others here, to hunt down and kill, any and all Teltermak they find." He cleared his throat. "I'm very tired of any of my fellow Owlamites being food for these…monsters. Since they can't leave us alone… destroy any and all of them…every one of them…on sight!" He looked around. "No more…trying to figure out anything regarding their cuisine or the potions. Just get rid of them."

The hunt for Teltermak on Satroco Isle did not take long. By the time they were finished, they had leveled fifty-four different Teltermak villages, towns and cities and the death toll was over 900,000. They also destroyed any industry and agriculture the Teltermak had been working on in those places. Satroco Isle was now uninhabited.

The destruction on Satroco Isle did not stop the carnage. Nine more Owlamites were murdered during the year 3452 while only two children were born. The search for more Teltermak continued all over the globe.

During the year 3453 another nine Owlamites were murdered in the same fashion while three children were born. In this year, the Owlamites found three more small hidden villages on Aerisau. The 16,000 Teltermak inhabitants of those villages were eradicated.

In 3454 another twelve Owlamites murdered, only one Owlamite child born. Another seven Teltermak villages found and another 19,000 Teltermaks dead.

In 3455 another eight Owlamites murdered, three of them children. One Owlamite child was born. 11,000 Teltermaks were found and executed.

Soolchakan could not understand why the carnage continued. Why were the Teltermaks so eager to grab any Owlamite, no matter what age, pick and choose which internal organs they wanted and then continue on? Why are the Owlamites so tasty to those monsters?

In the year 3456, another twelve Owlamites murdered and only two were born.

In the year 3457, seventeen Owlamites murdered. Five of the dead were children...one of which was only three years old. Only one child was born.

The global search continued for any and all Teltermaks. They were still out there hiding and murdering and eating Owlamites.

3458 brought about more tragedy. Twelve more Owlamites, including four children. One of the children, Banabee of the Sixth, was only two years old. In 3458, only three children were born.

The hunt for revenge against the Teltermak continued. Even though the Owlamites were able to kill thousands each year, while only losing one dozen or less, the murders seemed to go on unabated.

In 3459, seven more Owlamites died, including Jee the second husband of Mahanee. Only one child was born.

Bikaropin was getting more frustrated as the murders continued. The last time the Teltermak had pulled this stunt, they had used some kind of mind controlling machine in order to attract the Owlamites to certain places. It would home in on some electronic frequency that was being used in sending or receiving telepathic messages or some kind of synapsis in the brain was affected. He tried over and over to find if any machine like that was being used again, however, all of his attempts came up with nothing. He was using all of the technology of the spacecraft they had in #45, however, none of them came up with anything useful.

In 3460, thirteen more Owlamites were killed...four of them were children. Two Owlamites were born.

In 3461, three Owlamites died. Four were born.

In 3462, seven Owlamites died. Four were born.

In 3463, eight Owlamites died. One was born.

In 3464, twenty Owlamites died...four of them children. Two were born.

In 3465, five Owlamites died. One was born.

In 3466, six Owlamites died. Two were born.

Soolchakan kept on pressing all of the living Owlamites to stay together in groups. Do everything that they could to keep from being caught alone and being murdered. It did not seem to help at all.

From 3467 to 3472, fifty-four more Owlamites were killed. Sixteen of the dead were children...including one that had just turned one year old. In that same time frame, thirty-five Owlamites were born.

In 3473, twenty-one Owlamites died. Ten were born. Soolchakan was beside himself with grief in this year. Xana of the

Seventh had given birth to Aksonia of the Eighth. Two days later, both mother and daughter were found murdered. Later that same year, Vaha of the Tenth gave birth to Quagoha of the Eleventh. Nine days later, both mother and daughter were found murdered. There was no sign of a pattern to all of this. 263 Owlamites had been killed. Over one million Teltermak had been found and executed. The slaughter continued.

By the end of that decade, the death toll was at 385 Owlamites. No Owlamite was even counting the Teltermak deaths. Kill any Teltermak without remorse or hesitation. That seemed to be what they were doing to the Owlamites.

The next decade ended with the death toll at 559 Owlamites. The number of the dead kept rising with no clue as to how they were being singled out.

The thirty-fifth century ended with the death toll at 638.

Soolchakan pulled Bikaropin off to the side. "You've got to figure out something my son. Melasenia of the Sixth has just been born. She is the first child in fourteen years. The women…and the men are tired of burying their children…especially Mahanee. Mahanee has given birth to eighteen children…of which only four are still alive."

Bikaropin gritted his teeth. "I have fathered fourteen children by Inorim and Pyree. Both Inorim and Pyree are dead… as are *all* of my fourteen children. Mahanee is not the only one who is grieving."

Soolchakan closed his eyes and hugged Bikaropin. "Yes, my son. We're all grieving. It has to stop!" He stepped back from Bikaropin. "You are the smartest one of all of us. This is why I depend on you...in almost everything." He shook his head as a tear trickled down his cheek. "Take what you need. Do what you need to do, but, try and find a way to end this horrid slaughter."

Bikaropin sighed. "I will do whatever I can. I will...look at everything...again. I will do my utmost to...stop this."

Soolchakan nodded. He walked away with his head hung down in frustration and grief.

The year 3501 was another tragic year. Twenty-two more Owlamites died.

The year 3502, another twenty-two died.

The year 3503, another seventeen died.

In the year 3504, after another seven died (bringing the death toll to 706), Bikaropin went to Soolchakan.

Bikaropin stared forward. "Great One, I need to go to Zhagool...and look at the bodies."

Soolchakan frowned. "Which ones?"

Bikaropin bit his lip. "Uhm...all of them."

Soolchakan closed his eyes and shook his head. "What good will that do?"

Bikaropin took a deep breath. "I've been reading some

things on forensic science and pathology. I read things from the Chokchakchok people, the Zizzikinza people, the Jowfoonda people...and even the Doolood. They all expressed one very important thing, in common: The body of the victim is usually the best piece of evidence. There it is...displayed...saying: Look at what someone did to me! Find what you can on me! Use it to catch the perpetrator!"

Soolchakan looked off to the side feeling a little hurt. "Do you really think that...going to Zhagool and looking at the bodies...will help?"

Bikaropin shook his head in exasperation. "I'VE GOT NOTHING ELSE! You told me to do whatever I needed to do in order to stop the slaughter. The only thing that I've got left...that I haven't looked at yet...closely...is the bodies, all the bodies!" He cleared his throat. "I know that you don't like the thought of any desecrations being done to the bodies...but...I've run out of ideas. Maybe there is...*something*...on them...that will give us a clue... any clue."

Soolchakan leaned his head back and closed his eyes. "Do it," he said quietly. He opened his eyes and saw that Bikaropin was already gone. He spoke to no one at all. "There are only 92 of us left. I pray that you find something or that we finally find the last hiding place of those wretched Teltermak...before we're all dead." He thought for several moments on what he should do now. He sighed as he gave the order that all Owlamites would be living in the auditorium. They would all be there together. They would be there until the crisis was over...all except Bikaropin. If they were using some kind of mind controlling machine, again, it should not have the range to control Bikaropin on another planet... hopefully.

Bikaropin went to Zhagool to examine the bodies on 28 Zerbolud, 3504. The remaining Owlamites were banished to the auditorium on 29 Zerbolud, 3504. The only time that anybody left the auditorium was to be on duty watching the consoles for any outworlder that might be coming in. Fortunately there had been no attacks from outer space for quite some time.

Bikaropin examined the bodies of Inorim and Pyree. He decided that if anyone wanted to complain about which corpse he chose first, the bodies of his wives would prove that he was not attempting to insult others while leaving their bodies alone. He had no siblings so he was not sure what to do next. He shrugged and picked several others at random while a few were picked specifically.

Among the specific ones were Xana and Vaha. They had been the ones who had been murdered within days of giving birth. He also examined their two baby girls, Aksonia and Quagoha... and nearly went into shock.

The smaller bodies of the babies was more telling than any other thing he had discovered. He rechecked his findings. It came out the same. He quickly checked the list of the dead. Who was how old when they were killed? He started looking specifically for the infants. He found 9-year-old Welyish...same results. He found 9-year-old Fon...same results. He found 3-year-old Uyasalli...same results. He found 2-year-old Banabee...same results. 3-year-old Issa, 9-year-old Lamal, 9-year-old Urshmon, 9-year-old Choz, 1-year-old Quendar, 2-year-old Chama, along with fifteen other children 9 and under. All came up with the same results.

He checked the list of the ones who had died in the first war with the Teltermak. He found 19-year-old Yotam and 6-year-old Banabar. Since there was virtually no oxygen in the vaults and it was extremely cold, there had been very little decomposition - mainly desiccation, so he was able to find what he was looking for…or what was absent on these two bodies. He went to the body of 25-year-old Byrib and found the same results.

He decided to check the bodies of the eldest victims of each group. Of course Kiyalee and Chyning were the ones in the first group. He found the results were the same as the young. In the second group he checked the bodies of Maramee and Mymin. Once again his worst fear was confirmed. The first group was killed in one manner – the second group was killed in a different manner. There was only one conclusion that he could come up with that explained the difference and it was horrifying.

25 Consoray, 3504, Bikaropin Jumped back to the auditorium with his findings. He was still in his spacesuit when he arrived. Everyone covered their noses because even though there was no real decomposition in the vaults, the smell of death was still there. After removing his helmet, he smelled why he was being shunned in the manner that was happening. He immediately Jumped to another place in the gorge and took off his spacesuit.

He hung it up to let it air out and, hopefully, the stench would dissipate…maybe.

He Jumped back to the auditorium and immediately went to Soolchakan. Soolchakan was waiting with all kinds of apprehension and trepidation on his face. There was even more when Soolchakan saw the look on the face of Bikaropin.

"We need to have a *very* private conversation," said Bikaropin quietly. "Use your…*power* in order to…make sure that no one is eavesdropping on us."

Soolchakan's eyes narrowed as his suspicion grew. "Why?"

"I'll tell you…when we're discussing it…privately," whispered Bikaropin through his teeth.

Soolchakan silently ordered all of the other Owlamites to not listen in or interfere with the mental communication that was about to take place between he and Bikaropin. **"All right, what did you want**?"

Bikaropin swallowed hard. **"I know that this may be hard to accept but, we have…a traitor…among us.**"

Soolchakan glared at him in horror. **"Are you absolutely certain**?"

"I wouldn't state it if I had any doubts."

Soolchakan took a deep breath trying to control his temper. **"What makes you so sure of this**?"

"It…is the way that…they were killed."

Now Soolchakan looked confused.

"I looked at the way the ones who died in that first conflict with the Teltermak...and the way the ones were killed in this second mess. They're different."

"Okay, and how is that significant?"

"In that first conflict, the victims were drawn to the Teltermak by that...mind control machine. The victim Jumped to that location...and while still mesmerized, they were stabbed somewhere in front of the throat. Death was instant, or at least it happened very quickly. In the cases of the new ones...it especially shows up on the young infants, because the stab wound appears larger...on the smaller bodies...the stab wound...is to the back of the neck. Here, death *is* instant."

Soolchakan closed his eyes and shook his head slowly. "What possible difference could that make?"

Bikaropin stared directly into the eyes of Soolchakan. "Would you turn your back on a Teltermak...under *any* conditions? No! You would not! You have no trust in any Teltermak. You would turn your back to an Owlamite because you trust all Owlamites. All of the Owlamites, who have died in this second war with the Teltermak, were stabbed in the back, because...they trusted the person that was behind them...because that person *was...or is* an Owlamite."

Soolchakan stood there feeling a little nauseous. "Why... would an Owlamite turn on all of us? Why would an

Owlamite stab...a newborn baby...in the back of the neck?"

Bikaropin shrugged. "**This person knows only one method of murdering and is good at it. Why change your method...just in case the child wants to cry out**?"

Soolchakan was feeling even sicker. All of the centuries, all of the wars and battles that he had survived. Now, a traitor in the midst. A traitor, that was among his own children. A traitor who was responsible for 706 deaths. "**How do you suggest... that I expose this...vermin**?"

Bikaropin hung his head. "**Use the** *power*. **Command all of us to tell the truth. Find the traitor that way.**" He looked up. "**That is the only way to prove, one way or another, if I am correct. I truly believe I'm correct. I hope I'm wrong...but....**" He looked up and shrugged.

Soolchakan turned and slowly walked to the front of the auditorium. He took the four steps up to the stage and slowly walked to the center. He turned to look at the faces of all that remained of the Owlamites. He cleared his throat. "There is a traitor among us...according to what I have just been told. I hope that this is wrong. I hope!" He took a deep breath. "If there is someone in here...who has...been the one murdering...your own kin...come forward...NOW!"

A woman who had been sitting as far back as she could (without giving the appearance that she did not want to be too close) stood up. She started walking towards the stage with a rather strange gait. It looked as if she was being pushed by someone and was involuntarily stumbling forward. She staggered to a point directly in front of Soolchakan. She had a very tight-lipped look of aggravation on her face.

Soolchakan stared down at her in disbelief. "Mernier...of the Eighth. What have you been doing?"

She was doing everything she could to keep from speaking.

"TELL ME, NOW!"

She shook her head, still attempting to fight against the *Power*. "I...am the one...who has...been...killing...my fellow... Owlamites." She clenched her fists and teeth in anger. She moved her head around as she was desperately trying to not give any further information.

Soolchakan wanted to jump down on her and choke the life out of her. "WHY?"

"I...want...to be...the...*Voice of...Power*...but...you're standing...in the way."

Soolchakan looked away aghast. "If I remember correctly...there are still over 90 of us who are still alive and...60 or more...of those are older than you. You'd still have to kill all of them...before you could possibly become the *Power*."

"I...distracted...all of you...by...killing...many that are younger...as well as...the older ones."

"DISTRACTION? Is that all you have to say about the killing of Aksonia? The killing of Quagoha? The only thing that either one of them had done was...dirty a few diapers...

and all you have to say about that...is...A *CHOKWAD DISTRACTION?*"

"I...could...bring them...back...from the dead."

There were several gasps of horror and shouts of anger at her last words. Soolchakan held his hands up to quiet everyone. He stood there completely baffled. He had to think for several moments in order to get the correct question out. "Do you think that you...are God? Only the Great Maker can bring someone back from the dead."

She shook her head violently in order to keep from speaking.

"SPEAK TRUTHFULLY...AND WITHOUT HESITATION! TELL US ALL HOW YOU THINK THAT YOU'RE A GOD WHO CAN BRING SOMEONE BACK FROM THE DEAD!"

She stopped shaking her head and froze. She had a strange look in her eyes. She spoke in monotone. "You have the red stone. Bonarain has the blue stone. Those two stones, when the power is combined, you can bring someone back from the dead. The people who wanted to get rid of the stones put it in their writings. The cost of bringing someone back was just too high a price for them to pay. We...the Owlamites have a way of rejuvenating ourselves. That is why we live so long. We could bring someone back and... replenish ourselves. I could bring everyone back, who is younger than I am. I would be the *Power* and I would control all of them."

"To what end?"

"I would *make* all of the women give birth more often. In

a very short time, we could have millions of Owlamites…then billions…then trillions. We have the capability of taking over this entire dimension. After taking it…we could then take over all of the other dimensions. We could control every sentient being… anywhere in any dimension."

"And you start this idiocy by…killing your own?"

"It is necessary in order to become the *Voice of Power*." She snarled as she was forced to give the information on her plan of multi-galactic, multi-dimensional conquest.

Soolchakan scoffed. "And what about the blue stone? Bonarain has been missing for…" He looked up and did some quick mental calculations. "…over twenty-three hundred and eighty years. How were you going to find her…or the stone?"

"You obviously haven't done enough…to find her. I *will* find her. I will figure out a way to find her. No matter what it takes."

"She is older than you. What were you going to do… find her and immediately kill her?"

"If that's what it takes…yes!" She angrily clenched her lips shut.

Soolchakan had his jaws clenched so tightly that they began to hurt. "TURN AROUND! FROM THIS DAY FORTH, WHENEVER YOU ARE IN MY PRESENCE, YOU WILL TURN AROUND SO THAT I DON'T EVER HAVE TO LOOK AT YOUR FACE EVER AGAIN."

She spun around.

"From this day forth...your name is now Meurtrier (Traitor)."

She once again clenched her fists. She stomped one of her feet. "GO AHEAD AND KILL ME! I'd rather be dead than... be a servant to a fool like you who...doesn't have the courage to conquer...everything...and everybody! You have the power and capability...and you do nothing. You are worthless."

"From this day forth...you will not speak in my presence. You will remain silent. You will communicate... through somebody else. I will not ever have to listen to your voice again. I will not ever listen to your thoughts, again." He looked up. "Does this vermin have any siblings? Are her parents still alive?"

Mahanee stood up. "She is an only child. She is the daughter of Korint and Hypan. Both of them are dead."

Daykon stood up. "I...am an uncle. Korint...was my brother," he said sadly. "Chena is my daughter...my only... *still* living child. Did you want...either one of us to be the...go between?"

Soolchakan sniffed. "We need to discuss some things. We need to discuss it at length...before we do anything...in judgment." He cleared his throat. "Meurtrier, you will go stand in the corner in the main room of...your apartment. You will not harm yourself in any way at all. You will not attempt any form of suicide...even starvation. You will stay in your apartment until we pass judgment on you. You are forbidden from hopping or Jumping to any other dimension or place. You will stay in your apartment and you will not go anywhere. Now…GO…to your apartment and wait to be called."

The meeting (or trial) started in the auditorium.

Mahanee stood up and shouted. "WE SHOULD KILL HER! Exterminate that monster before she can do any other harm!"

"That's exactly what she wants," said Bikaropin. "She'd rather be dead than forced to live in some kind of prison thinking about what she is guilty of and how she'll never be able to fulfill her dreams of multi-dimensional or multi-galactic conquest."

Meffin scoffed. "So how are we going to stop her…in the long run? One day she could actually be the *Voice of Power*. Then what? She would have the power to change all of that…and make all of the Owlamites her servants and soldiers…and breeders."

"These are things that we need to contemplate before deciding on her punishment," said Soolchakan. "How do we punish her? How do we keep her from getting what she wants? She prefers death to imprisonment. If she is imprisoned instead of being executed, then as you say, one day, she just might become the *Voice of Power*."

Chena stood up. "I say we go ahead and give her the death she wants! Six of my children are dead because of her."

"We still have that mystery that she was talking about," said Bikaropin. "She stated that…with the power of the red and blue stones…combined…you can bring the dead back to life. I think that we should find out about this…before we perform any form of execution."

Zirgon stood up with a frown on his face. "Where did she get the information on the stones? How could she possibly know more about them than the people who were wearing them?"

"That's a very good question," said Soolchakan. "I've been wearing this stone for several…centuries. I still don't know everything that there is to know about it. I do remember that there were some computer discs that were in the craft that we got them from but none of us could translate them. We've always been able to read minds and get translations from the spoken word…or the active thought process. A written word tells us nothing. All we see is just so much unintelligible gibberish on the screen."

Sezer snickered. He stood up shaking his head. "Then someone needs to use the *Power* to force her to tell us how she translated the written word of…whoever it was that sent the stones to you."

"No," said Soolchana. She stood there looking thoughtful for a moment. "Before we let her in on the fact that we're following through on her statements about these stones having some kind of…divine power…we should read through her computer entries and…find out what she really does know about those things."

Everyone looked at Bikaropin. He looked up at the ceiling in a disgusted manner.

"I'll go check on her computer entries," sighed Bikaropin. "I'll see what I can find. I would like…a little assistance with this…search." He looked around at other faces. "If someone would be so gracious as to render assistance."

Korpem stood up. He nodded his head. "I'll help. I'm rather curious about this phenomenon. If she is telling the truth, then…I will once again be able to be with Na-Ima and Mymin. I'll be able to…see…and talk to…the five of my children that she murdered. I will gladly render whatever assistance I can."

"Me too," said Shashy. She had a tear running down her cheek. "I've lost Bak and all *ten* of my children. Any chance of bringing them back…I'd like to be able to be a part of that."

Soolchakan nodded. "All right. Bikaropin, Korpem and Shashy will go through her archives. If there is anyone else who can assist…go ahead. Let's find out anything we can…while she is still available…for questioning. We'll render a final verdict… later."

Hisang, Meffin and Pav went with the other three as well. They wanted to find out what they could about these stones. Between the three of them, twenty of their children had been murdered by the traitor. If they could be brought back through some magic of those strange stones, they wanted to be a part of that.

The traitor had to wait for more than two months while numerous Owlamites poured over her findings on the stones. While she was waiting, because of the orders from Soolchakan (using the *Power*), the only time she left the corner in the main room was to get something to eat or go to the latrine. Other than that, she had memorized every single nuance of the wall in front of her. She had no choice in the matter – the *Voice* had ordered her to stand there and wait. Stand, not sit. No matter how tired her legs became, she had to stand there doing nothing but…staring at a wall that was totally memorized. Wait for the final verdict while doing no harm to herself. Each day, her anger and hatred grew even more, however, there was nothing she could do, other than scream herself hoarse from frustration. The *Voice* had given a command. She, as an Owlamite, had no choice but to obey. The power she wanted was eluding her completely…and there was nothing she could do about it.

While all of the curious ones looked at the meager information, translated from the discs, on the stones, Bikaropin also looked at the information on the swords. After looking at this information he went to Soolchakan. "What *exactly* do you know…about the swords, Great-Grandfather?"

Soolchakan frowned. He looked down at the scabbard that was belted to his right leg. He loosened the leather thong that held the sword in the scabbard, took hold of the hilt and pulled it out. Immediately, everything in the room took on a red hue. The only colors that could be seen were different shades of red. "This is what I know," he said calmly. "I've been to some places… where they see the scabbard on my side and…some ruffian wants to challenge me to…who knows what." He chuckled. "As soon as I pull it out and everything turns red and the see the length of the blade, they've always backed down…or should I say they end up running away in terror. None of them want to mess with a magical weapon." He chuckled. "A weapon they know nothing about. Funny thing is, I don't know that much about it myself. I just let them run off in fear from the red hues."

Bikaropin looked a little nervous. "Have you ever used it against any opponent?"

Soolchakan huffed. "I haven't used it at all. I don't know what kind of properties it might have. I don't even know if it could cut hot butter."

Bikaropin let out a sigh of relief. "Please don't use it!"

Soolchakan was confused. "Excuse me? What for? Why not?"

Bikaropin shook his head. "I hate to explain it to you but… please…don't use that thing…against any opponent or…even to attempt cutting hot butter. Just *please*…don't use it at all. Put it back in the scabbard…and leave it there."

Soolchakan was now a little perturbed. "Explain yourself. Why should I *not* use it at all?"

Bikaropin sighed. "It…is difficult to explain….but I'll try. The stones, they represent good while the swords represent evil. They are opposing forces. You, Bonarain, Kiyalee and Chyning used the stones all the time for one reason or another. I don't remember any of you ever using the blades. The more you use the stones, the more control you have over them. The swords, however, cannot be controlled. They would control you. As long as you keep using the stones – not the swords – you keep your power over both. If you ever use the swords…they will start controlling you."

Soolchakan nodded. "As I recall…the ship that they were

on…was heading directly into our star Holgotho. If we hadn't intercepted that ship…it would have flown directly into the star and, with all of the stones and swords aboard and…"

"And it could have been catastrophic for all."

Soolchakan was totally confused. "How so?"

"The people who wanted to get rid of those things…were terrified of what the consequences would be if they destroyed them in their own star system. That's why they sent the ship into a star system they were unfamiliar with. If they destroyed that star system…it should not affect their home planet."

Again Soolchakan scoffed. "Four *chokwad* little stones and four *chokwad* little swords could…are you saying that they could have destroyed something…as large as a star? The star Holgotho?"

"That was the fear of the people who programmed that ship. They put the computer discs inside that ship to…if anyone did intercept that ship, they would probably have enough technology…to be able to translate the discs and…realize the danger of those swords."

Soolchakan nodded. "So…why not just destroy the swords and keep the stones?"

"No! That would leave the stones…unopposed. They are good and evil…in balance. Take away one and…the other one runs rampant."

Soolchakan sat gawking at Bikaropin. "Good running rampant. What's so bad about that?" He scoffed in disbelief.

"Then...we would have no point in...living...or doing anything. Everything is so bright and shiny and good. Everything is nice...and *boring*. Part of life is overcoming problems. That's one thing that makes you feel alive and good about yourself. If during your life...you never face any evil...there is no victory. Just...boredom and...no reason for any ambition of overcoming because...there's nothing to overcome. You become flaccid and lazy...stagnant."

Soolchakan cleared his throat. "So...by using...only the stone...I am overcoming the evil of the sword."

Bikaropin nodded. "To put it simply - yes." He frowned. "Uhm...where are the yellow and green stones and swords?"

Soolchakan looked down at the floor. "I buried them with Kiyalee and Chyning. I had no idea that...they might become more useful...for any reason."

"At least you know where to find them...if we need them."

Soolchakan sighed and nodded. "Yes."

"We're still working on translating the rest of what is there. Me...uh...the traitor was able to do a lot of translating. It is difficult to comprehend because...there are 34 different characters. 27 of them...we guess are consonants and the other 7 are vowels. We have no way of knowing...which one had what phonetic sound. She translated some of it, but there is, still, a lot more there and...I don't know if we can do it...without her help."

"You're not gonna get her help," said Soolchakan angrily through his teeth. "She cannot be trusted...with anything...ever again. I don't want her to have any knowledge of being *needed* to assist us in any way."

Bikaropin shook his head and held up his hands in surrender. "No objections."

After a lot of deliberation and decision making, the rest of the Owlamites were ready to hear the punishment of Meurtrier. Bikaropin, Korpem and Majim had been busy building the jail that she would be kept in, for life.

Soolchakan took a deep breath. "Some of this may be repetition but…I don't care. If it is repetitious…so be it. If it is not repetitious…then it needed to be said." He bit his lip. "Bring the traitor in."

Poolkiy, Korpem and Daykon brought her into the auditorium, backwards. She had to have her back to Soolchakan at all times because of his order. Soolchakan stood on the stage staring off into space as she was brought to the front. They stopped directly in front of Soolchakan.

Soolchakan smiled. "From this day forth, you Meurtrier… will be on your knees when you are in my presence."

She immediately dropped to her knees with a look of total hatred and anger on her face. She was obeying, however, she did not have to like it.

He started in on the written orders. "You are forbidden from doing any form of dimension hopping. You are forbidden from any form of Jumping. You are forbidden from attempting any form of suicide, including starving yourself to death. You are forbidden from harming yourself in any way at all. From this day forth, you are banished to a special ship in dimension 45. This will be your new home...for whatever length of time you have left to live. You are forbidden from sending any telepathic messages. We will be able to read your mind, but you will not read ours. You claimed that you would rather be dead than spend the rest of your life as a prisoner. Too bad! The only way that you will be executed is if...by some tragic event, you get too close to being the *Voice of Power*. Currently you are number 70 in line for the *Power*. If you ever get to 20 or less...then, and only then will I consider your execution. You will never obtain the Power as long as I have anything to say about it. You will live alone in your prison. We will observe you, but we will not talk to you. You are totally alone...for the rest of your worthless life."

She heard all of the orders and now the thoughts went through her head about how, now even more, she hated Soolchakan and everything he stood for.

Daykon was reading her mind, listening to the vitriol that was going through it. He sent a private message to Soolchakan. **"She hears you and hates you."**

Soolchakan smiled. **"Good. Let it eat at her."** He chuckled. "The ship that you are banished to has plenty of food, water...and sleeping quarters. You will live there without harming yourself for the rest of your life...alone. Someone may come and check on you from time to time but...don't think that we're going to get soft on you." He took a deep breath and steeled himself for some questions. "When you killed your own, why did you make it look as if the Teltermak did it?'"

Daykon shook his head. "She was selling...body parts... to the Teltermak."

"Why?"

Daykon shrugged. "Because they wanted them."

"FOR WHAT?"

"She doesn't know. All she knows is that those were the organs that they requested. Anything else...no interest at all."

Soolchakan sighed. "So that's why it looked as if the Teltermak were doing it. They got what they wanted." He was totally revolted by the thought. "They've become picky eaters...in their old age. They look at us as if we were some kind of walking buffet." He sighed and shook his head. "Daykon, take her to her prison."

Daykon grabbed Meurtrier and the two of them vanished. A few moments later, Daykon reappeared. "It is done."

Soolchakan nodded. "Then we are finished here. Everyone...back to living your lives...as you see fit. One exception to that rule...No more acts of treason. No one will ever even think about committing treason against us. If anyone wants to think about it...get that stuff out of your mind...RIGHT NOW!" He cleared his throat. "Have a nice day." He Jumped back to his apartment.

Meurtrier walked every hall of the ship she was on. She walked through screaming. The only thing she was shouting was how much she hated Soolchakan. She screamed herself hoarse as she listened to the echo of her own voice. Nothing else filled her mind at this time other than total hatred for Soolchakan and all of those who backed him. She had failed in her attempted coup and she had failed in being executed as well. She felt now that she was a total failure in everything and the only one to blame was Soolchakan. It never occurred to her that she was the maker of her own mess. Like any bully or ambitious tyrant, they always believe that they are totally in the right and if anyone disagrees, how dare they commit such an atrocious act? The bully is never wrong, it is always the victim that is to blame.

6

Every last one of the remaining Owlamites started looking at and studying this written language from that strange rogue spacecraft. No one was able to glean any other information about the legacy or capability of the stones or the swords. The traitor, it seems, was the one and only real expert on translating the written language and none of the other Owlamites wanted to give her any impression that they needed her assistance in anything. It just might make her believe that she was useful again. That was not going to happen.

Soolchakan read the part about the combination of the red and blue stones bringing back life. According to what he was seeing, that part was translated correctly, however, for some reason the other words in the other areas could not be so easily converted. He was beginning to wonder if the Traitor had just made that entire thing up or if it was really true. Until Bonarain and the blue stone were found, none of that mattered. There was no way of really checking any of this alleged divine, and incredibly strange, power of the stones.

Even if the body of Bonarain was found with the blue stone, who would he trust with the blue stone...or the yellow or the green? Mahanee was currently the second eldest living

Owlamite. Her daughter Hisang was third, while her son Poolkiy was fourth. If the blue and red were able to bring Kiyalee and Chyning back to life, would Hisang and Poolkiy then surrender the yellow and green stones back to their original owner...if they had been loaned in the first place? Soolchakan scoffed. Of course they would return them. If he had to use the *Power* in order to make them return the stones, the stones would be returned. Still, where was the blue stone? Where was the body of Bonarain? Is she dead or...alive or...?

After several years of fruitless searching of the strange texts, Soolchakan changed his mind about what they should be doing.

"All of us who are still here, still alive, start searching the entire planet. Anywhere that you can think of, search it. Look for any remaining Teltermak. Find them and destroy them. I'm tired of being constantly harassed by those monsters. They want us for food. I don't understand why they find us so tasty, but I'm completely fed up with their nasty ways. We are not livestock for their ghastly cuisine. They've been a constant nuisance to us since...that wretched firestorm weapon changed both of us...and many others on the planet. Seek out and destroy all Teltermaks. If you find a clutch of them that is too big for you to handle by yourself, call for help. All assistance necessary will be given in order to remove this pestilence from our lives without any remorse. We will still have shifts done here in the monitor room. We still have to scan the skies for outworld intruders. The rest of the time we will spend on eliminating the worst enemy that we have ever encountered."

With that, all but four Owlamites started the quest for the elimination of all Teltermaks. They took shifts in the watch room, scanning the skies, however, the quest to find all Teltermaks was the important issue at this time.

On the Aerisau continent, they found several communities of Teltermak in the northern wastelands of Tuvalow. Once again there were some of those potion plants. These plants were idle because they were currently short of that mysterious "critical ingredient" in order to continue manufacturing. There were some potions stored in a cooler...which were immediately confiscated. After the Owlamites were finished "removing" the citizenry and destroying the manufacturing plants, no ingredient, critical or otherwise, was important in these places ever again.

In the year 3818, an outworlder was spotted coming into the star system. Soolchakan initially wanted to just blast all five of the ships out of existence. Bikaropin informed him that some new technology would not hurt their inventory of "obtained" ships sitting in dimension #45.

All Owlamites went to see the five ships who were currently inventorying the vast mineral wealth of Bri (big surprise). After some quick perusals of the computer logs of the command ship, they found that this was an initial survey team that was coming here to conquer. After allowing them to send out a distress signal, that they were being attacked by forces unknown, all five ships were hopped to #45 and all crew members were "dismissed" in the appropriate manner. Now while Bikaropin studied the new technology, all the others went back to the elimination of the Teltermak.

There were small communities of Teltermak found on the Cifpasica continent along with North and South Chilamte. From 3504 till 3990, they found scattered small communities all over the globe. Each one was voided of all Teltermaks. By the year 4000, it was determined, hopefully, by all that they had eliminated the pestilence forever because they could not find any other communities that had seen or heard of Teltermak.

All of the Teltermak technology that had been found was confiscated and moved to some of the large Chokchakchok ships in #45. Those seemed to be the only ships large enough to hold all of that equipment. Now, Soolchakan was satisfied that the Owlamites were the only ones left on the planet who had sophisticated technology. All of the times that outworld invaders had attacked, they had always attacked any technology first. All of those attacks had literally blasted the vast majority of the planet back into pre-industrial and pre-electric times. Apparently the thickened rock in the gorge had shielded the Owlamite community from being explored by most of the outworld intrusions and was relatively safe…from most invaders.

After some study of all Teltermak technology and finding that it was somewhat inferior to anything that the Owlamites had obtained from outworlders, Bikaropin went to have a conversation with Soolchakan.

"Great Grandfather, now that we can't find any more

Teltermaks and...we're back to watching no one but possible outworlders...do you think that...we might be able to build up our population again?"

Soolchakan was a little surprised by that comment. "What was stopping us from procreating before?"

Bikaropin chuckled nervously. "It would have been a little difficult enough for...the women to...perform their searches...in third trimester. For any of the women...or men for that matter, to take care of a newborn...or child for...some 90 years would have been a great inconvenience."

Soolchakan hung his head. "It seems that...once again, I have somehow, inadvertently slowed our progress of repopulating."

Bikaropin shrugged. "No one faults you. The Teltermak have been a horrible threat to us...since long before any of us were born. They continually caused us no end to grief. You did give the orders that our top priorities were to scan the skies for outworlders and kill Teltermaks. Now that we can't find any more of them... we can move on."

Soolchakan shook his head sadly. "It is the year 4004 ATUT...and there are only 91 of us still living."

Bikaropin swallowed hard before making his next comment. "Yes, but...if we ever do find...the blue stone...and... Bonarain...then...who knows what the future holds?"

Soolchakan sighed. "If that part is true."

The next year in 4005 twelve new babies were added to the population. In 4006 Eighteen were born, in 4007 nineteen, in 4008 eleven and in 4009 three more. Just like that there were suddenly sixty-three very young babies all crying, playing and screaming in the gorge hallways. Soolchakan decided they were off to a good start…again…hopefully.

Mahanee, being the one who wishes to be the perpetual mother to as many children as can possibly be born, has now lost Zormun in the Teltermak War and Jee in the Traitor's War. Since Soolchakan decreed that you can only mate with others in your generation, she now turns to Bikaropin. He is her third husband and she is his third wife. Now, once again, Bikaropin has a living child.

Now came an era of watching all of those small babies turn into toddlers, then children, then adolescents and then adults.

The next children were not born until the year 4112. This was a bit of a celebration because two children born that year and they were the first two members of the thirteenth generation. Quinpar of the Twelfth married the twin sisters Betona and Bekona of the Twelfth. Betona gave birth to a son Moloter (*Event*). Bekona gave birth to a son Rotom (*Depth*).

Soolchakan was still wondering about how some of the mothers were coming up with the names for their children. He knew that they did not like the idea of taking a name that someone else already had. This is understandable…but…Depth? What was she thinking of when she named her son Depth? He would let her explain it to the child.

Citendali 17, 4160, another child was born. Noela of the Fifth gave birth to a girl she named Minnar (*Finest*). For

Soolchakan it was a little bittersweet holding the new baby girl in his arms. If Bonarain, Kiyalee, Chyning and all of the others were still alive, Minnar of the Sixth would be Owlamite number 1,000. Instead, with what was left over, she made just over 200 Owlamites that were still living.

Zerbolud 4, 4234 ATUT, a new generation was born. Moloter and Finacha of the Thirteenth, announced the birth of their son Rissokap (*Resolution*). He became the first member of the fourteenth generation.

Soolchakan, again, made a point of holding each new baby in his arms. He did not want a repeat situation like the one that the traitor had pulled on them. As he held each child he gave each one an order (coming from the *Voice of Power*). "You will never betray us. You will always remain loyal to the Owlamites that surround you."

At this same time, Bikaropin came up with a new idea. He had been studying the logbooks from the different outworld races. One of them discussed the use of trackers that were imbedded under the skin of their people. He had been using the mind reading ability. This was technological and could be done by a computer doing redundant checks any time of the day or night. That way they would know where each individual was and it would also send information on their condition. In the past, each time one of the Owlamites had been murdered, only Soolchakan had a general idea of where the victim was and once they arrived at the location they had to search for the body. These trackers could identify exactly where the body was. He gave this information to Soolchakan. After a few days of contemplation, Soolchakan allowed the "planting" of the trackers…as long as the program was changed to where only the Owlamites could find them. Bikaropin and a few others did some reprogramming and soon everyone had a tracker placed under their skin…in a place where the Teltermaks did not go to in order to obtain their favorite parts…just in case there were still some more Teltermaks out there.

On Whegire 25, 4341, Soolchakan once again had the pleasure of welcoming a new generation to the existence of the Owlamites. Rissokap and Okasan of the Fourteenth generation announced the birth of their daughter Osakisha (*Unmixed*). He contemplated the fact that this was Osakisha of the Fifteenth and because of the Teltermak and the traitor, she was only number 412 of the current living Owlamites. He prayed for peace and long life for all remaining Owlamites as he gazed into her big blue eyes.

Another new century had started. In the year 4502, Soolkan and Minnar of the Fifth announced the birth of the fourth set of triplets born to an Owlamite family. Junna, Aseki and Entazi, (three girls) were welcomed to the Owlamite world.

In the year 4526, Ohway and Osakisha of the Fifteenth became the parents of the first member of the Sixteenth generation. Tulivren 10, 4526, a boy named Iomyon (*A Cut Above*) was born. Soolchakan wondered how many more generations he would personally get to see. Bonarain was missing. Kiyalee and Chyning were dead. All of the second generation was dead. Meffin was the only one left of the third generation. More and more he hated the Teltermak...and the traitor...and what they had done.

In the year 4811, Iomyon of the Sixteenth, was grabbed as husband by the twin sisters, Shadeess and Shadazh. On Inamyon 28, 4811, Shadeess gave birth to a son she named Sondomon (*Executive*). Four days later, on Consoray 2, 4811, Shadazh gave birth to a son named Fulyom (*Administrator*). The seventeenth generation was here now.

The skies above remained empty of any enemies for a long time. Several of the Owlamites were getting a little upset over having to constantly rebuild and rework some of those spaceships in #45, however, they finally realized that if they did not rejuvenate those ships, then they would be back in ancient times just like the rest of the planet. They had become a little spoiled with the technology they had and did not care to do things manually, the way the rest of the planet performed their tasks.

The other thing that the Owlamites were doing was procreating. By the end of the year 4841 ATUT, the count stood at 2,239. Even though they had been going strong for several years, Soolchakan was still a little apprehensive about anyone getting complacent.

Then it happened. Bikaropin set off an alarm. The tracker that had been implanted in Queluck showed no signs of life. It also showed that he was located on the southeast peninsula of

North Chilamte. No one had a clue as to why he would be there.

Somehow, the trackers were not doing their job and Owlamites were being murdered again.

Twenty Owlamites, including Soolchakan, went to the location. Their worst fears lay there in a gory display. Queluck had been gutted in the same manner as all of the other victims of the Teltermak. Either the scourge was still alive or someone else was taking over the cannibalistic horrors of the Teltermak.

Queluck of the Thirteenth – born 4526…and murdered in 4842. He was a mere 316 years old…and the newest victim.

There was very little to celebrate during the year 4842. By the end of the year, four new Owlamites were born…and one hundred had been murdered in the Teltermak fashion.

Soolchakan continued in his new form of burial. No more funeral pyres. Instead he continued making a graveyard out of the huge vaults they had manufactured in the large moon Zhagool. It was getting rather crowded in some of them.

What he found thoroughly disgusting was that the Teltermak did not care who they killed. Piyashilla had disappeared with her two-year-old daughter Jamyliyma. Both bodies were found together…gutted. Mother and child were buried in the same coffin on Zhagool. There were four other very young children killed that year: One aged six, one aged twelve and two aged thirteen. Each one was killed along with their mother. Soolchakan was torn as to what he should do. It was the mother who had been lured away by…WHOM? Do you tell the children to disobey the parents…if they are going somewhere…and you are not sure where it is? The mother took the child and both get killed.

The trackers were working...somewhat, however, by the time the Owlamites were able to respond, the Teltermak had escaped with their...*treasure* (?). Bikaropin and a few others were working feverishly to find a way to speed up the process. Find a way to respond faster and maybe they could save a few lives.

The year 4843 was even worse for the Owlamites. Only two Owlamites were born while 111 of them died at the hands of the elusive Teltermak. Once again, six children under the age of 20 ended up being butchered with their mothers.

The year 4844 brought more tragedy as Bikaropin and others still tried to figure out a quicker response time to people Jumping somewhere else, only to be slaughtered. Only five Owlamites born that year while 102 were killed. Once again Soolchakan had the heartbreaking misery of burying four infants with their mothers and 26 more who were still children.

The year 4845 saw only six Owlamites born and 105 slaughtered. They were losing ground very quickly...again. This year they started searching the planet using what was left of their spy satellites. They knew what the Teltermak machines looked like. The machines that somehow were able to control the mind of one Owlamite at a time. Control that Owlamite in a manner that made them Jump to a certain location and just stand there while they were murdered. This turned up nothing. Apparently the Teltermak were able to somehow disguise the machine so that they were not able to see it from the skies.

The year 4846 was no better. Six Owlamites born and 106

killed. There seemed to be nothing that could stop or even slow the Teltermak from what they were doing…and how they were doing it. Nothing seemed to be working. This year was especially bad for Soolchakan. He had to bury thirteen infants on Zhagool. Every single one of them tore at his heart. He made several edicts, telling his people to not listen to…whatever the thing was that called them out. Even the *Voice* could not stop the massacre. He was feeling completely helpless against this overly persistent archenemy who somehow still existed and was completely hidden from detection by any and all means available.

The year 4847 came with only four new Owlamite babies and 102 killed. Soolchakan was a little puzzled at the women who, in spite of the risk, became pregnant during this war.

The year 4848 brought some puzzling things. There were several of the Owlamites who were attempting to see if there was a pattern to the people who were being taken. This year began with the normal horror of Panamishi (age 32) being the first one taken. This was followed by three unwed adults between the ages of 141 and 149. Then Gami (age 61). Then two more unwed adults, ages 130 and 133. The system was then blown when the next eight victims were two mothers with infants and four very young children. Then five unwed adults, ages 120 to 137, followed by a 76-year-old, followed by four more unwed adults, a 76-year-old, seven more unwed adults, followed by ten who were in their seventies. The rest of the murders were just as hard to figure out the rest of that year. There was no pattern. All totaled, the Owlamites gained 3 and lost 105. The tragedy continued on and on.

The year 4849 was no better. Five Owlamites born and 109 murdered. That made a total of 35 born and 840 lost in the eight years that this mess had been going on. There was no good news from their own scientific means of tracking or preventing any of the mess.

The year 4850 ended with no new results. Eight Owlamites born to 108 being murdered. Totals: Less than 45 born during the war and over 945 dead. One thing that looked like it was a kind of a pattern was the oddity of generations. Very few members of the fifteenth generation died. Of the sixteenth and seventeenth generation...no one had died. All of the dead were from four through fourteen. No one could figure out why the newest generations were being left alone...but no one was keeping any positive thoughts about it either. The only other thing that appeared to be a pattern was the fact that the number of deaths always quit after just over 100 – not really helpful. The Teltermak could strike from anywhere at any time.

4851 was a really lousy year. Zero new births and 103 deaths. Ten years of this nonsense and the Teltermaks were winning on all fronts.

Bikaropin gave Soolchakan a furtive glance. "I was wondering...if you've ever considered..." He stopped and cleared his throat nervously. "...what the...traitor said? What would be...the possibility or...probability of us...taking over in all of the dimensions?"

Soolchakan smiled. He walked over to Bikaropin and

backhanded him. He knew that he had hurt Bikaropin because his hand was throbbing from the strike. He did everything he could to keep Bikaropin from knowing that his hand was hurting – badly. "ARE YOU CRAZY? Do you have any idea what would have to happen? I would have to tell all of the women to start squirting out babies...EVERY YEAR! Yes, in a few centuries we could have billions of Owlamites...all over the place. We could take over...all kinds of planets and...cultures and...peoples. To what end? They become our slaves. They'd hate us. They'd serve us but they'd hate us and are constantly looking for a way to defeat us. Meanwhile, while we have them doing everything for us...we forget how to do it for ourselves. The bigger our expansion...the bigger our problems." He huffed. "And...all things considered, just exactly HOW do you suggest that we take over...in multiple dimensions...WHEN WE CAN'T EVEN FIND THOSE *CHOKWAD* TELTERMAKS ON OUR OWN HOME PLANET?!" He huffed again. "Over 13,800 years since the firestorm weapons changed us...and at least twenty-five generations prior to that... fighting the Teltermak. We're still fighting them! The ones that we're not fighting are the ones that we completely killed off... like the Axswain." He shook his head. "NO! I do *not* want to take over multiple dimensions because the bigger the empire - the bigger the headaches." He walked away grunting in disgust. "No thank you."

Bikaropin stood there rubbing his swollen cheek. He shrugged. "That's as good an answer as...any." He left the room.

Mahanee saw him in the hallway. "Did you get your question answered?"

He smiled weakly and rubbed his cheek. "Absolutely," he said flatly. "No more questions."

She smiled. "Good."

4852...eleven years and the Teltermak were still completely elusive. Only one new birth this year compared to 108 deaths. There was very little joy among the Owlamites as they kept on with their efforts to thwart the mysterious way in which the Teltermaks were luring Owlamites to their deaths. They had gone back to the original machines that had been used in order to find out...something. They were no help at all.

4853 showed no signs of the Teltermak letting up. This year had four births and another 109 deaths, bringing the totals, since the war started, 50 births and 1,268 deaths. Some were not calling it a war because, so far, everything had been very one-sided. An idea had been rolling around the halls that suggested that everyone should report in before they were going to make a Jump or a Hop. That way, if your internal transmitter gave different readings then that would be an indication of something wrong. It sounded like a good idea, however, there were still too many people to keep track of in all of their comings and goings. It did not help. Morale was sinking lower and lower.

4854 gave the Owlamites their first success at firing back. Veven noticed an uncalled Jump by Kiksama. She called it in and numerous Owlamites responded. They were too late to save her life, however, they caught the Teltermak in the act of butchering her. Soolkan, Pelox, Zuztay and Zenkin showed up first and sent five of the Teltermak butchers to different dimensions. Three of them ended up in #2 in the void of space. One ended up in #3 in the void of space. The fifth one ended up spending his last moments, vomiting to death, on the Stink planet.

Even though the father of Kiksama was dead, Kishay the mother was still alive and was able to extract a little revenge by destroying all of the butchering equipment that the Teltermak had brought with them. Bikaropin obtained another (newer form) of the mind machine used to lure Owlamites. He was not able to check on how it performed because the battery was burned out and he never did figure out how to replace this (unique and unusual) foreign form of a battery. The only satisfaction there was that now there were finally some Teltermak casualties and that they had not been able to obtain their vulgar prize…in this case.

The Owlamites were able to get to six other butcher jobs that year. Each one had more armed Teltermak guards who were trying to keep their people from being killed (and mysteriously vanishing along with their equipment). All butchers and guards ended up, floating in outer space, in various dimensions. Each time the Owlamites were able to confiscate more butchering equipment and mind machines. The curious thing was that in each and every case, the batteries were all burned out. They were never able to see the horrid machines in operation.

The year 4854 saw no new births. The usual 108 deaths did occur.

The year 4855 saw one Owlamite birth…and 109 deaths. Because of some people paying more attention to the monitoring of the Jumps, more Owlamite personnel were able to get to the slaughter sites very quickly. They were able to kill the Teltermaks at the scene and, in most cases, recover the Owlamite body, intact. The goal, which had not been reached yet, was to get there before the murder took place. They had not achieved that yet. What the Owlamites had achieved was that the body count of dead Teltermak was rapidly approaching the number of Owlamite dead. This did not bring anyone back to life, however, it gave some satisfaction in that the Teltermak were now suffering great losses as well.

The year 4856 saw one Owlamite birth and 110 deaths. It also had a bit of an awakening for the Owlamites. The Teltermak had to change some of their tactics in order to do their hunting. First, they put some snipers overlooking the butchering point. Those were found and taken care of with very little problem. Second, they revealed how they had been able to get away from the disembowelment points. They had watchers (and snipers) sitting in the conning tower of submersibles that were close to the shore. A great lack of imagination, and just pure anger, had not allowed the Owlamites to see that *all* of attacks had occurred on a beach area. It did not matter where the beach was, island, continent or a lonely sandbar - always on a beach. Even Bikaropin was embarrassed at not realizing this information before. Now, they were able to make the attacks even more expensive for the Teltermak when the submersibles were hopped into #45 as well. There were airtight compartments in the submersibles, however, that was a miniscule problem for the Owlamites – just let the monsters suffocate as their oxygen dwindled to nothing while floating helplessly in space.

The year 4857, again, saw only one Owlamite birth with 106 deaths. The Owlamites were getting better at showing up at the scene of the crime, just in time to keep the Teltermaks from obtaining their gruesome bounty. They Jumped to the location in Spy dimension, did a full reconnaissance of the area, found the snipers and any escape route, be it by land or sea…and then struck with passionate vengeance. It was becoming a very expensive undertaking for the Teltermak, but for some reason - they were relentless.

The year 4858 and the horror of the war drags on. One Owlamite born this year and 112 dead. The response time to the murder scene is getting somewhat better, however, they still have not been able to stop any killings.

The year 4859. Zero new Owlamites and 105 dead. Even with all of the equipment and personnel that the Owlamites have taken from the Teltermak, the murders go on unabated…and there is still no reason as to why they are so hungry for Owlamite flesh while leaving other races alone.

4860 has one new Owlamite and 112 murdered. Total Owlamite dead so far: 2030. The frustration tears on.

The year 4861 was not going so well. Soolchakan had just finished placing the body of Chadash of the Ninth in a tomb on Zhagool. She was victim number 52 so far this year. None of the women were pregnant so there was no chance of any new children this year. He could not blame them. The previous year when Kaluka of the Tenth had been mesmerized by the Teltermak, she had Jumped to the…location…with her two-year-old daughter Qualkipiy. The Teltermaks slaughtered both without hesitation.

He felt a sudden twinge in the back of his head. He winced. It was not painful, it was just surprising and rather uncomfortable. He shook his head and sniffed and thought no more of it. Then it happened again. Again he winced. He wondered if after some 13,900 years, his age might be affecting him somehow. The twinge happened again and again he winced.

Dawuni and Pinsong were nearby, both looking a little puzzled.

Dawuni spoke first. "Soolchakan…what *are* you doing?"

He looked at her equally puzzled. "What…are *you* talking about?"

She came toward him. "Three times you closed your eyes and all three times…that red stone of yours…lit up."

He looked at her skeptically. "Are you sure?"

Pinsong nodded. "Yes, it did. I saw it too."

He held the stone up and frowned as he stared at the translucent stone. He looked up at the two women and cleared his throat. "What kind of joke are you trying to play on me? It won't work."

Pinsong put her fists on her hips. "We're not joking! It happened!"

Dawuni nodded. "It did."

He stared back at the stone. The twinge hit him again. This time he was staring at the stone. This time he did not close his eyes when he winced. Now he saw it glow. The glow lasted the same amount of time as the twinge. Now he sat there staring awestruck at the stone.

Pinsong snickered. "Did you see it that time?"

He just nodded – still a little dumbstruck.

Dawuni clicked her tongue. "So, what does it mean?"

He shook his head. "I wish I knew. I...don't remember... anything like this...ever happening before. I don't know what... is going on...with me or the stone."

Pinsong looked a little shocked. "It's your stone...and you don't know what that thing is doing?"

Another twinge hit him. This time it was longer. The stone still glowed brightly, however, now he was getting some kind of image in his head. The imagery was like a bad dream. If it was true, somehow, the Teltermak were now using their machine to call him and this stone seemed to be protecting him. He tried to think of the names of people who were still alive. Then he made a different decision. **"All Owlamites everywhere. This is Soolchakan. I need you to...get your weapons and... come to the main auditorium...now."** He Jumped back to his apartment and retrieved his pulse pistol. He Jumped to the main auditorium.

People started appearing in the room. They were all Jumping in to their place in order to keep from hitting anyone else as they Jumped in. They all headed to seats as soon as they arrived.

Soolchakan could have cried. They barely filled the first five rows. Before this new mess with the Teltermak, there were over 2,000 Owlamites. Now there were just over 200. He steeled himself for what he needed to do. Twice while he was waiting for everyone to get seated, he had twinges. Both times the stone lit up - everyone noticed. He walked up onto the stage and addressed the remaining Owlamites.

"My children, I think…that the Teltermak have tuned in to *my* brain. I'm getting images…of where they are." He held his red stone up. "Somehow…this stone is protecting me from being under the power of their evil machine. I'm going to hop to Spy… and go there. This time, it doesn't seem to be a beach. It seems to be…some kind of cave or cavern." He looked around. "Mahanee and Hisang…you two are the oldest. You'll go with me. You'll find some landmark…in that place. You then come back here… and bring some others. It just might be in their main sanctuary. I guess that they've stopped attacking us on the beaches because it became too expensive for them. If it is a sanctuary…we can crush them. Crush them…there! In their own home. Maybe we can find…something that will help us find the rest. During the last twenty years, we've killed over 1,500 of those…parasites. Maybe now…we can finish the job…and be able to live our lives without…that pestilence bothering us ever again. I want only those…who are over 100 years of age. All the young ones…will stay behind." He looked off to the side in thought. "Bikaropin… you're the…only man…other than myself…who is older than the traitor. If we start running into trouble…or suffering any fatalities, I want you to stay behind and kill the traitor immediately."

Bikaropin nodded. "I was wondering when you were going to get around to that."

Soolchakan was a little surprised. "Get around to what?"

"You said that if it ever got to the point where there was less than 20 Owlamites who were older than her…she would be executed then…so that she could never become the *Voice of Power*."

Soolchakan sighed. "That was primarily a suggestion. I said that I would consider performing an execution, but, your point?"

"Currently…there are only *twelve* of us who are older than her. That is definitely below twenty." He shrugged. "When is she going to be executed?"

Soolchakan hung his head. "I'm still not ready to give her what she wants yet…or even let her know anything of the situation." He looked up. "Hold off the execution…at the moment. Just standby…to remove her…if it comes to that."

Mahanee stood up with tears in her eyes. "NO! He doesn't get to do it. I've had to bury…twenty-two of my children and two husbands…because of the Teltermak…and that…*thing*! Eight of them were murdered by *her* hand. Take Bikaropin with you and leave the traitor to *me*!"

Soolchakan stared at Mahanee for a while. He then nodded. He turned to Bikaropin. "You heard her. Any objections?"

Bikaropin shook his head. "Given the choice between killing the traitor or thousands of Teltermak…" He smiled. "I choose the second one. Even though I've lost twenty-five children…and three wives…between the Teltermak and the traitor…I'll go and kill Teltermaks."

Hisang and Bikaropin joined Soolchakan on the stage.

Soolchakan took a deep breath. "We'll hop to Spy…and then Jump to…" He shook his head. "…wherever these images are. To the rest of you…Bikaropin and Hisang will be back shortly to lead the rest of you to this…place."

The trio all hopped to Spy. Soolchakan concentrated on the landmark he had seen in that place and made the Jump. They definitely found themselves, not on a beach, but in some kind of nerve center. This was the first time, he could think of, any Owlamite had been called to a location that appeared to be in an underground cave or tunnel system. There was a rather musky smell of unwashed bodies in the air. There were Teltermaks all over the place sitting at computers, feverishly entering data or looking over something that was on a screen. The computer desks were scattered randomly because they were in some kind of cave where there was no form or way to organize things in neat lines or 90 degree angles. Desks were placed where there was room for them. There were all kinds of blocks under different legs of the desks in order to keep them leveled. There were long cables that were suspended from the ceiling that had leads dangling down and going to every desk. There were also a lot of different lights hanging from the ceiling that gave a great deal of bright light to the entire area.

Bikaropin snickered at the spider web of cables around the ceiling. "Safety first. Make sure that they're not a tripping hazard."

"You weren't joking," said Hisang. "I really...can *not* read their minds. Why?"

Soolchakan shrugged. "Either their skulls are too thick or...they don't have brains. We never did figure out why." He sighed. "Find a landmark and go back and get some of the others."

Hisang and Bikaropin vanished.

While they were gone, Soolchakan decided to explore this cave. He was not sure which way to go so he just shrugged, turned right and started walking. Another twinge in his head occurred, only this time it was more like a sledgehammer. He staggered as it nearly knocked him to his knees. The stone lit up the entire area with a brilliant red glow when it happened. He was closer to the source and the waves were much stronger here. He walked into a rather large area that seemed central to the entire area. Here the ceiling was much higher and there were three different levels, because of ledges, in which the computer terminals were located, with ladders going to each level.

In the center of this great room there was a large glass bubble. Inside the large bubble was a smaller glass bubble. Inside the small bubble, one single Teltermak was sitting on a very ornate throne. On the left armrest there was some kind of small keypad. The uniform this Teltermak was wearing was covered with shoulder boards, golden fringes, medals, medallions and other flashy ornamentation. There were five gold stripes on the shoulder boards. The man was using a microphone to give orders. He would hit some of the buttons on his keypad and say something into the microphone.

Being in Spy dimension, Soolchakan walked right through the bubble shields to find out what this overly dressed Teltermak was saying. He stood there listening while he visually checked the insides of the interior bubble completely. He listened as this Teltermak gave all kinds of orders about finding and gutting Owlams. He stood there ready to pull his pulse pistol out and dissect this Teltermak...slowly and painfully.

Problem: How do you obtain information from this monster about the never-ending desire that these monsters have for Owlamite flesh, before finally killing him? Plus, he had a new question: Why was he called to the nerve center and not some of the other beach areas, like almost all the other victims? Very strange turn of events that nagged at him. He wondered if he would get answers or...should he just slaughter all of these parasites?

7

Bikaropin called mentally. **"I've got the others shuttling personnel in here. Where did you want to start?"**

Soolchakan smiled. **"Start with the bottom of this silly looking inner bubble. I can see hinges in the floor. I think it has some kind of trapdoor, in case he turns cowardly and decides to run. Somebody get down there and see if it is an escape tunnel and what you can do to sabotage it."**

Bikaropin sent Cheesang down to check.

"It is an escape tunnel," sent Cheesang. **"He can drop through there, close it back up and make a good escape on this crazy looking sled...in any one of three different directions."**

Soolchakan nodded. **"Can you do something about the sled?"**

Cheesang giggled. **"I'd rather make sure that he can't fall through the trapdoor."**

Soolchakan sighed impatiently. **"Is that possible?"**

"That'll be easy. There're some pipes down here that were just thrown off to the side on the floor. I'll just place them under the trapdoor and join them into the wall. They'll hold very nicely as a brace that'll prevent the thing from opening at all."

Soolchakan grinned and nodded. "Good! So do it. Let me know when you're finished. I'll make my appearance then...and surprise all of these *bimyocks*." He grimaced as he felt another twinge and the stone glowed intensely.

Cymani had come up to the area. "Why do you need to make an entrance? Can't we just start removing the riffraff?"

"Not yet! I've got a few questions that I'd like some answers to, before we start cleaning house. I don't want them panicked - yet." He continued listening to the orders being given by the fancy uniform. "Also, let me know when everyone is here and ready to start."

Bikaropin was flabbergasted. "You want to talk to this *h'oolyach*?"

Soolchakan glared back at Bikaropin. "I want to find out something from these things. I want to find out why they think that we're so tasty while no one else is being bothered, or ending up on their dinner tables, by these *chogos*."

Bikaropin growled. "Is that supposed to make a difference?"

Soolchakan scowled at Bikaropin. "**I WANT TO KNOW!**" He scoffed. "**Now, put your gauntlets on because we're going to question that…IT!**"

"**If I'm going to touch that thing, I'm not going to use my favorite pair of gauntlets. I'll be back after I get another pair.**"

"**Fine! Go! Get the other gauntlets. Get back… real quick.**"

Bikaropin was gone for a very short time. He came back putting the reinforced gauntlets on as he looked to Soolchakan for instructions.

Soolchakan took a deep breath as he prepared himself. "**Get ready for…just about anything.**" With that, he hopped to Home dimension.

A very loud alarm went off and the attention of all Teltermaks in this large room turned to see their prey - Soolchakan.

The Teltermak leader stood up with a shocked look on his face. He put the microphone up to his mouth as he turned back to his keypad and punched a few keys. He looked back at Soolchakan smiling. "Army Leader, Quok, did we get finally him? Is this the big one?"

Another Teltermak, who had almost as much flashy embellishments on his uniform, walked up to Soolchakan with some kind of pulse weapon in his right hand and a photograph in his left. This one had four gold bands on his shoulder boards. He looked back and forth, several times, from the picture to

Soolchakan. "Yes, Ultimate Leader, Ootgreeg." He nodded with a big grin. "This *is* the one."

Soolchakan now had a few more questions. (1) Where did these things get this photograph? (2) He had heard the name Ootgreeg before...was this the same one he had heard about... over 13,000 years ago? If it was the same Ootgreeg, then they had a very long life span as well. He thought back to that meeting on that dusty plain from so long ago. A few words stuck in his mind. He scoffed. "Just exactly what is it that you *Oogoo* eating *Shkoks* want?"

Ootgreeg went pale and his jaw dropped. "Where did you hear that? The only one that I knew...that ever dared use that term around me...was one of my brothers! I haven't heard...that in...a very, very long time...not since he was murdered...while out on patrol."

Soolchakan chuckled. "I heard that from one of those Teltermak parasites. It was out there on the plains, between the cities of Owlam and Teltermuckity-muck...shortly after the firestorm weapons burned our city down...and eliminated a bunch of Teltermuck criminals...why?"

Ootgreeg snarled back. He turned to the Quok. "Get some help and seize that one. He's the big *Mombik* and we need to get a collar on him...NOW!"

Quok signaled five others who were standing off to the side. The quintet ran toward Soolchakan. Soolchakan shook his head, rolled his eyes and hopped to Ghost dimension. The quintet arrived at Soolchakan's location and started pawing at the air trying to grab the Owlamite. After a very short amount of time, all five stopped flailing their arms around and just stood there, surrounding him, panting, with shock and confusion on their faces.

Soolchakan shook his head. "No Teltermuck is allowed to touch me...unless I allow it. Right now...I don't allow it." He looked up in thought. "As a matter of fact...I will never allow Teltertrash to touch me. I have a few questions that I need an answer to before anything else happens here." He cocked his head to the side. "**Is everyone here who is supposed to be here**?"

Soolkan responded. "**There are 127 of us here. All who are 100 or over...except for Mahanee**."

"I don't answer questions to any stinkin' Owlam," snarled Ootgreeg. "I give orders to Owlams...and they obey. You got that?"

Chena was a little impatient. "**Do you want us to start killing them**?"

"**Not yet**," sent Soolchakan. "**Like I told him...I need some answers. I don't think that they'll be too cooperative if they notice a lot of disappearances. Everyone...pick one of the enemy and hold your position. I definitely want several of you looking at the computers in this room. This seems to be the prime headache center, so we'll get our best information here**." He gave Ootgreeg a smile. "No, I don't got that. Like I said, I want some answers. Nothing happens until I get those answer."

Ootgreeg clenched his teeth and growled. "GRAB HIM,

YOU *FONKS!*"

The five that were surrounding Soolchakan again tried to get hold, however, it was like trying to grab smoke. Their hands just passed through him.

One of the five turned to Ootgreeg. "Ultimate Leader, we can't seem to touch him. We're trying but…it is…as if he's not standing here…at all. We can't grab smoke!"

Ootgreeg got red-faced. "Either you grab him…or I'll have you all executed!"

Soolchakan laughed. "You stupid *chogo*! You are threatening them because they can't do something that you're incapable of as well? How dumb can you be?" With that he bolted from being in the middle of the arm-flailing quintet towards the one called Quok.

Quok raised his pulse pistol and pulled the trigger. He then stood there dumbfounded as the beam went directly through Soolchakan and killed one of the quintet as it burned a hole directly through his head. Quok looked helplessly at Ootgreeg as Soolchakan ran directly through Quok. Quok froze in terror.

Soolchakan now turned back to Ootgreeg with an arrogant look. "Now…before anything else happens, I have some questions that need answers. Are you ready to cooperate or…do I have to get nasty?"

Ootgreeg started jumping up and down having a temper tantrum. "GRAB HIM! GRAB HIM YOU *FONKS*! I want him chained up."

Soolchakan closed his eyes and shook his head in indignation. He opened his eyes to see the remaining quartet surrounding him once more and helplessly and vainly waving their arms through him. He looked around at each of the four. **"Somebody get rid of these four *moongfops*."**

Cymani responded. **"What is a...*moongfop*?"**

Soolchakan chuckled. **"Sorry, that's a Cacktash curse."** He sighed. **"Doesn't really matter though. Just get rid of these four...parasites."**

Four miths later, all four of the arm wavers vanished.

Numerous Teltermaks were now staring in shock, horror and confusion.

Ootgreeg was the first to find his voice. "Where did they go?"

Soolchakan gave him an evil smile. "They're dead!" He let his face go blank. "Now, are you ready to answer some questions?"

Ootgreeg glared back. "NOT TO SOME STUPID *MOMBIK* OWLAM!"

Soolchakan still stared back blankly. "My, such language. Is that the same mouth you eat with?" He waited for a moment. "You *Oogoo* eating *Shkok*." He did not wait for a response. **"Bikaropin, do you have your gauntlets?"**

"Yes, I do, why?"

"Go into that little central bubble and get ready to

backhand that *chogo*...when I give the signal."

Bikaropin snickered mentally. "**That'll be a pleasure.**"

"**Tell me when you're there.**"

"**I'm already there.**"

"**Okay, with the right hand...a backhanding...from your left to the right...are you ready**?"

"**I'm ready!**"

"**NOW!**"

As he gave the order, Soolchakan swung his right hand in a backhanding manner. Bikaropin connected with the jaw of Ootgreeg in the little bubble and nearly turned the man around. Bikaropin held back nothing in his swing. He hoped that he had broken at least one bone in that hard head. Ootgreeg turned back looking more angry than scared. There was a trickle of blood going down from a cut on his cheek.

Soolchakan smiled. "Are you ready to answer some questions now?"

Ootgreeg looked at Quok. "STOP HIM!"

Quok looked helpless. "What is he doing?"

Ootgreeg squawked. "I don't know how he...but...it was...uh...STOP HIM!" He almost sounded as if he were crying.

"**Okay, Bikaropin...this time it'll be a right jab. The target is his teeth...got it?**"

"Got it."

"Ready?"

"Ready."

"NOW!"

Soolchakan threw a right jab in the direction of Ootgreeg. Bikaropin landed a hard blow right into the teeth of Ootgreeg. Ootgreeg was unceremoniously knocked back into his throne. He was punched so hard that his legs flew up when he landed in the chair. Now there was a look of fear on his face as his lips were covered in blood…and he spat pieces of at least three front teeth out. After that, Ootgreeg started talking a little funny because of the damaged teeth.

Bikaropin mentally huffed. **"When this is over, I'm throwing these gauntlets away. They're all covered with that nasty…Ootgreeg."**

Soolchakan stood askance. "Are you ready to answer some questions now?"

Now Ootgreeg was looking scared. "THTOP HIM… THOMEHOW THTOP HIM!" He sounded more desperate than angry.

Quok fired his pistol at Soolchakan. The beam ricocheted off of the outer bubble and went directly into a computer on the other side of the room. The computer blew up sending sparks and debris in every direction. At least four Teltermaks were injured by the shrapnel…one fatally.

Quok, once again, looked helplessly at Ootgreeg with his arms held out wide, nonverbally begging for an answer.

Ootgreeg rolled his eyes and growled in frustration. "Pigure out a way to thtop him…without killing any of ourth."

Soolchakan puffed his cheeks out as he blew his breath out in frustration. **"This time…we grab him by the nose…with the left hand. Pick him up out of the chair and *kick* him in the family jewels…any questions**?"

"Just say when," responded Bikaropin.

"Nose grab…NOW!" Soolchakan reached his left arm up and acted as if he was doing the grabbing.

Ootgreeg let out a rather high-pitched howl of pain as he was forced to stand up. His hands went to his nose, however, he could not stop whatever it was that was pinching his nose.

"With the right foot…kick…NOW!" Soolchakan kicked as high as he could.

Bikaropin kicked Ootgreeg in the crotch, hard. Ootgreeg was lifted completely off the ground by the force of the kick. He grabbed at his groin, however he did not fall. He was still being nasally held up by Bikaropin.

Soolchakan chuckled. **"Let go of him**."

"With pleasure," sent Bikaropin.

Ootgreeg dropped into a moaning heap on the floor inside the small bubble as he held his hands to his groin.

Soolchakan cleared his throat. "Are you ready to answer some questions now?"

Ootgreeg looked up. There was blood dripping down his chin and tears rolling down his cheeks. He lifted a hand up and hit a button on the right armrest. He grunted and looked down at the floor. He hit the button again. He then started pounding on the floor. He grabbed the microphone. "Thomeone get thith trapdoor open! Help me! Thith ith crathy!"

Soolchakan shook his head. "I'll come back when you're more cooperative." He hopped to Spy. He looked around and could see a huge congregation of Owlamites who were all gathered around computers watching what was being entered on the screens.

Ootgreeg screamed. He looked around in anger. "GET HIM BACK...NOW!"

Soolchakan snickered. "Should I go back now?"

"NO," screamed Menola! "They're showing us how to use the mind machines."

Chejja looked at Soolchakan with a grin and excitement in her eyes. "We've learned more about these machines, in the last four mithist, than we ever knew before. Wait...for as long as you can...before going back." She turned back and looked at the monitor as the Teltermak in front of her was feverishly inputting commands.

Soolchakan shrugged. "Well, don't let it be said that I slowed any progress in education." He looked down as the red stone was flickering madly. 'This rock *is* protecting me,' he thought. **"Cheesang, are you still down below the trapdoor?"**

"Of course," she sent back. **"I've already sent five Teltermak to the Stink planet."**

Soolchakan nodded. **"Okay, good place for them. No one here is going to miss them at all."** He looked around and a thought hit him. **"Is there anyone here who is...not really busy with watching the computer inputs?"**

"I'm not that busy," sent Ahemeni. **"Why?"**

"We're in a cave. We know we're in a cave, but we don't know where the cave is. Go back to the gorge. Get...either one of the shuttles or a fighter. Come back here in Observation dimension. Then...fly straight up...and find out where on this planet we are currently geographically located."

Ahemeni giggled. **"That's a very good idea. I'll get it done right now."**

Nansing interjected. **"You may not believe how much information we're getting here. It is...wonderful."**

Soolchakan shrugged. **"Wonderful? Such as?"**

"Locations of every single hideout on the globe, along with numbers, on every single continent where these *h'oolyach* are hiding."

Soolchakan lifted the red stone up and kissed it. He smiled. 'Are we finally going to be able to get rid of...all of these monsters...I hope?' He wandered around the facility watching as each one of his children stared (and learned as they feverishly took notes) at the monitors of the Teltermak computers. He shook his head. 'We can't read their minds but...we can still glean information from them.'

Ahemeni finally called to him. **"Is there a good place to land my fighter...in the cave...without hurting anyone?"**

Soolchakan looked around. **"Yes. Land it inside that big bubble."**

One of the fighter craft appeared inside the big bubble. The canopy opened up and Ahemeni climbed out. She took her helmet off and looked directly at Soolchakan with a smug smile. **"We're in a cave...located in Satroco Isle."**

Soolchakan hung his head and his shoulders sagged. "All this time! These monsters were...going underground..." He looked up. "...IN SATROCO ISLE!" He sighed. "They always were good at...digging...and tunneling. I should've remembered that little tidbit." He grunted. He turned back to Ahemeni. "You can take your fighter back now...and thank you."

Bikaropin walked up to Soolchakan. "We found the complete roll call...a listing that gives all of their locations...their hideouts and...head count."

Soolchakan leaned back a little. "From the look on your face...I take it that...we are going to be...*very* busy."

Bikaropin sighed, closed his eyes and nodded. "Very!" He looked down at a sheet of paper he had with him. "This place here…is the main headquarters. They have four locations on each one of the seven continents. We have this Ootgreeg. He is Mister Big. He *is* the Ultimate Leader. Directly under him there are seven Army Leaders – one for each continent. They're in charge of the continents, however, they still command them from here. There is a Section Leader for each one of the twenty-eight hideouts." He snickered and shook his head. "This Ootgreeg likes to play favorites. He has nine children and all nine are either a Section Leader or Army Leader."

Soolchakan blew a raspberry. "Nothing like family favoritism is there?" He chuckled. "All of his family are in the top three officer ranks."

Bikaropin looked back at his list. "I could bore you with the total count of each officer rank…but…I'll just give you the bottom line." He looked up. "There current population is just over 3,100,000." He let the number sink in. "If we go with…ages as low as 89…which would include Sisitam…that gives us 138 Owlamites to do the job of getting rid of ALL of the Teltermaks… for good. That comes to an approximate ratio of 22,460 to 1." He nodded. "Yes, we're going to be very busy."

"After all of the torture these cannibalistic monsters have put us through…it'll be *worth* it," he said bitterly. He slapped a fist against his thigh. "They might have some kind of escape plan…at each one of these places…if people start disappearing."

Bikaropin smiled. "They do…but I've got that information as well."

Soolchakan looked around the cave. "Good! That planet,

Stink! It is going to get *very* crowded."

"Yes, it will." Bikaropin chuckled.

Soolchakan looked back over at the bubble. Ootgreeg had somewhat recovered from being ruptured. He was still on his knees, rubbing his crotch, hollering down at the trapdoor, trying to get someone to open it from below. **"Cheesang, are they still trying to get to that door**?"

"Yes, Sir. So far, I've introduced 23 of them to Stink."

Bikaropin shrugged and snickered. "Sounds to me like the place is already getting crowded."

Soolchakan frowned. "Do you think I should make another appearance…and see if he's more cooperative?"

Bikaropin shrugged. "That is entirely up to you." He grinned.

Soolchakan sent out a general call. **"How are we doing on the computer stuff? Do we have enough to continue on our own or…do we need more time**?"

There were several responses requesting more time.

Soolchakan nodded. "Why don't you go back up there and see if you can learn some more?"

Bikaropin simply bowed his head and headed for one of the work stations.

Suddenly the floor shook as they heard a muffled explosion.

It was followed by five more explosions that were equally muffled. Dust was coming down from the ceiling everywhere from the shock waves. Numerous people were looking around rather confused as to what had just happened.

Soolchakan looked around like everyone else trying to figure it out. "**What was that ground shaking that was going on, does anyone know**?"

"**This is Cheesang. I did it. Those parasites were starting to outnumber me and come in from all three directions…so I collapsed all three escape tunnels with hand-held bombs**."

Soolchakan grimaced. 'Another one of the tactics done by…what's-his-name…oh yes…Eeleeg. I should've thought of that one…as well.' "**Very good Cheesang. Are you able to come back up here now…or is there more damage to be done down there**?"

"**I'm going to go through the rubble in each one and set off another blast in each tunnel. That way…it'll take days before they can reach the trapdoor**."

"**Very good**." He shook his head. 'At least someone is using their imagination.'

They felt three more shocks and watched as more dust came down. This time a certain section of the floor buckled slightly.

Cheesang appeared outside the inner bubble, but inside the outer bubble. She looked around rather satisfied and walked out of the bubble.

Soolchakan smiled at her. "Are you sure that it'll take… days…before they clear the rubble?"

She smiled. "Right now, the main concern of the ones who were in the tunnel is to get all of the casualties out of the tunnels before they can start digging. All of those injured are in the way."

"Are there very many casualties?"

She shrugged. "At least eight in each tunnel."

Basabee broke in. "Hey, this Quok *bimyock* is on the radio to that…Ootcrud. He's informed Ootcrud that the tunnels have been collapsed and that he is totally trapped in his little protective shell. He's also informed Ootcrud that the oxygen is getting rather low in there."

Soolchakan smiled. "Perfect! Lack of oxygen and no escape plan. That should make him more cooperative."

Bikaropin snickered. "How long should we wait?"

"Until he's panting," said Soolchakan with an evil leering grin.

That did not take long. Ootgreeg was sitting on the throne breathing heavily. He brought the microphone up to his mouth. "Pind him. Bing him back. AND GET ME OUTTA HERE!"

Dawuni smirked. "That sounds more like begging than commanding."

"He might just be ripe enough," said Vymilla.

Soolchakan walked up to the outer bubble and made his

appearance in the cave – in Ghost. "Are you ready to answer some questions yet?"

Ootgreeg pointed at Soolchakan. "GAB HIM! TAKE HIM PRITHONER!" He immediately started panting harder.

Soolchakan huffed in disgust. He walked through the outer bubble shell and hopped back to Home dimension. The air inside this bubble was rather musty. Why not? There was no way to circulate the air trapped in this bubble. He heard several loud thumps as a few Teltermaks slammed into the outer bubble as they attempted an apprehension. He looked back and saw four Teltermaks on the ground with bloody foreheads. There were at least five others who were rubbing their chests or a broken wrist or arm.

He turned back to Ootgreeg. "Are you ready to answer some questions?"

Ootgreeg shook his head weakly. "Whaffor? All yer gonna do…is lemme die in here. Why thould I cooperate…at all?" His breathing was getting weaker.

Soolchakan hopped back to Ghost. He reached through the inner bubble, grabbed the microphone and pulled it to his chest. He smiled. He then threw the microphone back to Ootgreeg. "I *can* get you out. I will get you out…but only if you cooperate."

"Gemme out…then…I'll ather qethyonth."

"You are in no position to barter. You answer the questions…then you can come out." Soolchakan raised his hand as if he were going to backhand the man again.

Ootgreeg flinched. When he saw he might not get hit, he just glared back.

"Don't think too long. You might not have very long left. The air is getting very weak in there."

He closed his eyes. "Awright...awright!   Whatha quethyonth?"

"First...why do you think that you have all of us if you have me?"

"Thah woman...Mernier...thye thaid that...if we got you...you control eberybody. We could make you...make them... thurrender."

"We've dealt with her. She can't harm us again and she can't help you again...ever. Second...why are you constantly coming after us? Why is it that you find us so tasty that...your cuisine is unfinished without our flesh?"

Ootgreeg now looked somewhat surprised. "Whu? You crathy? We haben't...eaten anything...thentient...in over theven thouthand yearth."

Now it was Soolchakan who was shocked. "Then... WHY? Why are you...always chasing after us? Killing us...and gutting us? WHY?"

Ootgreeg managed a chuckle. "The pothions...ya *Thkok*!"

Now Soolchakan was shocked...and confused. "What do we have to do with the potions?"

Ootgreeg now looked at him in a patronizing manner.

"Whuddooyoo think the main ingredient ith in each of the pothions? *YOUR* GUTTHS!"

Soolchakan did not know whether to laugh, cry, puke or pass out.

Ootgreeg smiled. "Yeah, we take the heart. It hath the mothe pure blood. We take it, witha blood thtill in it...grind it up, mikth it with thothe other animal hearts...juth for tathte and you got a pothion that cyurth...juth about any ditheathe."

Soolchakan felt even more nauseous. "And the liver?"

Ootgreeg shook his head. "It ain't the liver. Ith that... little ekthtra gut you got thath under the liver and hooked to it. Thome kinda enthyme that gut makth. It can't be reproduthed thynthetically. You drink that one...and it addth yearth to your life. Some kind of youth...or longevity pothion." He laughed. "I drunk at leath eighteen dotheth of that thtuff. Any time I get to feelin' old, I juth guthle another one...and I'm full of pep."

"Oh, you're full of it, all right."

"The yellow bottle...that one helpth with thmarth. We gotta grind yer brain up. Mix it with the other thtuff. When you drink that thtuff...for about ten days...you are...tho much thmarter, you think clearer..." He laughed. "...you win more argumenth becauthe yer thinkin' fathter. I with I could get more of that thtuff." He grinned. "Now that we got you, I'm gonna have a never ending thupply of that thtuff...juth for mythelf."

Soolchakan was desperately trying to control his temper. He wanted to go in the little bubble and beat that monster to a pulp.

"The white bottles...witha aphrodithiac. That one ith gender thpecific. We gotta make thure which one ith which. We rip the thkin offa yer back. We look for a bunch of little white thackth. They look like thmall marblth. They got thome crud that comth out the back of yer neck. If we got the glandth of a man, we make a dothe that you feed to a dithobedient wife. Thye don't wanna do it. Tho you give her that...and thye'll wear you out. Thye can't get enough thex. If we get the glandth of a woman..." He sneered. "Heyyah men, ethpecially thothe who are old and impotent...they love it. They drink that thtuff and they'll attack anything in the houthe thath female." He glared at Soolchakan. "Ath I thaid, now that we got you, we can make yer femaleth thtart breedin' annually. That way we get more of you Owlamth fer butcherin'. Then...we really thtart makin' a real fortune."

Shashy sent to Soolchakan. "**Can I kill him now**?"

Soolchakan sent back. "**No, I have something special in mind for him. Killing is too good for him...at this moment. You can start killing all of the others...as soon as you're satisfied that you've obtained anything and everything we want out of their computers**."

Ootgreeg was looking desperate. "Are you finithed with your quethions?"

"No...why do you need all of those other ingredients?"

He laughed and wheezed while still panting. "Decorathion! Keep alla them people confuthed ath to exactly whath in the thtuff. We let the recipe get out...and when thomeone bringth all the other ingredients, we know what they want and we can charge more for it."

"Even though they brought something that you need."

"Nah, motha that thtuff we juth thow way anyway. It keepth life innerethting."

"It's nothing but a fabrication game."

"Yeah, but we get a good profit. Are you finithed with your quethtions, now?"

Soolchakan nodded slightly. "Yes…for now." He shook his head. "You said that you haven't devoured anything sentient for over seven thousand years…but…you are still ingesting parts of our anatomy. You are vomiting fabrications…even to yourself."

"GET ME OUTTA HERE!"

"Not yet. I am also wondering why you took all those other races and had them war against each other…to complete extinction of both. WHY?"

Ootgreeg grunted. "They were in the way. They didn't wanna cooperate with uth. They wanted to be the oneth in control. We didn't wanna lithen to them, we told them to lithen to uth. They refushed…we killed em by makin em kill each other. Whatha problem with that?"

Soolchakan turned away totally disgusted. The excuses were even more insulting than he had ever thought they would be. Don't conquer, just kill, all of them, for no sane reason whatsoever.

Ootgreeg tried to stand up. He was totally unsuccessful.

Soolchakan reached up and touched the inner bubble. He hopped it into Spy. Ootgreeg inhaled deeply as he was getting some air that was not quite so oxygen-depleted. He got up and charged (or rather stumbled) at Soolchakan – who hopped into Spy. Ootgreeg slammed into the outer bubble and slowly slid to the ground...groaning as he left a streak of blood on the glass. Soolchakan simply walked out of the bubble.

A Teltermak who was not dressed as elaborately as Ootgreeg or Quok started shouting about how the Owlam had escaped again. Quok went to a computer terminal and started keying in data. The red stone started flickering again.

Soolchakan stared at the stone for a few moments. He looked up. "Someone stop that *bimyock* from...whatever he's doing. It is *terribly* annoying."

Yakiss walked up to the computer operator and was ready to send him to the Stink planet. She looked down and saw a saucer sitting next to the keypad. She smiled as she reached down, hopped the saucer into Spy and picked it up. Since the only thing that was moving was his fingers, she moved the saucer into his neck where it was directly under his head. She hopped the saucer back to Home dimension.

Quok fell to the ground twitching a little. The saucer was porcelain. It was now joined in his neck directly under the head. It was cutting off all synapsis from the brain to the rest of the body because it was interrupting the nerves of the spinal cord. Since it was also blocking the esophagus, he could not breathe. He was, for all intents and purposes, decapitated, since nothing was getting from the head to the body. He lay there with his eyes wide open in shock. His mouth was opening and closing as if he were trying to say something.

Two other Teltermaks ran to his aid and were both rather speechless from shock when they saw the unusual collar protruding all the way around his neck.

His eyes finally rolled into the back of his head. The body twitches continued for several moments after the brain had died.

Ootgreeg had recovered...somewhat. He stumbled back to the throne and picked up the microphone. "Where ith that... *Protch?*"

Another Teltermak who was wearing four gold bands on his shoulder-boards walked up to the bubble. "Ultimate Leader... he escaped again. He also...killed...Army Leader, Quok."

Ootgreeg looked up angrily. "He...killed...my *thon?*"

"Yes, Ultimate Leader. Quok...is dead. Sir, we need to get a replacement for him."

Ootgreeg had a wild look in his eyes. "Army Leader, Gockthoyon, call Thection Leader, Prepkood. Tell him he juth got a promothion. Tell him to choothe hith replathement there from the Leaderth under hith command. He needth to get here... ath thoon ath pothible." He flopped back down on the throne and hung his head. "We're gonna make thothe Owlamth teach uth how to do that teleporting. We're gonna make them teach uth how to walk through wallths. Not only do we make a fortune off their gutth...we can come and go to any locathon we want...any time we want. We'll conquer everybody." He looked around. "Thomebody get on that computer and get that thtincken Owlam leader back here."

The Teltermak looked a little disgusted. "Yes, Ultimate Leader." He signaled another of the minions to get to that specific keyboard. He then walked over to a large array of devices. He punched a number on a keypad. A monitor lit up, showing a listing. He ran through the listing until he found what he wanted. He punched a number in on a different keypad. He picked up a device and held it to his ear. He started having a conversation with whoever it was on the other end of the line.

Ootgreeg sniffed. "How...did he kill Quok? How did he get a weapon?"

Four Teltermak picked the body up and carried it to the bubble to show Ootgreeg what had happened. Ootgreeg walked up to them and just stared at the saucer that was now a strange looking collar.

Ootgreeg stood there baffled. "How...he...what...how could he...do...that?" He shook his head in disbelief. "He ith gonna pay for thith...big time!"

One of the four responded. "If he can teleport himself...he can probably teleport other objects as well. Put them in a position like this and...even a simple saucer becomes a lethal weapon."

Ootgreeg stared at the body of his son. He closed his eyes and raised his fists in anger and pounded them against the inner side of the bubble. "GET THAT OWLAM BACK HERE... NOW!"

Soolchakan went to Bikaropin. "Who is Prepkood?"

Bikaropin looked at his list. "Prepkood is another one of Ootgreeg's children."

"So he replaces one of his children with another one of his children."

Bikaropin huffed. "Hooray for favoritism," he said sarcastically. "Soolchakan, your stone is flickering again."

"I know." He sighed. "Find a...less inventive way... to eliminate whoever is punching keys on the computer...that's trying to summon me."

Another Teltermak suddenly disappeared from the planet Hardooth and reappeared on the Stink planet. Now everyone in that room in the cave was a little apprehensive about going to that console. Strange things were happening to the people who messed with it.

Gockzoyon turned to Ootgreeg. "Ultimate Leader, I was able to communicate with Section Leader, Prepkood. He has informed me that his replacement at Neopaure Area 2 will be Leader, Yoxoyoo."

Ootgreeg looked indignant. "That ith ARMY Leader, Prepkood and THECTION Leader, Yokthoyoo."

Gockzoyon bowed his head looking embarrassed. "Yes, Ultimate Leader. I thank you for the correction. My apologies for my silly error."

Bikaropin snickered. "I wonder what he's really thinking."

"I wish I knew," said Soolchakan. "Did you get that update?"

Bikaropin simply nodded.

Soolchakan grinned as a thought occurred to him. He hopped to Ghost dimension, aimed his pulse pistol at the computer that seemed to be the one that was *allegedly* controlling his mind and fired. After the dust settled from the explosion, several parts just sat there sizzling. He turned to Ootgreeg, gave him a big toothy grin and hopped back to Spy.

Withkemi walked up to Soolchakan. "Okay, now that we've got the list of where their hideouts are. All twenty-eight of them. Should we start with the ones nearest to us on South Chilamte?"

Soolchakan shook his head. "No! We'll cast lots. We'll hit them randomly. That way they won't be able to figure out where we are. If we clean out all four on one continent quickly, even these *bimyocks* might be able to figure out where we really are."

Bikaropin looked at the list. "So…how do we start this… randomness?"

Soolchakan stared for a moment. "Twenty-eight pieces of paper…placed in a bucket. Someone is blindfolded and puts their hand in the bucket…pulls out one piece of paper, and, we attack… wherever that particular one is located."

Kellio looked askance. She smiled nervously. "What about this place? We can't leave them here…to coordinate."

Soolchakan sighed. "Kellio, Iscama, Dayet, Heerok, Cleef, Xoktiy and Cleezha…I think that you might stay here for a day and create some kind of disaster in here…that disables a lot of their communications systems."

The four men and three women named all smiled and looked around at all the equipment with sinister glee. All kinds of nasty thoughts went through their minds.

After the partial sabotage at the main headquarters, the lottery was prepared. The first piece of paper drawn was for Area 3 on Aerisau. After a quick reconnaissance of the area, it was determined that there were approximately 109,000 Teltermaks there. With the number of Owlamites, over 90, that worked out to about 795:1. The plan was to go in and find any and all Teltermaks who were asleep and get rid of them first. That way no alarm would be raised. Leave the shift that has just arrived at work alone. Go get the shift that is going to bed (or wait until they are drunk). Then go after the ones who are still remaining.

By the time the Teltermaks were down to only one third of their personnel, Shashy and Meffin had found some interesting things in the computer. They discovered there was an automatic alarm that would be sent to headquarters, at a specific time, unless someone shut it off. No actual communications between the area and headquarters was needed. As long as headquarters received the "no problem" communique, nothing would happen. As the last shift was being given free rides to the Stink planet, Shashy stood by the "no problem" switch and made sure that no one at headquarters (even though most of the people at Headquarters were not there anymore) got any other message than that one message, which was now a fabrication.

A group of rather exhausted Owlamites did some final sweeps throughout the massive complex to make sure they had cleaned it out completely. Once they were sure it was clean, Voyem, who was 87 years old and was not part of the attack, was assigned to stay there and do the honors of sending the "no problem" message at the appropriate times. Four other Owlamites - Ulaskeya, Yezhaza, Yozhazo and Unatami were brought in to learn that system. None of them were fully mature adults, however, being in their 80's, none of them were mentally deficient or immature. Now, there would be no alarm sent to headquarters and there would be four more who were trained on how to send the "all clear" signal.

The only Teltermak not sent to Stink was the Section Leader, Rubfisisk. When he woke up, he found himself in a very strange prison cell (on one of the spaceships in #45). There was no window in the cell, so he could not see out and find out that he was in a stranger place than he anticipated.

Of course, after the sabotage at the main headquarters had been accomplished, the remaining people in the headache center had enough real headaches and would have a problem responding to any alarm. They were working on repairing several arrays of computers that had inexplicably been burned up in some rather bizarre electrical fires. Another headache for them was the fact that as soon as something was repaired – oops - it suffered a new problem – usually worse. Not to mention the fact that when someone attempted repairs, they usually ended up getting electrocuted – even though the item was disconnected from any source of power. Of course, there was the other problem in that they had no idea where a lot of their personnel had gone…or why. They were all worried about that fact, however, Ootgreeg kept on screaming at them regarding the repairs. Mourn the dead and missing later, repair now.

The Owlamite attackers went back home and had a good slumber. When they awoke, another paper was drawn from the bucket. This one was Area 2 on North Chilamte. The plan worked again and Section Leader, Oovyotyut was grabbed. She is now a prisoner in #45. Now, however, they still had to replace the one who was sending the "no problem" signal from here. Quamissi was added to the list of ones who would be trained to send the signal. The personnel who were chosen for this, again, were not mature adults. So far all of them were in their 80's.

Soolchakan groaned when he realized how many of the younger ones would have to be used for the ruse. He looked at the list of Owlamites who were still breathing. The youngest that he might have to go to in order to continue the deception was Chab. His age was 56. He was still physically immature, however, at 56 he was no mentally immature moron. He remembered how most Heyyah were considered wise at the age of 40. By the time some were 56, many of them were old and feeble or forgetful. For someone to just watch and make sure that a message was sent should not be a problem.

Bikaropin gave Soolchakan a gentle nudge in the ribs. "We don't have to have someone sit there all day, just to hit one button. Get the timing at each station and have one person go to all of the locations on that continent, at the proper time, and hit that button."

Soolchakan did not have to be told twice. Excellent plan. Put that into play and it would take far less personnel to keep the ruse going.

He still had to think about the traitor. They could not afford to lose any other adults, especially the few that were older than she.

The next one that came up was Area 3 on South Chilamte. All Teltermaks were sent to Stink…except for the Sector Leader, Kolkakrik. He joined the other two Sector Leaders in that spaceship brig. One thing that was different about Kolkakrik was that he was one of the originals who had been there during the Algothon attacks. Apparently he had guzzled a few of the longevity potions as well.

Soolchakan could hardly wait until all 28 Sector Leaders were in that brig. Once again, though, the Owlamite attackers had to go back and get some sleep before the next assault. Hopping all of those thousands of Teltermaks, anywhere, was very taxing. The Owlamites were rediscovering how mental exhaustion can be even more of a strain then physical exhaustion.

Ficara, Area 4 was next. No problems, even when Sector

Leader, Uhbrabra was sent to the brig in #45. He was not happy but, among the Owlamites, who cares?

Neopaure, Area 4 was next. No problems there either. Sector Leader, Voovolokan now joins the group in #45. She is not happy either. Again, who cares?

Bikaropin found some communications going on with the next one that was pulled out of the bucket. It was: Lusaratia, Area 2. It seemed that the Sector Leader, Op-Op was one of the daughters of Ootgreeg and he liked to keep constant communications open with all of his children. Since one of his children had been killed at headquarters he was constantly checking on the rest of them, whenever he could get through. It seems that when Quok was killed, this was the first one of his children that had been lost in over 12,000 years. The five Areas that were commanded by Ootgreeg's children were removed from the bucket until further notice.

A new drawing is made and it comes up as Cifpasica, Area 2. Section Leader, Eelkwug is now in the brig in #45. He is screaming mad and making all kinds of threats. When his food is taken to him he gets it right in his face and must now lick it off of his face, shirt and the floor if he wants anything to eat. Now he is even less happy. AGAIN, who cares?

Cheesang went back to the headquarters to check on the progress in digging the rubble out of the tunnels. The one they were working on was nearly through…so she blew it up again with two hand-held bombs. When she got back to the gorge, she reported that since Ootgreeg had no proper toilet facilities inside the bubble, it was getting rather disgusting inside there. They had drilled four holes in the bubble with a diamond tipped drill bit in order to get some fresh air in there. They had destroyed twenty-two drill bits in manufacturing the four holes. They also put a tube through one of the holes in order for him to suck some soup through and get sustenance. Trying to break the bubble was nearly impossible. They had tried several times. They had gone to great lengths to make a bubble that was invulnerable. This was now working against them. They had imbedded the bottom of the bubble rather deep in the ground in order to keep someone from digging through. It was imbedded in flint and this was making it extremely difficult for them to dig under as well. All of their safety ideas were coming back to hurt them.

Back to Aerisau and Area 4. The Owlamites have successfully "evacuated" seven different areas. They have seven rather bewildered, and angry, Sector Leaders, including the newest "guest" Ongfok. He is more the quiet type, studying what he can in order to attempt an escape. The Owlamites do not worry and leave no guards because if they escape - where are they going? They are in dimension #45, on a spacecraft, that they have no idea as to how to start the engines and go...where? Besides that, the main bridge and engine rooms have been hidden from them even if they did get out of their cells.

Next is Lusaratia, Area 3. Another Section Leader is in the brig. He is Shkefko and, of course, he is just as surprised to find himself in this predicament.

Kymim came back to the gorge and reported that the prisoners were all a little confused as to why they had not been rescued yet. They were wondering if the silly Owlams had come up with some way of blocking the transmissions of *their* imbedded trackers. The question now is: Why are the ones at Headquarters not worried about the complete lack of signals? Apparently they are too busy trying to save Ootgreeg...or the computer that was watching the signals had been hopelessly damaged.

The Owlamites now realized that the imbedded tracker was not an original idea. It seems that the Teltermak had been using them for some time.

On to Cifpasica, Area 1 and taking another Section Leader, Boorgrook as prisoner. Once he has been established in a cell in #45, he informs the other prisoners that no one has raised any form of an alarm about anyone missing or any attack on any of the areas. He is surprised to hear how long the other leaders have been imprisoned in this strange place without any alarm being raised. The prisoners are starting to feel a little despondent, along with their confusion. How could those stupid Owlams be doing anything superior in warfare or anything else? The Teltermak are superior in all ways...aren't they? They had been listening to that specific propaganda for several millennium. Now, because of the situation, they were beginning to doubt.

The tenth attack places them back on Aerisau. Section Leader, Tok-Okot is now a prisoner in #45. Once again, the prisoners are informed that no alarm has been sent out. They are all a little baffled as to how the Owlams can do this. They are still not willing to admit that there is someone out there who just might have a little more intelligence than a Teltermak. That is just *not* possible...is it? Unless, of course, you are talking about those mysterious Ghost Assassins.

The eleventh attack goes wrong. Section Leader, Oofinich is taken prisoner, however, in his personal computer, he had another one of the "no problem" programs. He added it as an extra precaution and now, after going through, and demolishing, another fifty-five drill bits and finally breaking a hole large enough in the bubble, Ootgreeg is free and (after taking a much needed bath) returns to work. Headquarters has received an alarm. A general roll call is done on the sections and the Owlamite children who were watching the radios now have to retreat to the gorge. They do not know how to respond to certain security questions that were part of the system.

Since headquarters has no idea how the eleven areas that have gone silent were attacked, or how much damage there is, Ootgreeg calls for "Operation: Basic Hide".

Bikaropin got into the computer to find out what this means. He groaned in despair as he found out that it is an order for all personnel in those areas to run and hide. They are to maintain radio silence for at least two months. Headquarters will investigate to determine exactly how much damage has been done and will then pass out assignments for the personnel to get things corrected.

Dara J. Carr

Soolchakan feels his heart sink. They had the Teltermaks where they wanted them and yet again, many of the parasites may have escaped. Why is it always the Teltermak who are able to kill, hide and repeat their atrocities – because they are well practiced at this plan of hiding and evading.

8

Now the Owlamites had to start looking for the Teltermaks all over again. They had destroyed 11 of the 28 areas. That still left 17. Where do they start?

Bikaropin, Soolkan, Pelox and Lep, again, started digging through anything they could find in the computers. There had to be some protocol in there about running and hiding. The Teltermak Command had micromanaged all other aspects of the lives of their people, why should this be different? If they just ran and hid for two months, how could they get or give any update on the status of anything?

Soolkan found a hidden order that states that a team, of ten personnel, from other areas are to be dispatched to the silent areas for reconnaissance. Find out how much damage has occurred and report back.

For Aerisau, *that* is a major problem. Areas 1, 3 and 4 have been evacuated by the Owlamites. That leaves only area 2. They have to send a team to each one of the silent areas. Once this protocol was discovered, the teams had a welcoming party and they were never able to send in a report…because they joined their fellow Teltermaks on the planet Stink.

There were similar welcoming parties at each one of the areas that had been cleaned out on the other continents. The Teltermak headquarters received no reports from any of the silent areas at all. Now it is the Teltermak who are suffering all kinds of frustration. They are now thinking that those wretched Ghost Assassins are back at work. So far, they never once put the equation together where they blame the Owlamites of being said Ghost Assassins. Of course they are too bigoted to admit that the Owlamites could possibly have that kind of intelligence and tenacity.

Lep found another hidden program. The order for each one of the areas, during Basic Hide, was to depart their area, run and hide. What Lep found was a list of the acceptable hiding places. Each area had a list of 25 places they were to disperse their personnel. Each hiding place was supplied with enough provisions and equipment to keep approximately 5,000 personnel safe, fed and comfortable for 90 days. Once again, Soolchakan was amazed at the organizational skills of these monsters. All those supplies being stored at each location had been a massive undertaking. But, of course, they were very adept at tunneling and hiding things in tunnels.

Soolchakan also liked this new piece of information. The actual number of Teltermaks in each one of the hiding places came to approximately 4,600 per hidey-hole. That was a much easier number to handle, as far as cleaning the area out. Now all they had to do was determine which one of the 25 hideouts was the place where the Section Leader was living. Once they had the Section Leader, all other hideouts could be evacuated without being picky, while the Section Leader ended up joining the others, in the brig on that spaceship in #45.

Mahanee was still in #45, babysitting the traitor with mixed emotions. She had lost 22 children to the Teltermak. Eight of those children had been victims of the traitor. Her eldest daughter, Hisang, had lost ten children to the Teltermak, five specifically by the traitor. Mahanee was ready to exact revenge against the Teltermak, however, that included killing the Teltermak children as well, no matter how young they were. She just could not truly bring herself to committing that act without some horrible feelings of guilt. Her only compensation for her conscience was the fact that if any of the Teltermak children were left, they would grow up to be vengeful Teltermak adults. Final solution: Kill them all - without remorse. She did not have to be a part of that nightmare while sitting there with a pulse pistol in #45. The only regret here was that she could only kill the traitor once – if it came to that extreme measure.

The traitor did not know that Mahanee was there. There was a special room in the spaceship where the traitor had no access. This room had a monitor that showed the exact location of the traitor all the time. Mahanee had no trouble with the thought of killing the traitor. All she had to do was think of the eight children who had been stabbed in the back by the traitor. Drilling a hole through the head of the traitor, with the pulse pistol or with an electronic drill, would be a pleasure, however, she sat there thinking of ways she could possibly prolong death with some very painful damages done to the body.

Section Leader, Booboll was now in the dimly lit brig. He was the last of that rank in Aerisau. From Ficara, Section Leaders, Oobroo and Unchomich were now in #45. That left only Proop, because he was one of the children of Ootgreeg and in spite of the radio silent command left behind, Ootgreeg still contacted his children.

The next continent that was cleaned out was South Chilamte. Puprapo, Truhd and Zoozkrutch were added to the collection in the brig, while all of the rest of the Teltermak were "removed" from the continent. Seventeen down, eleven to go… and five of them were children of Ootgreeg.

The red stone started flickering again. Soolchakan had to put up with the thought that Ootgreeg was once again, attempting to summon and manipulate the *Voice of Power*. He quickly Jumped back to Satroco Isle, with a pulse pistol and once again destroyed the computer that was calling him. He sniffed as he looked around at the mayhem he had caused in their headquarters. Ootgreeg was fouling the air with a constant stream of curses at no one in particular as he surveyed the newly demolished mind control computer.

After wandering through the headquarters for a few more days, causing some more bedlam, Soolchakan Jumped back to the gorge. He was very pleased to find out that Section Leader, Shtug, from Lusaratia had been added to the collection in #45. Eighteen down - ten to go.

Next they cleaned out Neopaure. Section Leaders, Yoxoyoo and Duwud were captured. All of their followers died, in that same gruesome manner, on their knees on the Stink planet. Section Leader, Jih-In-In, from Lusaratia, was next. Then Swod and Dij from North Chilamte.

Now, the only Section Leaders not captured yet were the five children of Ootgreeg. The Owlamites had to be careful. They cleaned out all of the hiding places of the areas, other than where the Section Leaders were cowering. Yeema went to Satroco Isle and kept a close watch on Ootgreeg. She reported that Ootgreeg already had some new teeth to replace the ones knocked out by Bikaropin (not that anyone cared). Once he had finished his daily conversations with his children, the attack on the five hideouts commenced. This consisted of nearly 23,000 Teltermak that had to be Jumped to Stink and the five Ootgreeg offspring being surprised to find themselves in a large brig on a spaceship. The two sons: Proop and Urb are first. They wasted their breath with all kinds of vulgar insults. They then watched as the three daughters – Op-Op, Shushank and Nunkwothk - appear in the brig.

Once the children of Ootgreeg found themselves in this strange brig, they started demanding that the others assist in getting out of there and back to their original places.

Op-Op glared at the other Section Leaders (at least the ones that she could see from her cell). "Why haven't you done something about this? Apparently you've all been here longer than I have...and you're still in prison...why?"

Ongfok sighed. "Because we're waiting to determine what is going to be done with us...because we have no idea where we are."

"You get out of that cell and look out a window, ya stupid *mombik*," snarled Urb.

Ongfok glared back. "I HAVE! I got out of this cell. I got Uhbrabra out as well. We *did* look out a window. We looked out...several windows. We found out that...we are *not* on any part of Hardooth that I'm familiar with. We're on...some kind of ship...somewhere. We're just floating around. Every window that we looked out of, all we saw was the black of a night sky, without any stars, except for one big star. We also saw some other strange looking rocket ships that...are just sitting there, floating in space. I think that we're...in what is called outer space. I can't prove it, but I can't deny it." He looked at his fingernails and then back at Op-Op. "How do you suggest we commandeer this vessel? Once we do...where do we go? I'm open for any suggestions that you might have because...I...*WE*...are completely out of our element. We wondered why those Owlams left no guards. Once we did a tour of this ship. We know why." He shook his head. "We are completely lost with...no idea of which way to go...even if we did figure out a way to operate this ship."

Op-Op sank to her knees with a look of total horror on her face. "Outer space? That doesn't make any sense. No Owlamite is that intelligent."

Ongfok shook his head and scoffed. "Apparently they are. Because we are here."

Nunkwothk scoffed. "I don't believe you. I'd like to see this *alleged* outer space nonsense for myself."

Ongfok shrugged. "As you wish." He pushed the door

to his cell open. He smiled at Op-Op. "Don't worry, they're not locked. Since we have no clue as to where we are, the Owlams have no worries as to wasting their time guarding us. I don't know if they are aware that we can come and go as we please...from our cells, but...the only time they show up is...to bring another one of us in here...or bring some kind of slop for us to eat."

Op-Op pushed her cell door open. Nunkwothk, Shushank, Urb and Proop all did the same. Ongfok signaled for them to follow him. They spent nearly half the day (?) taking a tour of the parts of the ship that Ongfok was familiar with. The five children of Ootgreeg went back to their cells, totally despondent and baffled, awaiting for the Owlams to return and...do...what? Best thing to do was wait until the Owlams returned and then try some form of counter-attack. Then some form of coercion in order to... do... (?)

Now that all of the other continents had been cleaned out, after two and a half months of hard work, the Owlamites returned to Satroco Isle. The underground headquarters of the Teltermak was their very last hideout (hopefully).

The seven Army Leaders were quickly located. Three were related to Ootgreeg, four were not.

Gockzoyon went to his private quarters exhausted. He needed a nap. He did not realize that he was going to wake up in #45 in a cell between Shtug and Jih-In-In, both of which were in his direct chain of command.

Zidz and Blobsot went to a conference room, privately,

to discuss some of the problems. They were taken together and never finished their conference...on Hardooth.

Thoobwot was found in a closet, guzzling some kind of liquor. He finished a long drink, lowered the bottle and belched. He opened his eyes and was now wondering if it was the booze or reality when he found himself staring through prison bars at Section Leader, Zoozkrutch. When he realized that it was the second choice he took another long swig of the beverage. He lowered the bottle again and sank to his knees in shock.

Zoozkrutch scoffed. "I always did think you were a boozer. Now, I have proof. Now that it may be too late to do anything about it." He walked over and sat down on his cot (?), shaking his head. He sighed despondently.

The Owlamites did what they could to clean out as many personnel from the headquarters as rapidly as possible. Ootgreeg and his three remaining children were all concentrating on one computer and did not notice all of their personnel vanishing around them - until they suddenly noticed that it was unusually quiet in their cavern. They looked around in horror and surprise.

Ootgreeg picked up a microphone and started calling out, on a public address system, everyone who was still in the cavern should get back to their workstations. His voice echoes through the cave without any form of response from anybody. When they received no reply, the four of them pulled out their weapons and started looking around.

Soolchakan, Shashy, Chena and Cheesang were the only Owlamites left in the Satroco cavern.

Soolchakan heaved a tired sigh. "Don't worry, my children. There are only four of them left. That's only one each for us and...then...I pray that this planet has been cleansed of any and all Teltermak...now and forever."

Soolchakan grabbed Ootgreeg and Jumped him to the prison ship. Shashy grabbed Perposhk, Chena grabbed Hoffpoth and Cheesang grabbed Prepkood. Now Hardooth was clean (hopefully). Now, the only 36 Teltermaks, who were not orally dehydrating on the planet Stink, were all in a prison ship in #45.

Ootgreeg was briefed on the overall situation. "If those *mombiks* haven't locked the doors...why are you still sitting in those cells?"

Tok-Okot shook his head. "If they don't know that we know the doors are unlocked, we have an advantage over them. Small as it may be, it is still something in our favor."

Ootgreeg contemplated for a few moments and then shrugged in agreement because he could not come up with any better strategy...at the moment.

What the Teltermaks did not realize was that while they were discussing the situation, there were several Owlamites, in Spy, who were now locking the cell doors. All of the locking mechanisms had been "temporarily" hopped to Spy to keep the Teltermaks from hearing the very loud clanks as they were locked. Now they were being put back into #45 dimension. Once all of the locks were in place, all of the Owlamites went back to the gorge to get some rest before executing the final verdict on the Teltermak. Some of them were confused as to why Soolchakan was keeping his plans for that horrid enemy a secret. In actuality he had not fully made up his mind as to what he was going to do. He was mentally working on all of the logistics of it, however, he was really too tired to make any final decisions. Just get some sleep and make decisions after being well rested.

Soolchakan led the delegation of Owlamites into the brig. Several of the Teltermak prepared for a surprise attack as soon as they heard their captors marching in. Ootgreeg shouted the order and thirty-five Teltermak slammed into the locked doors at full force. Some were knocked out, some were dazed and some just sank to the floor with a rather confused look on their faces. Most had blood coming out of different abrasions on their heads, arms or chests...depending on where they had hit the unmoving bars with their bodies.

A few of the prisoners regained a few of their wits and tried to grab at the captors. The Owlamites just hopped to Ghost and now the Teltermak were just grabbing at smoke.

Ootgreeg snarled at Soolchakan. "You let us outta here... RIGHT NOW!"

Soolchakan huffed. "You are in no position to give any orders...*again*! Just like before, you're the ones who are the captives. We're the ones who have imprisoned you, along with all of your other high echelon personnel."

Ongfok grabbed at the bars of his cell and shook them violently...or at least made the attempt. "WE ARE TELTERMAK! YOU ARE OWLAMS! YOU ARE SUPPOSED TO OBEY US!"

Bikaropin shook his head. "Why? Why should we be, in any way, shape or form, forced to obey prisoners. This is one of the greatest cases of denial that I've ever seen. They're prisoners and the idiots still can't admit the truth."

"I'm going to educate them...rather quickly," said Soolchakan.

Yoxoyoo spat at Soolchakan. Her spit flew right through Soolchakan and hit Zoozkrutch. He was just as shocked as she when he got hit. Soolchakan just shook his head in a disgusted manner.

"We are going to alter our language," said Soolchakan. "There are many words that exist in the Owlamite dialect...that do not exist in the Teltermak dialect...and vice versa. We are going to add to our dictionary and inform these Teltermak of the changes." He took a breath and let out a contented sigh. "From this day forth...the word Teltermak will mean...parasite." He looked at Ootgreeg and smiled. "The word Ootgreeg will mean...manure." He chuckled. He turned to Bikaropin. "This is fun."

"What will be fun, is chopping up your guts for our potions," snarled Ootgreeg through his new false teeth.

"They're still in extreme denial," said Bikaropin flatly.

Soolchakan sighed. "Introduce two or three of them...to Stink. Let them see that the rest of their population is dead from dehydration...on that planet."

Nine of the Teltermak vanished as nine Owlamites each grabbed one and gave them a nice look at the Stink planet. They came back just a few moments later and now there were nine Teltermak, on their hands and knees, vomiting in a very loud and disgusting manner. Bikaropin had grabbed Ootgreeg. He had picked Ootgreeg because he had touched that one before and did not have any desire to touch any other Teltermak.

Soolchakan looked down at a little cheat-sheet that he had in his hand. He was looking at the names of Ootgreeg's children. He smiled. "Vomit! That's a good word." He picked the eldest daughter. "From now on...the word Hoffpoth...will be the Owlamite word for vomit."

Hoffpoth glared at him with total hatred. "Do you actually have the audacity to think that you're going to get away with this?"

Soolchakan turned to Chenny. "Take that loudmouth and give her a tour of Stink."

Moments later, Hoffpoth reappeared and was doubled over, hurling on the floor.

Soolchakan nodded slightly. "Which one of these pieces of garbage hasn't had the privilege of seeing Stink?"

"The other whelps of Manure," said Dawuni.

Soolchakan checked his cheat sheet. "Op-Op, Shushank and Nunkwothk." He smiled. "I suggest that you three *things* hold your breath. You'll get to see, first hand, the planet of Stink and all the millions of bodies of Parasites that are there. If they're not dead, they are certainly close to it. They'll be heaving their guts out in those last moments of agony."

Pinsong grabbed Shushank. "Hold your breath...parasite."

Shushank took in a deep breath and both women vanished. Moments later both women reappeared. Shushank had a look of horror on her face. She puffed her breath out and fell to her knees sobbing. "They...they're there. They're dead. Thousands of our people are...just laying there dead."

"Millions," said Pinsong flatly.

Passifi grabbed Op-Op and gave her the tour.

Sazara took Nunkwothk on the tour.

On her return, Nunkwothk turned to Ootgreeg with a bitter look on her face. "Bodies everywhere. As far as you can see... through that yellow haze...in every direction. None of them moving.

When Op-Op was returned all she could do was stare off into space in shock.

Perposhk shouted in anger. "IS THAT YOUR PLAN? YOU'RE GOING TO KILL US ALL WITH...POLLUTION?"

Soolchakan smiled. "No, Army Leader, Perposhk. I'm going to add your name to our dictionary...and it will mean... pollution."

Bikaropin was annotating the new words. "What about that whelp that was already killed. Quok...I think it was. What about him?"

Soolchakan contemplated. "Quok is...dead. That sounds good. Quok...means unnatural death."

Ootgreeg was seething. "I'm gonna make you pay for this.

I'm gonna keep you alive…after I butcher some of your parts. I'm gonna make the rest of your life be nuthin' but pain."

"That vulgar thing is still in denial," said Gry as he shook his head. "It actually thinks that it is going to survive." He shook his head. "What do we need to do to convince that thing?"

Soolchakan smiled. "Vulgar! That's the next of Ootgreeg's whelp. Prepkood! That means…vulgar."

"The next son is Urb," said Meelana. "What does that mean?"

Soolchakan looked at the faces of the captured Teltermak. "Defeat! Because that is what you Teltermak are now…defeated. That's a good one."

"The next one is Proop," said Gersom.

Proop slapped at the bars. "Do you really think that you're going to stick me with some trashy name?"

"Yes," said Soolchakan with a grin. "You picked it: Trash."

Proop growled and started shaking the cell door in anger. He was just wasting time and energy.

"Next is the daughter…Op-Op," said Bikaropin.

"Useless," said Soolchakan. He smiled and nodded at that thought. He checked his cheat sheet. "We have two more. Both daughters. Shushank…is a good word for…disease." He thought for a few moments. "Nunkwothk…means confusion."

Ootgreeg could not even form a sentence. All he could do was stand there making some unintelligible noises as he heard each of his children being renamed.

Soolchakan snickered. "I need a dictionary...or a thesaurus. I want to go through each one of the...still living... Parasites...and choose the definition of their names." He turned to his fellow Owlamites. "Are you ready to copy these down?"

They all nodded.

Soolchakan looked at the list. "I looked up each one of your names...as to what they mean in the Teltermak dialect. I've decided that they should mean something...totally opposite... or just something different in the Owlamite dialect. Gockzoyon will be vermin. Zidz will be scum. Blobsot will be obese slob. Thoobwot will be babbling fool. Tok-Okot will be mentally crippled or damaged. Booboll will be decay. Rubfisisk will be bastard. Ongfok will be abductor. Oobroo will be inconsiderate. Unchomich will be tumor. Uhbrabra will be debauchery. Shtug will be outcast. Shkefko will be criminal. Jih-In-In is a chaotic name so it will be chaos. Oofinich will be wicked. Yoxoyoo will be worthless." He looked at Voovolokon and snickered. "The name Voovolokon will be masturbation." He chuckled.

She huffed in disgust and turned away while clenching both fists.

He continued. "The name Duwud will be dullard. Boorgrook will be scornful. Eelkwug will be diaper rash. Swod will be stench. Oovyotyut will be incapable. Dij will be dumb. Puprapo will be failure. Truhd will be impurity. Kolkakrik will be scam. Finally…Zoozkrutch will be known as unidentified toxic lump."

Ootgreeg laughed. "You buncha *Spiknoks* really think that we're gonna answer to that nonsense? Here you are keeping us prisoner and you don't even have the courtesy to feed us any form of good food. What makes you think that we'll bow to anything you do or say?"

"You're not going to be answering to anything because you'll all be dead…or should I say…quok…very soon," said Soolchakan angrily. "For nearly 13,900 years, you monsters have been causing us endless grief. Now, we can finally rid ourselves and the rest of the world of you parasites. We already showed you that all the rest of your ilk is already rotting away on a different planet. The 36 of you are the last of the parasitic race to exist. We haven't fed you any good food, because any food given to you is a complete waste, seeing as how we've condemned all of you to death."

Ootgreeg snarled. "And just exactly *what* gave you the right to judge us?"

"SELF DEFENSE!" Soolchakan gave him a defiant fixed stare while panting in a loud manner. "For nearly fourteen millennium you monsters have been doing everything you can to kill us. Now, we finally have the absolute upper hand and we're not going to give it back. We're going to make sure that none of you ever cause us any grief ever again."

Ootgreeg laughed. "We didn't wanna kill all of you. We needed to keep you as livestock, to keep breeding so we could keep making our potions. We didn't have a reason to kill all of you off completely. Like I told you before, the stuff that comes from your guts can't be reproduced synthetically. We have to use the real thing. In order to get the real thing we have to have the real thing. No way would we have killed all of you. We needed fresh stock...all the time."

Soolchakan looked at Bikaropin in disbelief. "Those parasites actually think that we would have submitted to that *h'oolyach*."

Bikaropin shrugged. "Stupidity knows no bounds."

Soolchakan shook his head. "Very true." He looked back at the prisoners. "This is how you are going to be executed. We have a bucket. In this bucket there are slips of paper. Each one of you has your name written on one piece of paper. When your name is drawn..." He pointed at a large tube. "...you will be placed in that chamber. We will close this end of the chamber." He smiled. "Once it is sealed, we will then open the other end of the chamber and...you will be jettisoned into the void of outer space. Death will be practically instantaneous, unfortunately. I really wanted to make you suffer...but...if I did that...I might start to enjoy the thought of torturing before killing. I don't ever want to enjoy torture or killing. I only kill when it is necessary for the survival of me and my children. Torture is only necessary if I need to find out something. I've found out everything about you that I care to know. I don't want to know anything more about any of you. And I have no reason to allow any of you any kind of mercy."

Ootgreeg huffed. "And, you stupid pile of *protch*, you think that we're just gonna let you cram us in that thing without a fight?"

Soolchakan held his hands up and started rubbing his fingers against the thumbs. At first small sparks appeared and then small bolts of electricity. "Bikaropin, draw a name."

Meffin held the bucket up. Bikaropin closed his eyes and turned his head away as he reached in the bucket. He pulled a slip of paper out and read it.

"Abductor is the first one to be executed," said Bikaropin flatly.

Soolchakan thought for a moment. "**Oh *h'oolyach*! Which one is Abductor**?"

Meffin checked her list. "**That would be Ongfok**."

Soolchakan looked around at the cells somewhat confused. "**Point him out**."

Meffin walked over to the cell holding Ongfok. "Abductor, come forward."

He folded his arms across his chest. "My name is Ongfok. I don't go by any of your *fonk vogoth*."

Soolchakan pointed his fingers at Ongfok and the electric bolts shot out. Ongfok was knocked backwards and stunned as he hit the back wall of the cell. Soolkan, Pelox, Lep and Zuztay were waiting in Spy dimension. They hopped portions of their hands into Home and picked the dazed Ongfok up. Shashy and

Yeema were wiggling their hands and fingers as if they were doing some kind of kinetic spell. As the four men carried Ongfok, they hopped him into Ghost dimension in order to take him from the cell *through the bars* and to the jettison tube. Several times, Shashy and Yeema did some wild animated arm movements, in order to make a bigger show.

The rest of the Teltermak were all rather stunned as they watched Ongfok being knocked out, carried out of the cell, or floating in the air, right through the bars, and then helplessly planted in the tube. Once in the tube, they could see that there was a monitor on the wall, above the tube, that lit up and showed the inside of the tube. They waited until Ongfok recovered from the electric punch that had knocked him silly. He saw where he was and tried to batter at the door of the tube while screaming in terror. He could not be heard because there was no microphone inside the tube.

Soolchakan tried to make it sound ceremonial. "Abductor... for the repeated and habitual crimes against the Owlamite people, you are sentenced to death. You will not be allowed any final comment because no one cares what you have to say. Good riddance to you and may you rot in the lowest parts of the 666 punishments." With that he pushed a button on the wall near the monitor.

Ongfok was rapidly pulled out of the tube and the spaceship as the air inside decompressed in less time than it takes to blink an eye. Another button was pressed, the outer door closed and the tube was once again pressurized.

Soolchakan sighed. "Who is next?" **"Make sure that we know which one it is before we start looking around like a bunch of bewildered *bimyocks*."**

Each name was drawn and each one made a vain attempt at avoiding going peacefully. Each one got shocked and was carried to the tube, apparently by some form of magic. Stench (a. k. a.) Swod was number 27 to be executed. Now all that remained was Ootgreeg and his children.

Soolchakan looked at Ootgreeg and smiled. "Hey, Manure, I have something special for you and your family." He sniffed. "We're going to let you think about it until tomorrow. We held all of you back on purpose." He smiled. "Manure is going to get to see all of his parasite children die in front of him before…" He let his words trail off menacingly. **"Turn the artificial gravity off in this ship. Let them float around for the night,"** he sent. He Jumped back to the gorge without finishing the spoken sentence. He decided to add to Ootgreeg's suffering.

All of the rest of the Owlamites Jumped back to the gorge as well.

Vymilla was the last to leave. She hit the switch on the artificial gravity and all of the Teltermak were now floating around their cells with no way of controlling their movements.

Op-Op was near panic. "They got some *powerful* magic. No wonder we could never totally control them."

Ootgreeg looked away. "Shut up and let me think. There's gotta be a way outta this. We're Teltermak. There's no way that we can ever be outsmarted by a bunch of stupid Owlams."

Prepkood scoffed. "Why is it that they can't outsmart us? Because of your prejudices that you've been spewing all of these centuries? We *never* got control of them. We had to hide as we killed each one. So just exactly *how* did we ever outsmart them… in any way, shape or form?"

Urb felt he had to put his thoughts in as well. "Precisely who is it that is so superior? I've never seen anyone do what they just did. They used levitation to pick those people up, levitation to move them and…I don't know even what to call it when they made them float right through these steel bars. Can you do that? I don't remember ever seeing you do anything like that."

Proop broke in. "If we're so smart, why is it that, in order to become smarter, we have to consume part of *their* brains? Shouldn't it be the other way around?"

Now Ootgreeg was not thinking. All he could do was float and pout. His sons were correct. It apparently was the Owlams who were superior. 'I shoulda just left them alone,' he thought. 'Too late now.' Just sit (or float) here, feeling sorry for himself, and wait for his own execution.

Soolchakan walked through the preparation area of one of the Owlam potion plants. He saw Dawuni and Basabee placing some pans on the work table. He approached them slowly as they arranged the pans.

He felt a little guilty. "Is all the research done…and are you ready?"

"Everything is ready," said Dawuni solemnly. "Got all of this stuff fully prepared."

Basabee sniffed. "Now all we need to do is finish it."

He nodded. "Then let's go."

They Jumped to the prison ship. Zuztay, Zenkin, Yaspon and Pabon were floating around as guards in the cell area, hanging on to bars in order to keep from getting dumped on the floor when the gravity was reinstalled.

"**Turn the gravity back on**," sent Soolchakan.

All of the Teltermak grunted in pain when they hit the floor. They were now all making several groaning and growling sounds as they rubbed several bruised areas.

The Owlamites all smiled as Soolchakan led a delegation into the area. The nine remaining Teltermaks had been moved to adjoining cells in order to keep all of the riffraff in as small an area as possible. The place reeked of urine. None of the urine had been floating around because the Teltermaks did not want to float into an airborne pool of it. They had all soiled their linen in order to keep the urine corralled.

Ootgreeg looked rather disgusted. "Am I supposed to thank you for allowing me a little last moment with my children? Don't wait for any thanks, cause it ain't coming."

Soolchakan smiled. "I didn't do anything for you. This was arranged for my satisfaction…and pleasure. The last of the Teltermak…uh…parasite race…is the nine of you. All related. I did it this way so…you could watch…as each one of your whelps is executed. That will be the last thing you see here…before we implement your fate."

Ootgreeg scoffed. "So you're gonna shoot em out that hole. I've already seen that macabre mess. How is this gonna be any different?"

Soolchakan turned to Bikaropin. "Pick a name."

Once again, Meffin had the bucket. She held it up. Bikaropin reached in and pulled out a slip of paper.

He read it. "Useless!" He looked up. "Useless, come forward!"

None of the Teltermak moved.

Soolchakan sighed. He started the Electric Finger Spell. **"They're not going to make it easy are they? Okay, I don't remember, which one is it**?"

"The second female child," sent Hisang. **"The one called Op-Op**."

He walked up to her cell. Her eyes were wide with terror. She backed up to the wall and flattened herself against it. He threw the bolts at her. She grunted in pain as she was stunned by the electric charge and fell limp to the floor. Once again, four Owlam pall bearers (hiding in Spy) picked her up and brought her out of the cell, while two others put on a show as if they were moving her through magic.

In this case, however, she was not taken to the jettison tube. She was taken to a chair. The other Teltermak watched in confusion as leather bands moved by themselves around her arms and legs, strapping her to the chair.

Soolchakan turned to Ootgreeg. "We invented a new form of death when we executed that other whelp of yours. These others will get the same."

Menola was hiding in Spy dimension as well. She walked over to the stack of porcelain plates and took the top one. To the Teltermak, it appeared as if the plate was just floating in air. Yesati grabbed the hair of the victim, pulling her head back. The plate was now hopped into Ghost and placed in the neck directly under the head...and promptly hopped back into Home. Op-Op now opened her eyes and mouth wide in shock and panic. She could do nothing because, the same as had happened to Quok, all synapsis to the body were completely cut off. The esophagus was blocked so she could not breathe. The brain was receiving no new supply of blood. The rest of her body quivered because it was still alive, however, receiving no orders from the brain. After three mithist, her eyes rolled back into her head. Yesati let go of the hair and Op-Op's head slumped forward.

The Teltermak now watched as the leather bands opened up and the body fell to the floor. The body seemingly floated off to the side and vanished.

Soolchakan turned to Bikaropin. "Who is next?"

Bikaropin pulled out another slip. "Vomit."

Ootgreeg could do nothing other than shake the bars and stand there screaming as he watched each one of his children suffocate. His curses and condemnations were a steady stream of ignored vulgarities.

Shushank (a. k. a.) Disease was the last to go.

Soolchakan looked at Ootgreeg with no satisfaction in his soul. "Did you enjoy the spectacle?"

Ootgreeg was enraged. His teeth were clenched tight and his breathing was so forced that there was spittle rolling off his chin. "YOU MURDERED MY CHILDREN, YOU *FONK!*"

"YOU MURDERED THOUSANDS OF MINE, YOU *CHOKWAD!* Unfortunately all I could do was kill nine of yours. If there had been more, I would have given you the pleasure of watching them all die." Soolchakan stepped back and let his anger subside. "Now, you are the one and only remaining member of the Parasite race. I'm going to let you think about that for another day…before we show you your fate." He turned to Bikaropin. "Turn the gravity off." He vanished.

All the rest of the Owlamites vanished and once again Ootgreeg was floating in the air again. Now he was totally alone and did not even have his complaining children there to antagonize him. There was nothing to listen to except the echo of his own complaints and curses…and sobbing…while smelling nothing but his own excretions.

Ootgreeg floated for two days…without any food or water. When the gravity was suddenly turned back on, he hit the floor hard. In his weakened condition he could not even brace himself. There was a loud splat heard as his feces hit the floor as well. He had dropped his pants during any bowel movement and he attempted to stay on the opposite side of the room from that floating excrement. He looked through the bars and saw Soolchakan's boots. He did not have the strength or desire to get up.

Soolchakan looked down at his long-time foe. "I have a surprise for you."

Ootgreeg just grunted. Suddenly his eyes opened wide in shock as he felt something happening with his stomach. He let out an involuntary moan. He looked up. "Whu...wuzzat?"

Soolchakan grinned. "A little trick we learned, a long time ago in Algothon. They hung a traitor and we kept him alive for several days by...teleporting food into his stomach. We decided that he didn't deserve a quick death. We didn't let him die until he had gone completely insane and...our insults and torture no longer meant anything to him."

Ootgreeg scoffed. "So you wanna kill me...with a full stomach."

"We're not going to kill you."

Now Ootgreeg was really surprised. "WHAT? What... does that mean?"

"You'll see."

Ootgreeg was blinded. The light was suddenly tremendously intense compared to the previous very dim lighting. He rubbed his eyes as he sniffed. The air had a much better smell to it as well. He blinked several times as his eyes became accustomed to the light. He discovered that he was no longer in the brig area. He was in a rather large room, surrounded by thousands of the bottles of potions that had been manufactured from the Owlam "guts". He heard some clanking of chains and found that he was shackled, by the wrists and ankles, to the floor of this new room.

Soolchakan appeared in another area of the room. "Look around you. Does this look familiar?"

"It's...all of the potions...we made from you...Owlams."

Soolchakan nodded. "Yes it is. We decided to give them all to you."

Ootgreeg shook his head trying to grasp what he was hearing. "You...you're giving me...back...alla the potions? You're gonna let me...profit from them?"

"Yes, we're giving them to you. No, you're not going to profit from them. You are now on a different spaceship...in the same dimension as the prison ship. When I leave...you will be the *only* one on this ship. This ship has no propulsion system. It simply...floats in space at the whim of any gravitational pull. The only gravity, in this dimension, comes from the one and only star in this dimension. This ship will be slowly drawn towards that star. Eventually it will be engulfed in the heat and radiation of that star. Then and only then will you die." He smiled. "During the time that you're floating towards the star, the only thing that you will have as victuals...will be the potions. There is absolutely no other form of food on this ship. This ship has an air filtration system that operates on some long-life batteries so you won't suffocate. It has a waste disposal system so you can get rid of the empty bottles, as well as your favorite excretions. It has no windows. You will not know how close you are to the star. You will not know...until it gets extremely hot in here...that you are close to death. You will simply float towards your fate. The whole time, you will be able to contemplate how you have lost everything... because you refused to leave us alone."

Ootgreeg made an attempt at being facetious. "Do I at least get a change of clothing?"

Soolchakan chuckled. "You're going to be totally alone. You won't need clothing. You can run around here naked and stinking. There's nothing to clean your clothes with and there is nothing to clean yourself. Just you...and the potions. For the rest of your useless existence. You have *nothing* but your precious, disgusting potions." He chuckled. "Oh, by the way, that bunch you call Ghost Assassins...that was us...all the time. I thought that you'd like to know that tidbit of information before I leave you alone...forever." He vanished.

Ootgreeg squawked in surprise as the chains vanished as well and now he was free and alone, for the rest of his life - however long that was going to be.

Back at the gorge, Bikaropin stared in surprise. "You didn't tell him?"

Soolchakan was taken aback. "I didn't tell him...now. As you know, there are 32 special bottles. They will be easy access to him. After he consumes bottle number 32, of the 32, a recorded message will tell him that those 32 special bottles...the prime ingredient...came from *his* children." Soolchakan smiled.

"Tell him afterwards, otherwise he might never touch them. Once he has drunk them, he will have the pleasure of knowing that he devoured his own children."

Bikaropin shrugged. "Sounds good to me."

Bikaropin was on the Bridge of one of one of the ships in #45. He was staring at the death ship that was floating Ootgreeg to the star as it moved so slowly that you could barely perceive the movement. "**Soolchakan, this is Bikaropin. Can you hear me**?"

Soolchakan came back. "**Yes, what is it**?"

"**You know that it could take over 1,000 years before that prison ship floats into the star. What should happen if...he should figure a way out**?"

"**Where is he gonna go? Who could possibly rescue him? Besides that, if he does do something out of the ordinary, we can still smack him down and get him right back on course. There's no one in any of the dimensions who knows him or will help him. He is totally alone**."

"**I hope you're right**."

"**I'm pretty sure that I am. Plus, as I said, if he does do something remarkably unusual, we can always do a reset**."

Bikaropin just nodded.

9

Soolchakan called everyone into the main auditorium. Once again, he felt somewhat despondent over what he was seeing. Before this last round with the Teltermak the population had been over 2,200. Now, even with the youngest children the population of Owlam was less than 200.

He was glad that the Teltermak were finally gone. Their population was down to *one* and that *one* could no longer cause any more harm to anybody. He still felt rather empty though. Revenge was sweet, but only for a few moments. After that, there comes the realization that it is not as satisfying as one would think it would be. You can only kill your enemy once. His only real hope was that absolutely all of the Teltermak were gone from Hardooth and that no Owlamite would ever have to worry about being attacked and gutted by any Teltermak again. He was also hoping that the Teltermak had never divulged what the "prime ingredient" was in those disgusting potions.

He started his oration. "I know that we would all like to sit back and relax after what has just occurred. I would like that myself. The problem here is…in the past we thought we had completely wiped those monsters out…only to have them spring up somewhere else and…cause us more grief." He lowered his eyes. "We're going to remain vigilant. We're going to go back... regularly and check all of their hideouts. We're going to search for any sign that they are still around. In this latest fiasco with those monsters...we lost 2,082 of our...brothers, sisters, sons, daughters, mothers and fathers." He shook his head. "I do NOT want to lose another one of my relatives...to another one of those things. We are going to check all of those places and...some places we never checked before. We are not going to let any of them rest...if there are any that are still alive. We must remain vigilant in keeping an eye out for any return of any Teltermak... and kill on sight." He Jumped back to his apartment.

Soolchakan was sitting in the dining room sipping on some fruit juice when he heard a knock on the door. He sighed. "Enter."

Bikaropin hopped to Ghost and walked through the door. He hopped back to Home. He walked over and sat down at the same table. "Are you sure this is what you want?"

"I want to make sure that they never hurt us again. We thought we had them before but..." He looked off to the side and cleared his throat.

Bikaropin nodded. "In all of the other...instances...did we ever get any of the original ones? Did we ever get anyone in the upper echelons of rank? Do you even remember what their officer ranks were called?"

Soolchakan sighed as he looked in the glass at the juice. "The lowest was called Brass Standard. Next was Copper Standard, Silver Standard and Gold Standard. Then it went to

Icon Second, Icon, Icon Supreme, Leader, Section Leader, Army Leader…and finally Ultimate Leader."

"And in the past…did we ever get any of the top four?"

"Maybe…one or two."

"And also in the past, how many originals did we ever get?"

"Originals?"

"You know, someone like you who was originally there, when that Algothon firestorm attack, that you told us about… occurred. How many did we ever get before?"

"Again, maybe one or two…until lately."

"This time…we got 36 in just the top three ranks. We got fifteen originals in the top three ranks. According to what I've found in the computer, we got over 800 who were originals…most in the top *five* ranks."

"I know. I would still like to make sure that we got all of them. There could have been someone who…was hiding somewhere else…for whatever reason. We keep looking until we're all sure. In case you didn't notice, all of the places that they had to hide, primary and secondary, they were all underground. Those monsters love living underground. They are tunneling fools. We can't see that from the air. We have to keep looking for tunnels, caves and caverns."

"Okay." Bikaropin stood up and departed. He did not feel as if he had accomplished very much in this conversation, however, seeing as how Soolchakan was over 10,000 years old before Bikaropin was born, that was a lot of experience with the Teltermak that he could not argue about. The search would continue. Those monsters had been incredibly elusive for a very long time. It could happen again…not likely…but…

After five years of searching, once again, Bikaropin went to Soolchakan with a certain look in his eyes.

"You're doing it again."

Soolchakan looked up a little surprised. "Doing…what?"

"Ever since the end of that last Teltermak war…there haven't been any new Owlamites born. This is the year 4866. That last Teltermak has enjoyed five years of at least a 1,000 year journey. All of our searches and proof say that he is the only Teltermak that still exists. I think that some of your despondency is, again, stopping the women from having any…desire…or need…or want. That war is over. Let's start anew."

Soolchakan growled in frustration. "You can't blame everything on me."

Bikaropin shrugged with a questioning look on his face. "Who else could possibly stop all of the women from procreating… without some form of physical force?"

Soolchakan huffed. He took in a deep breath. "If there are any women who wish to have children, you may do so with my blessing. I realize that it adds an extra burden, being pregnant while we are doing all of this searching, but…the search is necessary in order to assure our safety. We still need future generations in order to keep going. Have children…if you want to." He cleared his throat. "Satisfied?"

Bikaropin smiled. "If they don't have any children now, I, now, certainly can't blame it on you."

"Anything else?"

"Yes, I wanted to inform you about the computer systems that the Teltermak were using. It is so…archaic…compared to what we have."

Soolchakan snickered. "They never had the opportunity to obtain newer and more sophisticated equipment like we did. All of that outworld technology that was designed to move spacecraft from one star to another. We have the better technology but… the originals from the Algothon attacks…they still remembered computer technology. They never let it die. I remember… all of those attacks from outer space…they always attacked the most advanced technology first. They killed the most intelligent minds…first. They would do everything they could to demolish any modernization that we had in order to accomplish their conquest. It seems that since we have the vast majority of our technology underground…as did the Teltermak…that is how it all survived." He looked thoughtful for a moment. "Of course, there was that one bunch…who did find us in the gorge. They wandered around there…and murdered several people…before we destroyed them."

Bikaropin nodded. "Yes, we did have to rebuild and replace that…array out in orbit…several times."

"Up until we hopped the array into Spy dimension. Then we're the only ones who can see it."

"Yes. I don't think that we'll have to worry about anyone else taking over that horrid potion manufacturing." He looked off to the side a little disgusted. "Because of their greed, in holding onto a monopoly, they never wrote down, or entered any of the information in their computers, as to exactly what the..." He shuddered in disgust. "...*main ingredient* was...in those potions."

Soolchakan scoffed. "Hooray for stingy and selfish ideology," he said sarcastically. "If they never shared it with anybody then we can rest easy, knowing that the secret dies with... Manure...in a few hundred years."

"Bikaropin nodded and sighed.

In the year 4867, three new Owlamites were born. In the year 4868 there were none. In the 4869 there were two new additions.

Soolchakan figured that it might take a little while before many of the women were ready to try again. He really did not wish to push them. The women were the ones who would go through the most headaches (and body aches). It was their decision to make...or not. If someone had been expecting a flood, they were now disappointed. A trickle was better than nothing. The trickle was so small that between the end of the second Teltermak war and the end of the forty-ninth century ATUT, only twelve children were born. By the end of the century there were 222 Owlamites.

The fiftieth century did not start off with a bang. Between 4901 and 4911 only two children were born. Still, Soolchakan still did not wish to push any of the women. He let them take their time thinking about all of the possibilities. In the year 4920, several women decided to start having children. It became a bit more popular after that.

Soolchakan was still puzzled over the fact that during the last Teltermak war, none of the Owlamites from the sixteenth or seventeenth generation were ever mesmerized by those mind machines. Since he was not the one to figure out riddles, he once again turned to Bikaropin. "Why is it that the later generations… were not affected?"

Bikaropin shrugged. "Maybe…after all these generations, with all the things that the women can do to a child in the womb… maybe they've perfected the brain to where those generations ignore that kind of thing."

Soolchakan shook his head. "I really wish I could be sure."

Bikaropin grunted. "Do you want me to turn one of those *chokwad* things on to find out?"

"ABOLUTELY NOT!" Soolchakan looked away in horror. "As a matter of fact…I want those vulgar things dismantled. I don't want anyone to ever know that those things existed."

Bikaropin smiled. "Destroying is easy. I'll get a few others to assist. We'll have the parts scattered all over the place… and make sure that any schematic is turned to ashes and the ashes are trampled to dust."

Soolchakan nodded. "The sooner the better."

The year 4962 brought the birth of the eighteenth generation. Inamyon 23, Sondomon and Ditishi became the parents of Rinnboz (*Wield*). Soolchakan welcomed this new baby boy to the world with a smile, while secretly inside, he was grieving and wishing that Bonarain, Kiyalee and Chyning were here to enjoy the moment. Once again, he asked himself the question: How many more generations would he see before some kind of old age or another attack from outer space took him to his grave? He also wondered if they would ever get lucky and find Bonarain…with the blue stone.

By the end of the fiftieth century, the population had risen to 323, including 74 in the fifteenth generation, 91 in the sixteenth, 32 in the seventeenth and 6 in the eighteenth generation. 119 covered all of the other fourteen generations. The question still remains unanswered as to why the newest generations were never affected by the mind machines. Soolchakan was not sure that he ever wanted to know the real answer as to why. Maybe it was because the repairs that had been accomplished on each fetus had brought about more perfection as each new generation came about…maybe.

In the year 5050 ATUT, Soolchakan was musing over the population being back up to 454. The adults (who were not pregnant) were going all over the planet, still searching for any kind of new trace of those wretched Teltermak.

Suddenly one day, Hisang, Cheesang and Dawuni came to Soolchakan, all looking horrified. They were all talking so fast (and at the same time) all he heard was a bunch of excited babbling. At first, Soolchakan thought they had found a new nest of the Teltermak. Then he started hearing words like: Sacrifice, altar, temples and false gods. He was hearing most of what they were saying, however, he was not hearing anything that was intelligible.

"QUIET!" He now saw three women with their lips clenched shut. "One at a time, please…starting with the eldest." He looked, wide-eyed, at Hisang because he knew that she was the eldest of the trio.

Hisang smiled nervously. "Thank you." She cleared her throat. "There's this horrible thing going on out there. Someone has built…what they call…holy places. They seem to be everywhere. These things are…places where they worship gods that…no one thought about, except in some of those ancient myths and legends."

Soolchakan shrugged. "Any…particular one that… worries you?"

"As a matter of fact, two different gods. Skabilt and Hiv."

He started running those words through his mind. He had heard of them from, a lesson in mythology, a long, long, long time ago. The only one that he could remember, with any clarity, the most was the legendary King of the gods – Red Sssorg Masnie Nie. He was not a god of anything in particular, he was just the King who ruled in the 21 Paradises. He was the one who settled squabbles between the other greater gods, lesser gods and demigods. "Okay, who *exactly* are Skabilt and Hiv?"

Hisang looked a little disgusted. "Skabilt is supposedly the god of the underworld. He controls all of the 666 punishments of the lower realms. Hiv is the god of evil...any and all evil acts committed by...anybody."

Soolchakan now felt a little disturbed. "And someone is worshipping those two mythical monsters?"

"Yes," said Cheesang. "And they're sacrificing *children*... on altars...any children of any race to those...things."

He closed his eyes and sighed in disgust. "Wonderful," he said sardonically. "Why is it that someone always has to come up with the worst possible things to get attention? Why can't they... go with something nice?"

"They might not get the attention that they really want," said Dawuni.

"They could spread all kinds of fear with the evil," said Hisang.

"You said...everywhere." He shook his head. "I need something...a little more specific. Exactly where? Exactly how many?" He took in a deep breath and let it out slowly. "I need to know just how much it affects us...if at all."

Ahemeni had come into the room as well. "They will take any children...by force. They don't care whose children they lay on that unholy horror of an altar. Any child will do – as long as they're prepubescent."

He nodded. "And that could be quite some time in pre-adolescents...especially for our children."

"It could be the same for a lot of the Elf races," said Dawuni. "Ours are not the only children who mature slowly. Numerous others age slowly as well. None of them age as slowly as us...or live as long, but...again, those, so called, priests...don't care whose children they murder...as long as they can put some innocent child on the altar."

He closed his eyes. "How often do they commit these murders?"

"During any equinox they kill at least one in each of their temples," said Hisang. "During the High Holy Day, in the middle of Citendali...they usually make a festival of slaughtering at least 20 victims...in every single temple."

He looked up at the calendar. The date was currently Citendali 16, 5050. The High Holy Day, where every religion in the world celebrated something. That day fell between 15 and 16 Citendali. The slaughter had been accomplished already. It was four full months before the Fall Equinox so there was time to prepare for any action that he might take. "Show me where this mess is taking place."

Hisang quickly strode up to him, grabbed him and Jumped.

Soolchakan looked around as he found himself in a very large, very dark sanctuary. There were numerous tall candles along all of the walls that did not take away from the gloominess of the room. In the center of the room there was a large golden table. This was probably the altar where the victim was tied down and murdered. The stench of contaminated and decomposing flesh gave him the main clue to this activity.

In the east side of the room, most of it was taken up by a gigantic, dark marble statue of a male figure that had three sets of horns growing out of a bald head. The statue was in a seated position and there was a big grin on the contorted face. In each outstretched hand there was, what appeared to be, a child that had been mangled.

There were four children in the room who were mopping up blood from around the sacrificial altar. They were all weeping as they continued their labor because there was an overseer who had a whip who was encouraging the children to hasten in their labor.

The overseer was dressed in a dark red robe. He had a ruddy complexion and he was barefoot.

Hisang pointed at the overseer. "He's a Perek Elf. I don't know if you remember or not, but, they all have that dark skin and they have retractable claws on both their hands and feet."

"I've come across them before. I didn't remember what they were called but…I do remember that they're not very nice."

Hisang nodded. "Some of the priests here are Perek, others are Heyyah while others are Bloynid Elf."

He was a little shocked. "Bloynid? They…usually stayed on Aerisau. *What* are they doing here?"

Hisang grunted in disgust. "Where there's a temple to Hiv, you'll find the Bloynid. They're the ones who have been pushing the worship of Hiv and Skabilt." She sniffed. "Dawuni said that she thought she saw a Fastern Elf here as well."

Soolchakan rolled his eyes. "Why don't we bring out *all* of the nasty ones? Did you see any P'Lalfan or Shan-Ad Elf?"

She smiled. "No, I don't remember seeing any of those." She sighed. "Is there anything that we can do...here...to get rid of this atrocity?"

"How many of these places are there?"

"We know of three here on South Chilamte and four on North Chilamte. We have some suspicions about Aerisau...but no proof yet."

He nodded. "We have a little over four months before the Fall Equinox. Find all of them and then we plan and strike and end this idiocy."

"What if we find some other...atrocities...along the way?"

He hung his head. "Each thing as we find it. One catastrophe at a time...please!"

Mahanee, Hisang, Bikaropin and Shashy came in with reports. For two months the Owlamites had been going all over the planet. They had found numerous temples where 94 different gods were worshipped. There were sacrifices and devotions that were required for each one. Livestock, food, money, jewelry, time and lives of sentient beings – usually children.

He looked at the list that had been drawn up. The gods fell into three echelons: High, middle and demi. The high gods had to be worshipped even if you did not like them. The middle gods were worshipped if you had a career in their area of influence: Aantir covered musicians, Blyteni covered metallurgy or blacksmiths, Fisken covered archery, Hasa-Oon covered farmers who raise different crops, Koshim covered carpentry…and several others. The demigods were equally limited. Blad covered wine, Crotra covered poetry, Kazabilo covered singing, Oorped covered competitive sports, Rokiyi covered gambling and one who covered the manufacturing and drinking of spirits (other than wine) named Dahlee-O-Onka.

"This is ridiculous," said Soolchakan. "In…history classes…I heard of some of these…things." He shook his head. "Some of them…I've never heard of before." He scoffed. "Look at this! There are four different gods who deal with war. Votiquep, a high god who covers all war. Then there are three middle gods: Waldaka who covers ambushing an enemy, Zeljik who covers attack and Treko who covers counterattack."

Hisang looked up from her copy. "Is it possible that this… King of the gods…Red Sssorg Masnie Nie is…the Great Maker that you've taught us about?"

Soolchakan shook his head in disgust. "No, absolutely not. According to the myth, he just sits there, on his extremely obese butt, settling squabbles between all of the other gods. He has nothing to do with what happens here on the planet. The Great

Maker, on the other hand, stands alone...as the one and only true God. He watches over all of us. He is totally ubiquitous." He clenched his jaws. "He seems to have been forgotten, in favor of all of these...fabricated beings."

Shashy cleared her throat. "Are we going to...try to lead the people back to...the Great Maker?"

"We should," said Soolchakan flatly.

Bikaropin looked around. "So where do we start...with getting rid of these false gods?"

Soolchakan looked up. "We start with any god that requires the murder of innocent children. Children are the future. If you murder your children – no matter what the reason – you've murdered your future."

Bikaropin shrugged. "That means that we start with Skabilt, middle god of the underworld and Hiv, the high god of evil. Right now, they're the only ones that require the sacrifice of children...any children...or any living sentient creature."

Shashy rolled her eyes. "That alone is a daunting task. There are 220 temples to Hiv and 151 to Skabilt. That means that each time there's a required sacrifice...371 children are murdered...planet wide."

Mahanee shuddered in disgust. "Multiply that by at least 20 on the High Holy Day."

Bikaropin looked sick. "That's...7,420 children...in one day!"

"That's unacceptable," said Soolchakan flatly. "There are only 454 of us...including babies. We can't expect the babies to go out and help us...nor can we expect mothers with infants to assist so...with only...51 days till the Fall Equinox, where they kill more children...we've got to get busy crushing those horrid cults. If we don't...that means that the deaths of those children could be on our heads."

Bikaropin raised his eyebrows. "Where do we start?"

Soolchakan shrugged. "Which one is geographically the closest to us?"

"There's one in Peegruch...just a little south of the High Country cliffs," said Shashy.

Soolchakan nodded. "Sounds like as good a place as any."

Shashy looked a little guilty. "Should we really be interfering with the lives of other peoples?"

Soolchakan gave her a dull look. "7,420...*children*...just on the High Holy Day. Do you want to rethink that again? How many children did you lose in all of the Teltermak wars? Another good question: How many of those sacrificed children are related to the rotten garbage that kills the children on those heinous alters? They probably have some rule about their own children...being exempt from the atrocity."

She looked down and shuffled her feet a little. "I lost... seventeen...of my own children. I lost two husbands."

"And that was wars" said Bikaropin. "This isn't war, this is just...*horrible*!" He cleared his throat and looked a little confused. "I don't think that starting with the closest one will work for the best."

Soolchakan looked up expectantly. "You have a better solution?"

"Time zones." Bikaropin smiled. "The different murders will take place at different times...depending on the geographical location and when the sun comes up over that specific spot."

Mahanee looked a little surprised. "Good point! That way...we don't have to try hitting all of them at the same time."

Soolchakan nodded. "So we point them out...in the order that they'll be waking up and...starting their heinous ritual. That'll work."

Leegkoy, 31 Consoray, 5050. The Owlamites had listed all of the places in order of being attacked and had landmarked where they were going to show up. They had memorized all of the "priests" at each site in order to determine who the primary (and most fanatical) murderer was. They all went to their starting points and waited for the sun to come up in that particular spot.

Astekoy came all too soon. The Fall Equinox and the first day of the year 5051. The day that the two cults would be thwarted in committing their murders.

Soolchakan wanted to be the one who started it all. He stood in the sanctuary of the temple. At the moment, he was in Observation dimension. He was dressed completely in white with a hood and a mask over his head. If he was going to show himself he did not want anyone recognizing him or his race.

This temple was located in the eastern section of Dreeland on the continent of Cifpasica. This was the place where the day started on the planet - in accordance with the location of the International Date Line. He watched as the High Priest walked in, doing some ceremonial rituals as he walked in. He had the long, ugly looking dagger in his right hand and he held it out at arm's length, with the tip pointed up, as he walked up to the altar. He was mumbling some kind of strange noises as he headed for the altar. Soolchakan came up behind him and lightly tapped the right shoulder of the priest. The priest was momentarily distracted as he felt the touch. He looked off to his right and behind him in order to see who touched him. When he saw no one, he went back to his ritualistic mumbling, though looking a little confused. What he did not realize was that when he was touched, his right arm (along with the dagger) had been hopped into Ghost.

A small Heyyah girl was dragged into the sanctuary by two other priests. She was naked, sobbing and pleading for her life. Her pleas fell on deaf ears. Two other priests were at the altar, preparing the ropes that would hold the victim in place. She was practically slammed onto the altar and tied down while still sobbing, struggling and pleading for her life.

A man and a woman were then ushered in. They were being watched very carefully by several armed men wearing leather armor that was the same color as the robes of the priests. In looking over the rituals of this cult Soolchakan found out that the parents of the child, to be sacrificed, were given the "honor" of a front row seat, unless the child was an orphan. Then no one got the honor of being there. There would be nothing standing in the way of the parents seeing their child slaughtered…to the glory of Hiv.

Soolchakan decided to see what was in the mind of the monster who was about to perform the ritualistic murder. After a few moments he shook his head in total disgust. This priest was doing nothing but mumbling gibberish. He had seen several other priests do this same thing so he was following their lead. He had been told that it was a song of praise to Hiv, however, he did not know the words. He had prayed to Hiv several times and had asked why Hiv never spoke to him personally.

Soolchakan smirked as he sent a telepathic message to the priest. **"I do not like to talk to any of you *bimyocks* who murder children**!"

The priest stopped his mumbling and looked very startled. He looked around to see if anyone else was reacting to what he had heard. He cleared his throat and whispered. "Great and mighty Hiv…is that really…you?"

"Of course it is you stupid piece of carrion. Who else would waste their time talking to a rotten *bimyock* like you?"

The priest swallowed hard. "But…why do you say that… you don't want children? That Bloynid Elf…he said…"

"Nothing that was worth listening to. He's a Bloynid! I don't recognize his authority."

The man shook his head in confusion. "No! This is a test!

You're testing me! I will do…what needs to be done for your glory. I have no problem with it."

The high priest turned to the main doors of the sanctuary and motioned to two other priests. The doors were opened and a large congregation of people of mixed races were forced to enter the room. They were all being pushed and hurried into the room, being prodded with spears, in order for there to be many witnesses to the sacrifice. The temple guards were also carrying some very large axes and whips that they were using to push people along.

Soolchakan growled to himself. 'Okay, *bimyock*,' he thought. 'I gave you a chance. You had to go and be stupid.' He waited for the moment.

The priest started his mumbling again. He looked down at the crying child tied to the altar and raised the dagger, point down. The parents of the child started screaming for her life. He closed his eyes and did a little more mumbling. The terrified cries of the child echoed throughout the large room. He came down with the dagger, aimed directly at the heart of the child. The dagger and his hand went through the child…and the altar. The girl screamed (and peed all over the altar). The parents screamed. Then there was some mass confusion because no one saw any blood as the priest made several more attempts at stabbing the girl.

Soolchakan looked over at the statue. **"Okay, Hisskey… blow it up**!"

"Yes, Sir," sent Hisskey. She hit a button that activated both of the small explosives.

The hands of the grotesque statue were blown completely

off. The noise was deafening as it reverberated inside the sanctuary. The attention of everyone in the room was on the statue and the damage that it had just suffered.

Soolchakan took that moment of confusion to grab the dagger away from the priest, hop the dagger into Home dimension and ram it into the chest of the high priest. With his eyes wide from shock and pain, the priest sank to his knees and slowly expired.

Enmeez and Arungpon cut the ropes holding the sacrificial girl. She sat up looking down at her chest, looking very confused as to why the dagger had not harmed her. She then looked at her shocked parents. She started to crawl off of the altar and head for her parents. Two of the priests grabbed her and held her in place. They had both been looking at the cut ropes wondering how the cuts had happened.

Soolchakan had jumped up and was standing in the middle of the altar. He hopped himself to Ghost dimension. Now, everyone who was in the room saw the ghostly apparition. He pulled out a sheet, hopped it into Home dimension and wrapped it around the terrified girl.

The two priests made an attempt at stopping Soolchakan from covering the child.

Soolchakan scoffed. **"The one to my right is first**." He flipped his right hand in the face of the priest as if to rudely dismiss him.

Arungpon was standing behind the priest. When Soolchakan flipped his hand, Arungpon grabbed the robes of the priest and as violently as he could, threw the priest back away from child and altar. When Soolchakan flipped his left hand at the other priest, Enmeez yanked the robes of that one, throwing him away from the altar. Arungpon and Enmeez now had clubs in their hands. If the priests made any attempt at getting close to the girl, they were going to get clobbered…by something that they could not see at all.

Soolchakan picked the panic stricken child up and attempted to calm her. "**You are safe now. No one is going to harm you**."

The tear-stained child's face changed from terror to terrified confusion. Soolchakan started slowly walking toward the surprised (and somewhat stunned) parents of the child. He reached them and handed the bundled child to her mother who tearfully accepted her daughter. "The Great Maker does not like this idiotic slaughter of the innocent." He then hopped to Spy dimension. "**Okay, Hisskey…hit it!**"

With that, Hisskey poured a very strong acid over the head of the statue. The sizzling sound could be heard very easily because no one was speaking. They were all too amazed at what they had just witnessed.

Soolchakan quickly ran back to the altar, hopped up on it and hopped back to Home dimension. He was trying desperately to keep from laughing as he saw the faces of the horrified priests. "ALL WHO ARE HERE, LISTEN AND HEED! I REPRESENT THE GREAT MAKER! I DECLARE THAT THIS *THING* CALLED HIV…IS A FALSE IDOL. NEVER BOW DOWN TO IT AGAIN! NEVER WORSHIP THAT THING AGAIN! IT IS AN

INSULT TO YOU AND TO THE EXISTENCE OF THE GREAT MAKER. DESTROY ALL WHO DECLARE THEMSELVES AS PRIESTS OF THIS FALSE IDOL!" He grunted in disgust as he saw that no one was moving. "WHEN I SAID YOU SHOULD DESTROY THOSE PRIESTS...I MEANT *NOW*!" He hopped to Spy.

The soldiers in the red leather armor immediately turned their whips and axes on the priests. When the rest of the throng saw that the soldiers were now on their side, the priests were now the ones screaming in pain as they were disarmed of their daggers. They were then stabbed, hacked, beaten, stomped, bludgeoned and whipped to death.

The mother of the girl ran from the riot, holding her daughter close. The father, after seeing that his wife and daughter were safe, jumped in, enthusiastically, on the destruction of the priests and the unholy sanctuary.

Soolchakan looked for his children. **"One down, 370 to go. Let's get to our next destination**."

Enmeez, Hisskey and Arungpon all Jumped with Soolchakan to their next target.

The way things had been set up, there were 70 teams of four people. That meant that each team only had to take out five or six temples. It made things much easier for all of them that way and they were able to destroy all of the temples to Skabilt and Hiv in that one day.

Over 27,500 priests of the two evil deities were killed in that same day. It was rumored that over 2,000 escaped by shedding their ceremonial robes and donning any rag they could find, even if it was inhabited by unknown vermin.

The people who "assisted" in destroying the temples were able to find and ransack the vaults and coffers of the temples. An untold amount of wealth was redistributed back to the people who were cheated out of it as the Hiv priests had demanded gold as well.

When the last temple in the westernmost island of Roonifim was destroyed, the Owlamites celebrated over having ridded the world of the murdering cult while the Bloynid were licking their wounds and grieving over the fact that they had lost their main source of income. They were trying to determine who did this horrible thing to them, however, since all occurrences seemed to be supernatural, they were completely lost. They had to retreat to their original home in Aerisau and think of new ways to extort money.

While the Perek had been a major part of the cult, they had not been as financially dependent on the offerings as the Bloynid. Still they were doing what they could to determine how the overthrow had happened, however, they could not come up with any rational or natural explanation either. Divine intervention seemed to be the only answer, even though most of them did not believe in or follow the Great Maker.

Soolchakan hoped they would not have to do anything like that again. As he had stated, he did not like to kill, however, he would if it was necessary.

They started looking at all of the other false idols that were being worshipped and wondered how they should get rid of them. Hopefully they could get rid of them without the mass slaughter of priests like they had with the two very evil deities.

Soolchakan now had the idea of going on a campaign to rid the world of any false idol. Even if they seemed benevolent and good for the people, if the deity came from legend with no proof, he did not like the idea of any worship of those false gods growing. This kept the Owlamites rather busy for quite a while.

10

The Owlamites spent the next few decades desecrating all kinds of pagan temples. They did check closely to see if any of them required the sacrifice of sentient beings. Those had to go first. Since the destruction of Hiv and Skabilt, they found no one willing to murder children or adults in their rituals...so far. The next goal was to get rid of ones who demanded exorbitant amounts of wealth. They were the ones who were destroying the local economies and turning most of the citizenry into financial slaves to the pagan religions and the nobility.

For some strange reason, every time they destroyed some pagan temple, another one would sprout up nearby. The priests of that particular god kept on coming up with some excuse that the people had not been loyal enough and since another one had to be built, it would be placed in a more deserving area...and the people would have to pay for the construction thereof. The Owlamites realized that this was going to be a long and formidable task (more closely resembling a quest) getting rid of all of the false idols.

In most cases, after creating chaos and destruction in some of these places, the Owlamites liberally distributed books that gave a full description of the history and call to worship for the Great Maker. Many of the aristocracy and priests of the pagan religions did not like the confines of that belief. It gave them very little wiggle room in forcing people to worship the God their way as well as what could be done with any wealth acquired in the coffers of the temples. They did not like the fact that there were too many rules that allowed the lower class any kind of equality in the eyes of the God.

All wealth, in the coffers of the Great Maker, was to be used to assist the sick, the widow, the orphan, anyone who was destitute because of circumstances beyond their control and the upkeep of the temples (without being extravagant). The information was very strict about not giving anything to freeloaders or just keeping the money for the greedy purposes of the nobility (or some greedy cleric). The nobility did not like the people having their own kind of savings because that kept those people from being reliant on the higher ups and made many people self-reliant thus independent. This meant that in most cases the nobility was not needed for a great many things. They wanted the people to be dependent on the nobility for everything. The nobility wanted bigger government where they controlled all aspects of life and the lower class had to bow to all demands at even the slightest whim of the aristocrats.

Pelox and a few others came to Soolchakan. "Sir, are you really sure that we're doing the right thing…in destroying all of these temples…to all those gods? Are you sure that they're… false?"

Soolchakan shook his head in disgust. "Think about it! How many different gods have we assaulted or insulted? Don't you think that if that, so-called, god were real…don't you think that they would have done something against us by now? Any – *ANY* – deity that is worth their divinity would have surely taken retribution by now. Have we suffered any form of supernatural punishment…of any kind? Have we suffered any punishment of any kind at all? Any god of evil would be going all out for revenge in the most insidious and painful method possible. Where are they?"

Withkemi cleared her throat. "How about the fact that I've lost four of my children to those horrible Teltermak? Isn't that some kind of divine punishment?"

He glared back at her. "How many of those children were lost *before* we started destroying those temples? All of them… right? How many of your children have been lost since we started destroying the temples?"

Withkemi looked a little guilty. "I lost four children… before. I've lost…none of my children since we started the destruction."

Soolchakan calmed down. "Right," he said softly. "The Teltermak cost us dearly. These…false gods…have cost us nothing but the time that it takes to ruin them. If you look at all of the history of each one, any punishment to anyone, who dared to defy the god, was dished out by the clerics, or their private armies who pushed that religion. Find one time, which can actually be proven, where there was some kind of divine intervention or punishment by that particular deity…that can be *proved.*"

Iomissa scoffed as she shook her head. "We've been at this

false god clean-up for about twenty years and…we're still going strong. Like you said: No deity worth their divinity would have allowed that to happen."

Iscama looked worried. "But we've kept ourselves hidden," she said. "What happens if that deity is real…and they reveal us to…their clerics?"

Cleef threw his hands up in frustration. "If that deity were real, it would have exposed us by now! We haven't been exposed, so, any deity where we've been constantly insulting their existence and assaulting their temples and clerics…they don't have the power to stop us from that desecration…thus…NOT REAL!"

Soolchakan nodded. "And so, we will keep on doing it until someone can prove that those deities are real." He became very serious. "And there *will* have to be some kind of supernatural incident in order to prove that reality."

Each one of the Owlamites vanished as they Jumped back to their own apartments.

In 5080, Idonbrok and Mipi of the Eighteenth, announced the birth of the first member of the nineteenth generation - A boy named Yamshono. Soolchakan felt very good about yet another generation while he still grieved over the disappearance of Bonarain and the deaths of Kiyalee and Chyning.

In the year 5150, Bikaropin came to Soolchakan. Soolchakan sighed despondently because he saw the look on that face. It usually meant that there was some kind of bad news somewhere.

Soolchakan smiled. "What is it now?"

Bikaropin shrugged. "They waited 100 years...and now they're doing it again. The Bloynid and the Perek are reopening temples to Hiv in central Aerisau. They're being cautious about it because they're hiding in the background while they use Heyyah as their clerics."

Soolchakan sat there with his teeth clenched. "They're hoping that everyone forgot about what happened...especially Heyyah. Cover up the history with some garbage story and you can make anyone forget anything. I hate historical revisionists." He leaned back in his chair with his eyes closed. "How many temples have sprung up?"

"Four. All of them in central Aerisau."

"That's still a big continent." He grunted in disgust. "Let's go take a look."

Bikaropin and Soolchakan held hands and Bikaropin Jumped them to Aerisau.

"We're in the northern part of Monokland. All four temples are in this area."

Soolchakan nodded. "So how many months before they commit another murder?"

"They've started doing it every Tadkoy. They're trying to make up for lost time."

Soolchakan was livid. "ONCE PER WEEK?"

Bikaropin nodded.

"Get everybody above the age of 100. Make all of those outfits that we used the last time. We're going to make sure that…SOMEONE…remembers what happened. We're going to devastate all of the Heyyah who are participating voluntarily. We're taking out any Bloynid or Perek who are involved. We're going to make sure that the Bloynid and the Perek remember *this*…forever!"

Bikaropin returned to the gorge and informed all of the marching orders. There were 455 Owlamites who were 100 or older. With only four temples to take down, each was going to be assaulted at the same time. 113 at each location would be able to cause significant damage to the memory of Hiv and in the memories of the Bloynid and Perek.

The Bloynid had a normal life span of about 500 years while the Perek lived about 350 years. Since the previous murders had taken place only 100 years ago, most of those monsters could still be alive while the Heyyah were not. That meant they would get two lessons regarding false deities. Soolchakan hoped they would not have to give the lesson a third time, however, considering how hard-headed the Teltermak had been, this might not be the last time.

With every single one of the Owlamites dressed in white linens (and each one assigned to the rescue of a child was carrying a sheet) they converged on the four temples at the same time. The four leaders of the raids were Soolchakan, Mahanee, Bikaropin and Shashy.

"**Their architect isn't very original,**" sent Bikaropin. "**All four temples have the same floor plan...including dungeons.**"

"**That should make our jobs a little simpler. Not too much of a recon,**" sent Shashy.

Soolchakan was in the dungeon of his target temple. "**I've found fifty-three children here. It's a good thing that there are over 100 of us. We can get the children and... ahem...remove the vermin clerics at the same time.**"

Mahanee looked around at her targets. "**What about their armies? There's more than 400 troops at this location.**"

Soolchakan had an evil grin on his face. "**When we're in Ghost dimension, those armies are going to be helpless against us. They'll have some tales to tell...at least the ones we leave alive, will have a tale to tell.**"

"**I think that you may have the main one,**" sent Bikaropin to Soolchakan. "**There are only thirty-one children here at mine.**"

"**I've got twenty-nine,**" sent Mahanee.

"**I've got thirty-three,**" sent Shashy.

Soolchakan took another look around. "**The only thing that's important about the count of the children is...we**

get ALL of them out...no matter what."

Bikaropin did a quick inventory of the naked, crying children. **"They're not picky about who they take. I've got a few Barratokefin Elf and Grod Elf children.**"

"I've got eight Plyskenlil Elf children here," sent Mahanee.

"Race is unimportant," sent Soolchakan. **"We're here to get all of the children out, even if they're P'Lalfan Elf.**"

"I hope they realize that we're here to help them," sent Shashy. **"I've got a Shan-Ad Elf girl here...and she already has her *fangs*.**"

"Just make sure that whoever helps her...has some armor on and remembers to do everything he can to soothe and calm her," sent Soolchakan. **"Now...stop talking, put your hoods on and let's get the situation resolved.**"

All of the Owlamites hopped from Spy to Ghost. The guards at each location were rather stunned at the sudden appearances of the semi-transparent figures. They were surprised, however, they got over it quickly and sprang into action (most of them at least).

As soon as they had hopped, there were some who were assigned to the different children. They reached down, touched the naked children and hopped them into Ghost as well. When the children saw the apparitions, at first, most were terrified. When they were touched, the chains suddenly fell off and they were wrapped in soft, warm linen, most were now in shock but showing signs of being rather hopeful.

The guards started swinging their weapons, which consisted mainly of big ugly looking footman's maces. Now they were surprised again as the maces went harmlessly through the strange white phantom creatures. They were even more aggravated when their weapons went harmlessly through the children as well. There was a lot of noise as the large maces were clanging off of stone walls…and maiming other soldiers.

The children were terrified of the maces at first. After seeing the thing go through them, harmlessly, two or three times, they calmed down, however there was still some trepidation, confusion and wonder on their faces.

At least one of the troops at each location had the fortitude to start ringing the alarm in order to awaken everyone and get reinforcements. The reinforcements were just as helpless as the ones who had been there already. As a matter of fact, it started getting so crowded that the troops, while attempting to stop the invaders, were bashing each other, even more, with their big maces and causing more panic, pandemonium, casualties and fatalities in their own ranks. They tried forming Heyyah walls to stop these weird interlopers. When the phantoms simply walked through them, there was a large mixture of emotions going through the heads of the soldiers (and a large amount of urine dripping out of their uniforms).

The Owlamites carrying the children slowly headed out of the cells in the dungeons and started ascending the stairs with their loads. Each one was reading the minds of their burden, trying to soothe the child and to figure out where and to whom the child belonged. Of the 146 children, it was found that 33 of them were orphans who had been living in the streets and were pulled in here because nobody wanted or cared for them.

Iomyon was the one carrying the fanged Shan-Ad girl. At first she had made a feeble gesture at biting her benefactor. When she was covered in a clean, warm, comfortable sheet, she calmed considerably and was now thinking all kinds of bewildered thoughts about this person or thing…who was slowly carrying her out of the dungeon. She was a little upset because she could not see a face, however, getting out of that cold dungeon was something that she was not going to fight. She had not been sure who this ghostly figure was, however, when she saw that the forces of Hiv were against it, she gratefully accepted the rescue…in spite of her confusion.

Soolchakan sent out a message after getting some briefings. **"Take the orphan children to any temple of the Great Maker. Communicate with the priests there, mentally, and order them to take care of those children. All of the others…see if there is any way that you can find the parents."**

Fortunately, finding the parents of most of the children was easy. The parents were upstairs in the sanctuary, pleading for the lives of their children. When they saw their children in the hands of the ghostly figures, they cried out to them and the children responded. The clerics, in the area, now made attempts at stopping the parents from getting to their children and were promptly backhanded by someone or something they could not see. Even after getting slapped down, however, some still made attempts at stopping the parents and got backhanded again... and again...and again. Usually it took at least three times being knocked down before the Hiv clerics got the message to stay away...or down. Only a very few had to be knocked unconscious in order to keep them down.

The Owlamites who were not caring for children were now causing no end of grief to the temple guards and the clerics. They were tripping them, knocking them down, slamming them into walls and...temporarily sending them to the planet Stink. After getting a lungful of the Stink gases, they were brought back and added to the problems as they started puking all over the place. Several of the guards and clerics ended up slipping in those messes and going down hard, in the very nasty puddles.

Once all of the children were out of the temples, the Owlamites started getting rid of the clerics and guards permanently. Some were sent to Stink, others were sent to random dimensions where they were thrown into the void of outer space. A few were shoved into walls of the temple and were joined with the stone. Soolchakan had decided they needed to leave something behind that appeared to be supernatural. If a body was half in and half out of a wall, that would leave a lasting impression behind...especially if they died slowly and painfully.

Soolchakan had ordered that all of the clerics were to be done away with. Any survivors should be the guards. They now had to be picky because all of the Bloynid or Perek guards were to be eliminated. The only guards that were to be allowed to survive had to be Heyyah. They allowed at least seven to live at each location, preferably the lowest ranking ones.

The altars and all of the wealth at each location was seized. No one would be allowed to profit from this mess (except the parents of the children taken).

The walls at each temple were damaged by removing certain pieces, here and there, and making them look rather dangerous if you went anywhere near that wall, column or arch. The ugly, grinning statues of Hiv were all sitting in random places on the planet Stink.

It only took three days to get all of the children back to their parents (or in the case of the orphans, in the care of the priests of the Great Maker). Even the Shan-Ad girl was reunited with her parents. While the Shan-Ad did not care for any form of worship of the Great Maker, they could not argue with what they had all seen as Iomyon had safely delivered the unharmed girl back to her parents…and then promptly vanished into thin air.

The story of what had happened at the Hiv temples spread out all over the continent very rapidly (with great assistance from the Owlamites). Many thought it was just rumor until there were all kinds of witnesses to the event. Merchants who traveled all over the continent and told of what they had personally observed were quite common and since all of the stories were consistent and no one was grabbing children for Hiv anymore, it became very believable.

Soolchakan returned to the gorge with his children, hoping they would not have to worry about Hiv cults any more…or at least not for a long, long time.

The year 5195 arrived and so did the birth of the twentieth generation. Yamshono and Deem of the nineteenth generation became the parents of a boy named Grannkon. He became number 917 of current living Owlamites.

The end of the 52nd century ATUT had the population of the Owlamites up to 938.

The 53rd century went by without any new enemies from the sky or the ground. At the end of the year 5300 ATUT, there were now 1,655 living Owlamites. The future was looking rather bright for all...at first.

It was found that the Bloynid were once again attempting to resurrect their hideous religion and worship Hiv with the sacrificing of children on Aerisau. This time they had waited 150 years before trying to bring it back. It was also found that the Kalawb-Rahanan-Or were trying to start a group of religions on Lusaratia. These dealt with the god of ruling, authority and law. Comt was the god of ruling, Bordig was the god of authority and Kenhimni was the god of law. It seemed, according to the Kalawb-Rahanan-Or, that all three required a sacrifice of wealth - a great deal of wealth.

There were currently 940 Owlamites who were 100 or older. Soolchakan wanted only those to participate in the destruction of the Bloynid atrocity. This time, there was only one temple to Hiv (that they knew of). Hopefully it was the only one. They used the same plot of rescuing some fifty-five children. The different thing this time was that no one (wearing those blood red outfits) was to be left alive. Bodies of Bloynid, Perek, Heyyah and a few other races were scattered around the temple grounds. All of them were hacked to pieces or smashed and left for carrion eaters. This statue of Hiv joined all of the other statues on the Stink planet. Etched in granite, on the inner wall of the temple was a warning that this had better be the last time this happens or else all Bloynid and Perek were going to die.

Now on to Lusaratia and the other mess that was being created there.

The Kalawb-Rahanan-Or people were another Elf race with milky green skin. They were a short race of people, usually standing only about 120 Teck in height. They had a rather nasty attitude and looked at any other race as a lower form of life. There was one other race of Elf that was allowed to be clerics of these religions and that was the Weesak. They stood about 168 Teck in height, had tan skin and they had ten fingers on each hand. Both races were very greedy and were doing everything they could to push this religion and force everyone to "give" offerings to the gods – massive offerings. The offerings had to be precious metals, precious stones, elegant furniture, crystal ware and anything else that was expensive. The two Elf races made it sound as if anyone who did not give was being disrespectful to the gods and should feel guilty about their blasphemy. The temples coffers were quickly filling up with all kinds of riches (labeled as holy relics).

The temples were in four places on the northwestern fringes of Lusaratia. They were in groups of three, one for each god, and the rituals of sacrificing wealth to the gods occurred twice per month. The clerics decided that to take all of the wealth of the area would not be productive to a long term situation. Just bleed the people slowly of all of their wealth and make them dependent, if not terrified of the gods.

Soolchakan did some inspections of the vaults in the temples. He found the High Clerics each had their own private vault. In each case, they loved to wander through the vaults adoringly gazing upon all of their acquired wealth. The clerics said that all of these items were now holy relics, however, they were not shy about having many precious gems reset in rings and pendants and claiming them for themselves. After reading the minds of many of the clerics, Soolchakan and the rest of the Owlamites found that these clerics did not believe in the gods themselves, they just worshipped wealth and greed.

Bikaropin came up with a plan on taking the wealth away from the clerics. Do not remove the items from the vaults, just hop them into Spy or Observation. The plan was that in the back half of the room, all items were hopped to Spy. In the front part, near the door, these items were hopped into Observation. This way, if they wanted to go back and claim the items for themselves, you hop to Observation in the back of the room without any danger of *joining* with any of the items. Hopping to Spy in the front of the room offered the same safety.

There were numerous fancy tables and chairs all over the vault area. As soon as the original owner was dead (or deemed unfit to visit a cleric's home), the furniture would be moved to the home of the cleric. Certain very large diamonds were traded to temples in other areas in order to assure that the original owner did not see a cleric wearing one of those items. It would give the whole thing away, or at the very least, make them suspicious of what was really going on.

Soolchakan lead a force of 237 Owlamites who were going to start the mayhem in the three temples that were the furthest east in Lusaratia. Once again, the three eldest Owlamites: Mahanee, Hisang and Bikaropin were the leaders of the other three groups.

Each temple had six High Clerics. The reason for this was so that not one of them had to be out of his or her private vault for any great amount of time. One out of six days, each one took turns as the primary upstairs, performing ritualistic thievery. The seventh day, all six of them led in the worship of the deity (and the thievery of the wealth of the unwilling worshippers).

Soolchakan did a little mathematics. Six High Clerics at each temple for Comt, Bordig and Kenhimni. Eighteen High Clerics total at each of the four locations of the triple houses of thievery. 72 of the primary thieves in all four locations. He shook his head as he realized just how quickly they could drain the economy (any economy) of the area. They were taking in all kinds of wealth and giving nothing back. If someone was poor, well, that was just too bad. According to the High Clerics, you had better come up with something otherwise you were committing a blasphemy. They were not concerned as to how you came up with it, however, you had better come up with something, or they would send some of their army of followers after you…and take what little you had…even if they had to leave you naked in the streets. He sighed. Yes, this is a real benevolent set of gods, he thought sarcastically.

The first temple that Soolchakan went to was for Comt. He checked in the main office to see who the six High "thieves" were. He also checked on certain things about the races that they were dealing with. The Kalawb had a normal life span of about 750 years while the Weesak had a 300 year life span. Three men and three women were in charge here. Chontumik was the number one thief. He was a green-skinned Kalawb-Rahanan-Or. Two of the women, Epimnin and Yayhiya were also of his Elf race. The other three were Weesak – Natsanaya (female), Selzoolon (male) and Vog (male).

Today, it was Chontumik's turn to be the one in the sanctuary, giving the blessing to the people (and blessing himself by stealing as much as he could off of them).

The process they followed was to obtain as much as possible on their day of "receiving" the tribute. The loot was taken downstairs to the massive vaults. No one was allowed inside the private vaults except the six clerics. The assistants would carry all of the booty down to the main hall and the six clerics would move the heavy stuff into the specific vault that was the current destination. The assistants were never allowed inside because they might start getting (just as) greedy and that was not allowed until they became one of the high clerics.

Three Owlamite women - Zhiva, Evadee and Vira - walked up to Soolchakan.

Zhiva chuckled a little. "When do we start with our

pilfering?"

Soolchakan sniffed. "We start with the vault of that main thief, Chontumik. He's upstairs committing more larceny. His vault is currently...unoccupied. We can hop all of that stuff without raising any alarm, at the moment." He took a deep breath and shook his head. "After that, we go to the next ranking one - Epimnin. Even though she *is* in there, we start hopping stuff... anything that is behind her back." He thought for a moment. "No! We've got enough people here. We can hit the other five vaults all at the same time...once we clean out...Chontumik."

The three women all giggled.

Evadee grinned. "Shall we start passing out assignments along that line?"

He nodded. "Absolutely," he said flatly. "I'll let you all know when to start on the other five vaults. Right now Chontumik loses all of his...goodies." He smirked. "When he gets back, maybe he'll blame the other five for the missing items."

It took quite a while to hop everything in the room into Spy and Observation. They had to touch an item in order to hop it and there were several hundred thousand objects in the big vault. When they finished, Soolchakan hopped back to Home dimension, looked around and realized that this room was bigger than the vaults that they had "dug" on Zhagool, which were currently being used as mass cemeteries – at least until he could find Bonarain or the blue stone. They left nothing but the twenty sconces on the wall. Four of the torches were currently burning. This would give enough light for someone entering the room to see that everything had been taken.

He heard someone humming as the vault door was being opened. He realized that he was in the front part of the room, so he hopped to Spy to await Chontumik and see the surprise. The door was pushed open and Chontumik backed in humming and pulling a large wheelbarrow full of coins, golden flatware and golden plates. He stopped, went back to the hall and backed in again with another wheelbarrow full of goodies. He stopped to catch his breath as he stared, grinning, down at his new haul. He suddenly stood up straight and looked to his right. He saw empty space. He turned to his left. Same thing. He spun around with a look of total horror on his face. He cut loose with an ear-splitting high-pitched scream that echoed throughout the empty room. He took several steps forward, then raced to one of the sconces. He took a burning torch and ran to the far end of the room, making all kinds of unintelligible noises as he ran.

Soolchakan chuckled. "**Someone take care of those two wheelbarrows. We want *all* of his stuff gone**." He watched as the two barrows vanished. Whoever else was in this room was in Observation.

Chontumik raced back to the entrance and again let out with a scream when he saw that his fresh take was missing as well. He ran out the door, still holding the torch, and hollered at the guards. "WHERE IS IT?"

Soolchakan heard a confused voice respond.

"Where is…what…your Holiness?"

"EVERYTHING THAT WAS IN MY VAULT! WHAT

HAPPENED TO IT?"

Soolchakan walked to the entrance to watch the conversation.

A large Heyyah man was standing there looking bewildered. "No one has entered but you, your Holiness. I don't know what you're talking about."

Chontumik was seething with rage. "LIAR!" He backhanded the tall guard with his free hand. He then let out an agonized groan, dropped the torch and started rubbing his pained hand with the other, while letting out a few more moans of pain.

The guard looked uninjured, and totally oblivious, from the slap, while Chontumik's hand was in agony. Soolchakan was laughing uncontrollably at the scene as it unfolded in front of him. Chontumik stopped shouting as he rubbed the pained hand with the other while grimacing and breathing erratically.

The guard looked at three others who had walked up to find out what was going on. He shrugged and turned back to Chontumik. "Your Holiness, if you could…explain what is going on…then…maybe I…or we…can assist you."

Once again Chontumik grunted in pain as he rubbed his hand. "The room…is EMPTY! When I left if this morning…it was FULL! Where is my treasure…?" He stopped himself and shook his head. "Uh…where are the *holy relics* that were housed in here?"

All four guards shook their heads.

"No one has been in there save you, your Holiness," said

one of the guards.

"We had a shift change at midday," said another one. "Perhaps we should talk to the morning shift."

Chontumik looked up angrily. "PERHAPS, my foot! Call them! CALL OUT EVERYONE!" He walked across the wide hall to another vault door. He knocked on the door with his right hand and instantly cried out in pain. He once again rubbed the injured right hand with the left. He turned his back to the door and started kicking the door repeatedly.

The High Cleric, Epimnin finally opened the door. "What is going on here? Who dares to disturb me...oh...Chontumik, you. What do you want?"

Chontumik turned to her. He got up close and whispered through his teeth. "Someone got into my vault...and robbed me. They stole everything...*everything*!"

Epimnin was stunned. "But...how," she whispered back? "It took all six of us to get that huge banquet table in your vault. How could anyone...?"

"I don't know," he snapped. "All that I know is...my vault is...EMPTY!"

Soolchakan looked around at some of the other Owlamites. **"Why is everyone standing around doing nothing? Get in there and get everything moved. It'll add to the confusion...and then we'll all get a good laugh as we watch what happens."**

The Owlamites dispersed to the other vaults.

Soolchakan smiled. 'This is going to be fun to watch,' he thought. 'Take the wealth from a greedy miser and watch them go insane. Nothing quite as funny as a bankrupt miserly thief.' He walked into the entranceway to Epimnin's vault and saw things disappearing. He grinned. He closed his eyes. **"Mahanee, Hisang, Bikaropin. Have you started the chaos at the other sites?"**

Mahanee came back. **"This is hilarious. They're going completely screaming mad crazy."**

Hisang answered. **"They've already executed three guards here. Even though they can't prove a thing."**

"I've never seen anyone so angry in my life," sent Bikaropin.

Soolchakan smiled and sighed. 'It's working,' he thought. He went back to Chontumik and read his mind.

'I know that someone here had something to do with this. I'll search them out if I have to tear this whole building down, but I'll find him…or them…or…whatever,' thought Chontumik.

"I took your treasure," sent Soolchakan.

Chontumik looked around rather surprised. "Who…who said that?"

"I did, you *bimyock*."

Epimnin looked confused. "Who said what?"

Chontumik was even more surprised now. "You…didn't hear that?"

Epimnin huffed. "Hear what?"

"I'm talking to you, not her."

Chontumik clenched his teeth. "THAT! DID YOU HEAR THAT?"

"I hear you babbling," said Epimnin. She shook her head and huffed at him.

"I'm talking to you in your mind. Come, join me in your *empty* vault."

Chontumik turned to Epimnin with a very strange demeanor. "Uh...excuse me for...uh...I'm going back to my vault to...think." He quickly walked back to his vault.

Epimnin rolled her eyes and huffed. She walked back to her vault shaking her head in disgust. When she turned her gaze to the interior of her vault, she let out a blood curdling scream regarding what she saw - or did not see.

Chontumik ignored her screams and walked in his vault. He looked around at the huge empty room and nearly started crying. "Who are you?"

"I represent the true God."

"Uh...which...god?"

"The only God, you *doovoft*."

Chontumik was baffled. "Comt?"

"Phony."

"Bordig?"

"Phony."

"Kenhimni?"

"Phony."

Chontumik snarled. "Then…WHO?"

"The Great Maker."

"That…is…IMPOSSIBLE!"

Soolchakan sighed. **"This vault is empty, and you say impossible? How? Why**?"

"But…the Great Maker…is not interested in wealth. He's only interested in…some kind of idiotic purity and everyone getting along with each other through love and understanding and everyone being equal in his eyes. He wants us all to be nice to each other. He wants us to share our wealth with…those who don't deserve it. Widows? Orphans? The destitute? Why should I waste my treasure on garbage like that?"

"Your treasure? You claimed that everything in here was holy relics. Since everything in here is holy relics, The Great Maker claimed it as such. That's rather hypocritical of you to try to claim holy relics as your personal treasure."

They heard more loud shrieking coming from the vault of Epimnin. Chontumik rushed out of the room headed for her vault. Epimnin was running around in her vault screaming at things in order to stop them from disappearing.

Soolchakan got a giggle because he was in Spy and he was watching several of his children as they were going about touching and hopping things to Spy. Most of the things near the door had been hopped to Observation, however, there were still a few things that had not been hopped yet. He hopped to Observation to see who was doing the damage in here. He saw Quiptap standing in the middle of the room near a very large armoire. She had her hands out and was admiring a group of rings. Rings on each finger with a variety of precious gems in the settings.

Soolchakan snarled a little in disgust. "What are you doing?"

Quiptap looked up from her displayed hands and smiled. "Just looking," she said with a mischievous grin. "They're so pretty."

He grunted. "Put them back."

Off to his right he heard another voice. "All of them?" Nanpin was standing there admiring several different ostentatious and elaborate necklaces.

He shook his head. "Yes, all of them. We are going to make an attempt at getting these things back to their owners."

Sazhaki came up to him from his left. "Of course we are," she said dryly. She held up a ring with a huge emerald set on it. "And of course, all of them are going to be completely honest about it. Every one of them is going to try to claim *this* beauty."

He gave her a disingenuous smile. "Don't forget…we can read their minds and tell whether or not they're telling the truth."

Nalzomim held up a longsword with a gem encrusted scabbard. "Who makes things like this? Only the elite and filthy rich can afford something like this…superfluous thing. Then when they get it…what do they do with it?"

Ewiki laughed out loud. "Do what they do best, show off! They try to outdo their friends with foofaraw that is more gaudy, garish and showy than what their friends have."

Shoz held up an item that puzzled most of the people in the room. "Yes, they show off but…I don't even know what this thing is." He held it up higher. "Can anyone tell me what this thing is?"

Witbilly snickered as she looked at it. "That is a tool that is used to properly tune certain types of stringed instruments. I don't ever recall seeing one of them made out of gold before, but that is what it is."

Shoz huffed as he took a closer look at it. "Toys for snobs!" He tossed it onto a table and went back to hopping goodies into Observation.

"That's what a lot of this stuff is," said Emelami as she held up a solid gold serving spoon. "Snobs had it designed and manufactured and now these greedy phonies who worship a phony god took it away from them."

Soolchakan shook his head. "I had no idea that there were this many stinking rich people in this area of Lusaratia."

"That's probably why they started this mess here," said Zobra. He shrugged. "Where else can you get stinking rich this easily? You go to an area where there are a lot of stinking rich people and figure out a way to legally steal all of their material wealth."

Soolchakan sighed. "Quit eyeballing all of the baubles and just get everything into Spy and Observation. We'll try to figure out the correct owners later. For now, leave these…marauders… with nothing but the clothing on their backs."

"No," said Azzaki. She grinned and grabbed the cape that Epimnin was wearing. She hopped the cape into Observation. Then she grabbed the sleeve of Epimnin's dress and hopped that to Observation. Now Epimnin was standing there with nothing but some loose fitting pantaloons and shoes. Then she lost her shoes…then the pantaloons.

Chab grunted in disgust. "Was that necessary?"

Azzaki shrugged. "Why not? They wanted everything. The best thing to do is leave them with nothing - *absolutely* nothing."

"Good idea," said Soolchakan as he nodded. He went to Chontumik and stripped the Kalawb Elf of everything he was wearing. He chuckled and then sent a wide message to all his children in all four locations. **"When I say strip them of everything…that even includes the blemished underwear that they're currently wearing as well. Leave them with absolutely NOTHING!"**

Mahanee, Hisang and Bikaropin all came back with responses that agreed with the idea of taking absolutely everything.

Now there were six High Clerics in the hallway all

screaming for someone to bring them some clothing…any kind of clothing. There were some fifty very confused guards who complied with the request (with several of them trying to hide their giggling).

Chontumik looked down at the raggedy loincloth that he was wearing. He looked up and called out. "Messenger from the Great Maker…please stop this!"

Epimnin looked at him as if he were insane. "Who are you talking to?"

"Someone who talked to me earlier. He said that he was a messenger from the Great Maker," said Chontumik sadly. He looked up as if pleading. "Messenger, please, tell me why you're doing this?"

Soolchakan shrugged. **"You claimed that all this stuff was a collection of holy relics. Since it is all holy and dedicated to God, you have no right to keep it…any of it. That is only right**."

Chontumik wailed on. "But…why can't we keep any of it?"

"You claimed all of those things to be holy relics. Since when do you have the right to horde and play with any holy relics?"

Selzoolon broke in angrily. "If you are in communication with some…supernatural messenger…since we're clerics as well, why can't we hear this…messenger?"

Soolchakan scoffed. **"Because I was carrying on a**

private conversation with Chontumik," he sent to all six of the High Clerics.

Now the other five were standing there with shocked looks on their faces.

Natsanaya was the first to find her voice. "Who…or what was that?"

"That was the messenger from the Great Maker," said Chontumik sadly.

"The Great Maker doesn't exist," said Selzoolon indignantly.

"Then whom are you communicating with?"

Once again the five others stood there with confused stares.

"The six of you have claimed that all of the items in the vaults were holy relics. That means that you have to surrender them to the Great Maker. Any more questions?"

The six High Clerics were left with nothing more they could say or argue about. All of their treasure was gone. They had claimed that it belonged to God and now God took it (even though it was a God they did not believe in). End of discussion. When they later found out that all of the other temples had been drained of their treasures as well, they found it very difficult to make the argument that the Great Maker did not exist. They had started this entire worship of Comt, Bordig and Kenhimni, while not believing in them. Those three gods had not claimed any of the treasure at all. This messenger had claimed all of the treasure in the name of the Great Maker. Now what do you do? Anything you claim, you cannot keep. It all goes to the Great Maker...or at least someone who is claiming to be a representative of the Great Maker.

Chontumik decided that he was going to consult a wizard in order to determine just how holy and supernatural this alleged messenger was. Soolchakan did not worry about this inquiry...at first. Most of those wizards were frauds anyway. How could they do anything that could assist in this investigation?

Shortly after cleaning out the temples of Comt, Bordig and Kenhimni, in 5308 ATUT, Korrero and Lalmora of the Sixteenth became the proud parents of the fifth set of triplets born in the Owlamite race. Two girls - Yalreema, Yarleema and one boy – Yurlon of the Seventeenth.

11

The High Priest Chontumik was not finished with his skepticism. He hired a highly experienced wizard to find out what had happened in the vaults. There were numerous other High Clerics of the triple order who were interested in just exactly how all of their illegally obtained riches had just vanished into thin air. They were following along with Chontumik and this wizard.

Mortonim of the Seventeenth had been assigned to periodically go to the temples and find out if the Kalawb and the Weesak were attempting to rob the people of the areas again. He found out about the wizard and reported to Bikaropin.

Bikaropin headed for Lusaratia and the temple where this wizard was going to perform his incantations. He arrived to find the wizard negotiating his price.

Chontumik seemed a little upset. "Great Wizard, Shenngren, I appeal to you. I don't have the money now…with me. But if you find out where all of the treasure went, I assure you that you will be paid most handsomely."

Shenngren looked unconvinced. "I am paid in advance or I don't do anything at all. I thought that I made that quite clear. I have been swindled before and *that* is not going to happen again…

EVER!"

Shenngren was a very tall Heyyah. He had long flowing white hair an equally long beard but no moustache. He was dressed all in dark brown leather with some very shiny bracelets and several flashy rings on his gnarled fingers. He had three different necklaces that did not appear to be there for show. He held a staff that was almost as long as he was tall. It had several strange glyphs etched in the length of it and on top was the head of some strange looking, reptilian, fanged creature that Bikaropin could not readily identify.

Chontumik was looking rather impatient. "Look... whoever did it...they stole gems, gold and silver coins, along with furniture, flatware, plates, platters and other items, all worth millions. When all of that is found and recovered, I assure you that you will be paid much more than you asked."

Shenngren grunted in disgust. "*Again*...I've heard that one before."

Selzoolon walked up glaring angrily. "If you don't help us, I assure you that the wrath of Comt will be coming down on you."

Shenngren snickered. "I have the protection of the god of magic – Nepekeep. As long as I am loyal to him, your threats are an empty waste of hot air. As I said, I want payment in advance or forget it."

Yayhiha pulled a pouch out from under her ragged dress. "Here! I hid this from the thieves. I'm sure that there is enough in there...to at least get you started with your investigation. I can always get more…if needed."

Bikaropin huffed. 'You sneaky little *bimyock*,' he thought. He sent a quick message back to Soolchakan informing him of the deceit.

Chontumik looked rather hopeful. "Is there enough there?"

After counting it Shenngren placed the pouch inside his shirt. "Barely! It is enough to get started. But if you desire a thorough investigation, you had better get more." He walked into the vault belonging to Epimnin.

The clerics all followed.

Shenngren looked back at them looking thoroughly disgusted. "I need to be alone in here so I don't lose my concentration. You people will be a very unwanted distraction."

The clerics all turned with their jaws clenched tight. They went to the door, turned around and stood silently while watching the wizard.

Shenngren sighed in disgust, shook his head and turned his back on them. He took a deep breath, leaned his head back and started concentrating.

Bikaropin started doing some hardcore mind-reading on this wizard to find out what he was actually doing. He saw some very strange imagery forming in the mind of the mage. It was nothing like he had ever experienced before.

Shenngren's eyes rolled back in his head. He turned around slowly with his arms stretched out wide. He was mumbling some kind of incantation as he turned.

Bikaropin sensed some new kind of imagery going along with what had been there before. It was rather confusing, however, he did everything he could to commit it to memory and comprehend what was happening.

Shenngren started talking slowly and quietly. "I see... someone...whom I have never seen the likes of before. No, several of them. Men and women. They are touching items... all items in the room. The items are still here. You just can't see them. The people who took them...are not...wait...yes, one of them is here now." He held his hands in front of him and started walking towards Bikaropin.

Bikaropin quickly Jumped to a spot directly behind the wizard and slapped the man in the back of the head as hard as he could. "That should be a big enough distraction to break your concentration," he said irately. It was – it did.

Shenngren placed his left hand on the back of his head and looked around angrily. The clerics were all still standing in the doorway and were nowhere near striking distance. He now knew that he had been smacked by...the presence. The imagery was not in his head now. There was anger – and jealousy. He knew that whoever it was that had slapped him had some kind of magic that was equal, superior or unknown and that was something that Shenngren did not want to admit to or put up with. He was going to have to deal with this...entity. He was going to have to steal the knowledge of that entity and obtain the magical skill in order to improve himself. He had to figure out a way to enslave this unknown entity.

Bikaropin shook his head and Jumped back to the gorge to make a quick report and see what instructions were forthcoming from the briefing.

"We have a new danger," said Bikaropin. "I tried to understand the imagery that was in his head but it is so...*different*. We can do all kinds of things with the imagery that we have already, but it all seems to follow a certain pattern...if you will. What was in the head of that Heyyah was so radically different than what we're doing...or have been doing."

Soolchakan sat there pondering and worrying. "How could we have missed this? This is something that...this Heyyah has been doing for some time...obviously...because he is elderly." He looked up. "You said that he is an elder...Heyyah?"

Bikaropin nodded. "Yes, he's...obviously somewhere around late 70's or early 80's. He doesn't act like an elderly Heyyah though. He seems to have more energy than any other Heyyah that I've seen, especially of that age."

Mahanee let out a guilty chuckle. She smiled and flushed. "I think that I've been paying attention to this, but, I didn't tell you. I thought that you were more interested in attacks from outer space and Teltermaks and...other possible sources."

"This is a source that I should have been told about long ago," said Soolchakan. "How long have you known about it or been watching it"

Mahanee cleared her throat. "I think about…800 or 900 years now," she said with a red face.

"It's longer than that," said Hisang. She huffed. "A *lot* longer!" She turned to Soolchakan. "She first told me about it shortly after I turned 3,000 years old. I'm now 4,711 years old."

Soolchakan gave Mahanee a patronizing look, while she had a look of confusion on her face.

"It couldn't have been that long," said Mahanee desperately. "Could it?" She shook her head and huffed a few times. "Where has the time gone?"

"It *is* that long," said Hisang emphatically!

"I agree," said Meffin. "I remember you saying something about it before just before Hisang turned 3,000. You were talking about her age and you were talking about those magic things they're doing."

Soolchakan huffed. "WHATEVER! It doesn't matter when it was. I'm aware of it now and I'd like to find out as much as we can about it…to see if there's any danger to us. If he can sense us in a different dimension…we have no place to hide from any attacker. I don't like that at all."

Bikaropin sighed. "I've heard certain rumors about different people on different continents. They are talked about with an air of awe. I just thought that it might be a bunch of *h'oolyach*. Now, it might have some bearing in fact…plus that Shenngren was worried that it might be someone who is equal to him…in magical abilities."

"So start checking on some of those names and see if there is something to it," said Soolchakan. "We don't need anyone sneaking up on us and taking over...like the Teltermak were attempting to do to us."

Yesati and Fwensa were assigned to keep an eye on the wizard who was trying to find the treasures for Chontumik. They were disturbed over the fact that he could sense them. They found the easiest way to confuse the issue was hop to Spy and go stand inside the wall of the vault with only one ear and eye on the outside of the wall. This way, when Shenngren sensed them, he was feeling a wall with his hands and getting even more confused over the location of the beings (while getting some ribbing from the clerics as they watched him fingering and molesting the wall). If he ever started getting into their heads with his incantations and spells, they just slapped him and destroyed his concentration. Any disruption or major distraction was devastating to the spell and he had to start all over again. They also discovered that he could not sense them while they were in Observation.

The seven eldest Owlamite children – Mahanee, Hisang, Bikaropin, Shashy, Meffin, Yeema and Chena went to the different continents, each with a team of younger Owlamites and started looking for all of the strange arcane people that were legends, or even rumors, among the inhabitants of the different continents.

It took almost ten years to accomplish most of the searches and a lot of the information together, however, they were finally satisfied that they had enough to speak about all of the arcane arts with some modicum of expertise.

Meanwhile, even after all of that time, Shenngren was still trying to find out what had happened in the vaults. He was now doing it, without pay, because he was frustrated over the fact that there was someone who could perform magic that he could not understand and did not have. He coveted this strange magic in the worst way. He would do anything, by fair means or foul, to obtain the knowledge, no matter what the cost, or how long it takes to get what he did not have…even if he had to figure out a way to mentally or verbally communicate and control this entity.

Bikaropin started reading the report to Soolchakan. "We've found that there are ten different types of magic. We've been able to follow and watch and they're in four different areas. First of all is magic itself. It is in three categories, depending on which one the person, Elf of Heyyah, shows themselves capable of performing or mastering. This one has three of the types. The major one is called Coalescent Magic. It *is* the most powerful according to what we've been told and observed. It consists of performing magical stunts, using both inner mind manipulations as well as some outer, I guess you could say, chemical reaction or enhancement." He cleared his throat. "The second part of this one is called Circumambient. Not quite as powerful, however, there are some very nasty things that can be done to an enemy… using this craft. Most of this magic is outer and consists of the use of chemicals, baubles and other equipment, as well as some very strange physical animations. The third part is called Hyperphysical and it is extremely rare. It requires certain…mental talents. This one, it can only be performed by those who are born with a certain mental talent. Unlike the first two, it cannot be taught. You can either do it or...not. The spells that can be done using this force are...totally from within and...can leave an individual totally exhausted, mentally, after performing some of their stunts."

"So this one is completely magical," observed Soolchakan.

"Yes. It seems to operate outside the laws of physics in all three cases."

Soolchakan nodded. "Next?"

"The next one is rather confusing because...this one is done by members of the clergy. It is done by Elf or Heyyah... in the worship of gods that...*you* have claimed are false. I don't know how they get their powers but they do have these capabilities and they claim that they're getting their supernatural abilities from their gods." He looked up fearfully. "I know that you said that the Great Maker is the only true God, but...these people are getting powers...from somewhere."

"So, we'll have to study it further for some kind of proof... one way or another," said Soolchakan thoughtfully. "Continue."

Bikaropin smiled. "Yes." He looked at his paper. "This one is broken down into three categories as well. The first, and most powerful, is called Orthodox. It seems to be all encompassing and is done only by the most dedicated ones...the ones radically dedicated to their religion. I've been looking at the gods that we've been...foiling and...it seems that there are those who worship Comt, Bordig and Kenhimni and...they have powers. The Kalawb-Rahanan-Or and Weesak...only seem to be in it for the money and...they don't have any of these powers. The ones who really worship those gods and truly believe in them...they are not in it for the money and they do have these powers. The second part of this religious magic is called Environmental. All of their powers and spells come from nature, elements and...worship of the environment along with the use of certain different natural items from nature. The third, in this case, is also Hyperphysical force. Again, just like the magic forces, this one cannot be taught. You can either do it...or not."

Soolchakan nodded again. "Magical...non-religious and religious. All right, what else?"

"This next area is used by Healers or...those who curse. The Healer uses spells that are called positive restoration. They can heal...just about any disease or...broken bones...and sometimes even severe mental problems. They make that drug Tuzine, which you talked about so much...obsolete. The second part of this magic is called...negative destruction. If you want someone cursed or killed by disease, you call on one of these...cursing assassins. They kill through curses, nasty disease or driving one to suicide." He shook his head. "The third part of this one is very confusing. It is called commingling adversity. It is a combination of the other two. It has positive healing and destructive cursing and I don't understand why anyone would want to do both."

Soolchakan huffed, looking rather confused. "So this is either good, bad or...mixed up."

Bikaropin nodded. "That sums it up pretty good."

"That's nine - what is the tenth?"

Bikaropin had a sickened look on his face. "The last one is disgusting. I don't even know why they call it magic at all. It is called...Demimondaine. The only ones who perform this vulgar stuff...are courtesans. If they want to get information from someone, either for themselves or for a client, they give certain drugs to their victim. These drugs seem to destroy any desire to keep secrets and...in order for the drugs to work and continue working...they have to keep the blood pressure up...using all kinds of sexual stimulation. There's nothing magic to it...just drugs and copulation...or molestation. For some reason it still gets into the magical category because those who don't use it, don't know that the whole thing is all about using certain types of drugs."

"If you don't understand something completely, it can seem like magic," said Soolchakan with a smile. He stroked his beard. "Is there any chance that this stuff is a danger to us...or a chance that we can learn how to use these things?"

Bikaropin shrugged. "It can be dangerous to us. If we want to learn it...or any of them, we need to start learning how to understand and use the imagery."

Soolchakan hung his head. "Where is Bonarain when you need her?"

"Uh...what do...you mean?"

He looked up. "It was always Bonarain who figured out and explained any of the imagery that we couldn't understand. She has...had a talent for it and...no one else could match her. She could always simplify the most complicated things and make them seem so easy."

Bikaropin sighed. "After all this time…are you sure that she's alive?"

He sighed. "Until I see a dead body, or have proof of her death, I can remain optimistic." He leaned back in his chair. "That stuff that you just gave me…I hear the topic headings. Do you have some…specifics…under each one of these main headings of magical abilities?"

Bikaropin smiled. "That information takes up a lot more than one piece of paper. As a matter of fact…it uses over 400 pieces of paper."

Soolchakan closed his eyes and groaned. "Bring them in." He opened his eyes and sighed. "It'll make for some interesting reading."

It took several days for him to pour over the information. A lot of it was boring and repetitive. Some of it was amazing and some of it was horrifying. Some of these wizards and clergy could actually hop to other dimensions as well. It was not clear which ones they had found, however, it was clear that they were able to do so…with a little more difficulty than the Owlamite way. They could still hop. The strange thing there was the fact that no one talked about hopping to the void of outer space in another dimension. This made it even more confusing as to which dimension they were hopping to or from.

One thing that Soolchakan found doubly disturbing was the fact that this Shenngren was still attempting to find who was responsible for the thefts in the treasure vaults. He was not worrying about being paid by the Kalawb or the Weesak, he wanted to find out who this entity was that was more powerful than he was and get their spells from them. The second thing that was disturbing was that according to the ones who were keeping an eye on Shenngren, he did not seem to be aging at all. For any Heyyah, this was unusual. Either he had obtained one of the Teltermak longevity potions or there was a spell that stopped aging. Soolchakan sent a message to the spies to see if they could find out which one it was.

Somebody finally got tired of watching Shenngren do all of his boring incantations and decided it was time to put an end to the nonsense. As Shenngren came close to the Owlamite, who was standing inside the wall, a hand came out of the wall, hopped to Home, grabbed Shenngren by the beard, hopped his face to Ghost, pulled his face into the wall and then hopped his face back to Home, where his face joined with the wall. It did not take long for the wizard to suffocate. The clerics eventually had to carve the rest of his head away from the wall and get rid of the body before something really catastrophic occurred.

Soolchakan also sent messages out to all of his children. Keep searching for any other spells that were not in the 412 pages of material discovered so far. There could be spells that were not used very often and could be even more dangerous than the dimension hopping capability of some of these wizards and clergy.

Bikaropin poured over all of the spells listed in the 412 pages and found that there were numerous spells that were listed more than once. Several people had listed observing spells being performed by different wizards, clergy or healers and had not consulted others when listing the observations. He had to come up with a committee that started reading through all of the documentation and remove the repetitious information.

Menola, Passifi, Ahemeni, Vymilla and Fwensa were given the task of reading through and comparing. It took them nearly three months, however, when they finished finding and removing repetitions, the number of pages was reduced to 161. All of the new reports that came in were given to the five women and they either added or rejected, depending on what was already on the listings.

Again the years went by. After a certain point, any new addition to the listings of the spells was rare indeed. It usually occurred when some wizard or cleric figured out a way to invent a new spell. This was a rather unusual situation.

One thing that aided in determining if anything was new was to start spying on some of the temples (Orthodox or Environmental) to see if the clergy were coming up with anything new and also spying on any of the hidden colleges of mages (Coalescent or Circumambient). The Healers had their special schools for any new medical personnel. The ones who dealt with Negative Destruction were usually hidden covens where they secretly trained new assassins. Of course, very few secrets could ever be kept from the Owlamites, for very long.

The only one that was not spied upon constantly was, or barely at all, of course, the Demimondaine. This, again, was not really magic. The ones who practiced it tried to pass it off as magic, however, it was all a situation of drugging a victim and then keeping their blood pressure up by continuous sexual acts. Observing this bunch was nothing more than watching some repetitive, boring pornography. The prostitutes who practiced it were only trying to gain information that they could use to blackmail some of their "customers". This way they could obtain money without having to resort to submitting to more debauchery.

The spying continued through the 54th century. Even Soolchakan went out on a few missions, just to keep in practice. He not only wanted to stay in practice at spying, he also wanted to observe some of these spells being taught and practiced first hand.

In the year 5362, Grannkon and Feheela of the twentieth announce the birth of their son Irinthion of the twenty-first. Another new generation has arrived on the scene.

This year made Soolchakan think again about this wizard Shenngren. That man had gone through those vaults for well over 40 years. He had appeared to be somewhere around 70 to 80 years old when he started. He should have been well over 110. He had been going strong and showed no signs of giving up on finding the culprits and learning their magic…all the way to the end. At first Soolchakan wondered about the ages of those clerics of evil and greed until he remembered that they were all of two Elf races who had a much longer lifespan.

The phony clerics, in those temples, grew rather tired of

getting no results from Shenngren (not to mention the fact that he ended up dead). They brought in other wizards and as a result this situation was getting a great deal of unwanted attention. The Owlamites were finding that they had to interfere with several very powerful wizards and this, again, only made those wizards all more curious as to who was performing these incredible stunts. Every time the Owlamites gave the wizards an irritating (and sometimes painful) setback, it only made them more stubbornly determined to find the truth in order to obtain new spells and powers.

Soolchakan decided that the curious wizards all needed a few episodes of visiting the Stink planet. Maybe that would change their minds. It only deterred a few of them. The rest of them became even more determined, especially since they now saw that there was a strange new regurgitation or sickness spell involved with this mess, which they might use against an enemy. Get your opponent on all fours upchucking and they cannot concentrate on any hostile spell against you. This would mean instant victory for you and enslavement of your enemy.

Another thing that came from all of this spying was that the clergy all claimed that they received their spells as divine gifts from their gods. Since Soolchakan did not believe in all of these other gods, he had to find out where they were actually getting their spells from. This brought in a new round of intelligence gathering. The Owlamites could not find any form of divine intervention in these spells or where they were coming from. It definitely required more investigation – that so far, the Owlamites did not even know how to start investigating the situation.

The Owlamites were not leading boring lives as they

constantly spied on others and still had to keep an eye on the stars for any other outworld invaders. Usually it was the pregnant ones who stayed in the room where all of those star-gazing monitors were.

Time went by and finally came the end of the fifty-fourth century ATUT. The count of the living Owlamites was now up to 2,922. The search for knowledge of the spells and their origins continued unabated. Soolchakan was determined that they had to know as much as possible in order to maintain the survival and secrets of the Owlamites.

He was rather amazed at the fact that they had not been discovered by the wizards and clergy yet. The only reason that he could think of as to why they had not been found out was the Dragon Force of High Country. Apparently, no one in High Country was interested in what was in the gorge and since no one else was able to get into High Country, they were still safe from any outside marauders.

12

In 5403, Palsalan of the Eighteenth claimed the very last apartment on the first level. Now, all of the first level was occupied...for the first time since the Owlamites had first moved to the gorge so many centuries ago. Most of the second level was occupied. For some reason, all of the children wanted apartments on the upper levels. Soolchakan was the only one who lived on any level other than the first or the second. He was still too stubborn to move because he preferred to stay where he had first moved to in the gorge. It was too much of a headache to move to a different one, especially since he had acquired so many treasures over the centuries and was still using more than one apartment. There were still 164 apartments on the second level that were unoccupied so it would be quite a while before that level filled up. Soolchakan was sure that it would fill up before anyone tried to claim an apartment on the third level.

Soolchakan started going out on more of the scouting missions himself just to have something to do. He had been feeling rather useless just sitting there giving out instructions. How could he really expect all of his children to do all of the work while he just sat there getting bored and waiting for something to happen, and then hearing about it after the fact, and then making another boring entry into his huge set of memoirs. If he was out there in the world doing some of the exploring for himself, he just might find out a few things either before or while they happened. That might make for some more interesting (or at least less dull or repetitive) entries into the memoirs.

Knowledge of the mysterious arcane arts was increasing, however, no one could really comprehend the imagery that was coming from all of these spells. They could see the results when some wizard, clergy or healer cast a spell. They could not comprehend how or why the spell worked. They still did everything they could to commit the imagery to memory and take specific notes on what happened when and how the spell was cast.

In the year 5450 ATUT, Nerron and Ulstafa of the twentieth wed. They took the very last apartment that was vacant on the second level. While apartment 2-571 was, in reality, not the only vacant one on either the first or second level, they were still considered to be occupied. Ever since the word came out that the red and blue stones, working together, could bring someone back to life, no one picked the apartments that had been occupied by the ones who died in the two Teltermak wars and the traitor's war. They were all hoping to see this phenomenon and therefore did not claim the apartments that had been claimed by the victims.

In that same year, when Kredzodo and Tajahing of the Eighth wed and had to start claiming an apartment on the third level. When the daughter of Tajahing, Elahema was born, that brought the population of Owlamites that were breathing to 4,253.

In the year 5451, five more newlywed couples moved into the third level. The population was still, thankfully, growing.

At the end of the year 5473 ATUT, the population was now at 4,671. Yes there were still more Owlamites and a few more women who were pregnant, however Soolchakan wished that the population could grow faster. He still refused to make any attempt at forcing women to get pregnant. They suffered physically during a pregnancy and he allowed them to decide when to get pregnant. While gritting his teeth, he swore to himself that he would do everything he could to not use the *Voice of Power* to influence any of them. He did everything he could to keep this promise. He remembered the animosity and problems that had been created when Chyning had been tricked. He really did not want to see that happen again.

Soolchakan was out doing some of his wanderings. He had been called back to the gorge to welcome a new arrival into the Owlam population. A girl named Lootama of the Twenty-First. She brought the population to 4,683. Once he had done his traditional holding of the newborn, congratulate the parents and give the newborn a private message against any act of treason, he headed back out to wander. Why not? No other baby was due for several weeks.

He was doing some travel on foot around North Paselter.

A couple of decades ago, the King of Paselter had become the father of twin boys. When twins were born, the midwives were supposed to tie a red string around the right ankle of the first-born. They had neglected their duties in this case and no one knew which of the boys was eldest...by just a few moments. Since no one knew which one was the elder, the King had a last will and testament that ordered the kingdom be split between the two boys equally. Dolomon was King in North Paselter and Dolomot was King in South Paselter...and there were a few rumors of the two bickering back and forth among themselves.

Soolchakan decided that he did not want to get involved in any of the politics of the bickering twins. He just liked going around and looking at what had become of the area that used to be his home. The City of Owlam was located in what was now North Paselter.

North Paselter also had custody of the Turgon Wall. After all this time, the great wall was still the only thing keeping those vicious Turgons confined to a specific area. All the countries of the world continued sending their long term detainees to the wall. Why not? It kept them busy at the wall fighting Turgons and the country they were sent from did not have to watch or care for them. If you refused to fight the Turgons when they attacked the wall, you ended up as Turgon fodder. That was the way the death penalty was carried out at the wall. Even after all the centuries of killing Turgons...there were still Turgons attacking the wall... somewhere...almost daily. They must breed incredibly fast.

Soolchakan was wandering around in a wooded area near the ancient location of the city of Owlam where the trees had definitely come back after the destruction from the Algothon attack. He smiled as he looked up at the very tall trees the Owlamites had brought in from other dimensions. He marveled at the massive trunks of the trees. It was early autumn and most of the leaves were turning all of the different bright colors as they succumbed to the inevitable death of any leaf. There was a chill in the air as the sun sank over the horizon in the west. He was thinking of going to some other warmer area while it was night time in this area, then he heard some people talking and saw the glow of a campfire… and he decided to get nosy.

There were eight people gathered around the fire. Three Heyyah men, two Heyyah women, one Kalash man, one Wokig man and one Wokig woman.

'Interesting group,' he thought. 'Three different races and they're all sitting there peacefully cooking some large bird.' Time to read some minds and see if there is anything worth looking into. It turned out to be *very* interesting.

The largest of the three Heyyah men was named Homproon. He was a tall muscular man who just looked dangerous. He was an assassin who worked for some intelligence gathering spy ring for North Paselter. He had been trained in some strange martial art where he could punch or kick with 20 times the power of a normal Heyyah. His hands and feet were absolute lethal weapons. From what Soolchakan could glean from this thoughts he was 36 years old, so he was just in his prime as a spy and assassin. For some reason he kept on looking at one of the other Heyyah men with hatred…wanting to rip him apart.

Sitting next to Homproon was the Kalash. He looked like just about any other Kalash man and he was about 320 years old. His name was Lomonit and he worked for the same spying organization as Homproon. The task for Lomonit was just intelligence and data gathering. He would only kill if necessary for survival. He had some pretty nasty thoughts about the same Heyyah male that Homproon wanted to exterminate.

Next was another Heyyah named Avendolo. Yet another spy who worked with Homproon and Lomonit. He was another who was assigned to gather intelligence. He also had some pretty nasty thoughts about the same Heyyah as his two colleagues.

Next was a rather attractive young female Heyyah named Imahana. She was a Demimondaine prostitute. Her talent was to use the Demimondaine talents to gather intelligence and blackmail information. She used her talents for the same spying organization as the others. Her thoughts about the Heyyah, targeted by the three men was one of love.

Now the target of the love and hate. Sitting next to Imahana was a Heyyah man named Bathak. He was another member of the spy organization. This one, however, was not as hateful as the others. He was also a man who was not very sure of himself. He also had some very lustful thoughts about the two women that were sitting on each side of him. He could not get his mind (or eyes) off of their ample cleavage.

Next was the other Heyyah woman. She was Namahiff. She was older and more experienced than the other woman and another member of the Demimondaine prostitute group. Like

Imahana, she was supposed to use her talents to get intelligence and blackmail. She also liked Bathak very much – like, but not love.

Then came the two Wokig Elf. They were husband and wife. They both had that large blonde mane around their heads where every hair was neatly in place, even though no one ever saw a Wokig combing their mane. He was Tonzozo, she was Hihikass. They were also members of the same spy organization and both of them had some pretty nasty thoughts about Bathak.

Soolchakan was doing everything he could to get more from reading their minds, however, there was just too much bitterness aimed at Bathak. The only way that he could possibly get anything he wanted was to start talking to them and get them to think about certain other subjects…like why is a group of North Paselter spies sitting here in North Paselter and not spying on someone else… somewhere else? What is so special in North Paselter? He sighed, hopped to Home dimension and walked toward the camp.

All eight of the people around the fire stood up as they realized that someone was approaching. Weapons were drawn by all of them except Homproon who clenched his fists.

The Kalash was the one to speak. "Who's there?"

Soolchakan kept on walking. "Just another traveler who wants to stay warm on this cold night. I was wondering if I could join you…staying warm." He immediately got readings from several of them. They looked at him as being some half-breed. Apparently none of them had ever seen an Owlam Elf before and the shape of his ears was foreign to them. Their first thoughts was that he was half Kalash and half something else. They also were very suspicious and cautious about this new meeting.

Tonzozo took a step forward. "Do you come in peace?"

Soolchakan smiled and chuckled. "I would be a fool to come here alone...and attempt any attack on you...since there are eight of you, who seem to be rather familiar with each other, and only one of me." He nodded and stopped. "Yes, I come in peace." 'I come on a very nosy, but peaceful exploration mission,' he thought.

Homproon placed his hands behind his back. "Then come forward and let us see you better and get acquainted."

Soolchakan started walking towards them again. He noticed that the two Wokigs and the Kalash were looking around to see if anyone else was coming up to surprise them.

Homproon motioned for Soolchakan to sit on a log near the big assassin. The Heyyah was thinking that he would be ready to kill in case anything was amiss with this tall-eared stranger.

Soolchakan sat down with a smile. He reached into his cape and pulled out a pouch. He held the pouch up and smiled. "I have some meat jerky in here...if you care to imbibe. I know it will not be as tender or tasty as that bird you're cooking but it is edible and, unlike the bird, it is ready *now*." He opened the pouch, pulled a piece of the jerky out and stuffed it in his mouth. "Does anyone want some?" He tried gleaning some of their thoughts.

Lomonit sat down on the other side of Soolchakan.

All were highly suspicious, however, the fact that he had

eaten one of the pieces of jerky made them feel a little better about partaking of the jerked meat. The pouch was passed around and each took a piece of it and all chewed slowly on the tough meat.

They started introducing themselves. All except the female Wokig and the Kalash. Soolchakan introduced himself as a traveler who had come into this area for some nostalgic reasons.

Avendolo stopped chewing for a moment. "Are you from around this area?"

Soolchakan smiled. "I used to live near here." He hung his head. "Certain situations arose that kind of fouled that situation." He looked up. "I was part of a team of engineers who were tasked with strengthening the Turgon Wall." He shook his head. "We moved from here to there...along the wall...in order to do this... rather large undertaking." He paused for a moment attempting to find anything out about the Turgons from their thoughts. None of them were thinking of anything other than listening to his oration. He continued. "By the time we finished, this area had been claimed by others and...our homes no longer existed...and the thieves had claimed all of our properties."

Lomonit narrowed his eyes. "I'm 320 years old and...I've never heard of this maintenance team that you talk about. I helped as a guard at the wall...in my younger days."

Soolchakan smiled. "You're *only* 320? No wonder you've never heard of our endeavor." He chuckled. "We did such a good job of it...no one has been needed to do any repairs on the wall... since we did what we did." He sniffed. He looked back down at the pouch of jerky that had come back to him. He pulled out another piece and stuck it in his mouth. "We finished our repair job…" He looked up in thought. "…well over 600 years ago." He scoffed mildly. "No wonder that none of you have heard of it."

Tonzozo still looked suspicious. "Did you have to get involved in any of the fighting with the Turgons…while performing your duties?"

Soolchakan shook his head and smiled. "Oh no! That was for the prisoners. I remember that while I was working… there were only two attacks that occurred in my area. I and my team stood back…while the prisoners fought those snarling beasts." He looked off to the side in thought. "Rather frightening experience…at the time. Now I can look back and just remember that it happened. My life was never in danger but…during one of the attacks, one of the beasts did top the wall." He nodded. "The guards went after the thing with those great, heavy battle-axes they had. That beast killed two prisoners as it topped the wall and severely injured another before it was…hacked to pieces."

All eight of the spies were thinking about the wall, the Turgons and…Soolchakan could not believe what was coming from their thoughts.

Hihikass was the first to speak the thought. "Have you heard about the Turgons now? Have you heard about how they're getting smarter?"

Soolchakan had to be careful about not giving away what he had found in their thoughts. He gave a very apprehensive look. "How can any dumb beast get smarter?"

"The Turgons now have weapons," said Avendolo.

Soolchakan scoffed. "Weapons? They've never been able to master a weapon of any type…even one as uncomplicated as a club. That was our observation at the time. What weapons could they possibly be using?" He chuckled and shook his head.

"Catapult," said Homproon simply. "There is an area where they've brought several of the things up near the wall."

Soolchakan shook his head. "No, that's impossible! As I said, they don't have the brains to master a weapon as uncomplicated as a club and you're talking…a sophisticated catapult? How!?" He scoffed.

"We don't know," said Lomonit. "We only know that we've received numerous reports from at least five different respectable and reliable sources. The catapults are there. Several of them. So far, the beasts haven't fired them and…also according to the reports, with at least fifteen of the things, in firing range of the wall, there is only one that is aimed in the correct direction… so far."

"And they have yet to load and fire any of them," said Hihikass.

"I may have to go and see this spectacle for myself," said Soolchakan. "It sounds just too incredible to be true…but…if it is true…where did they get the knowledge to build one…or several, let alone attempt to get the thing near the wall, aim or fire one?" He scoffed. "Also, how did they come up with the intelligence to get them all in the same area?"

Avendolo was now a little curious. "You said that you were part of a team – who else was on that team?"

Soolchakan smiled. "My wife…Bonarain. She was part of the team."

Hihikass looked around. "And where is this Bonarain?"

Soolchakan shook his head sadly. "Don't know. She… vanished…disappeared and I don't know where…or how."

Homproon smiled. "There are certain types of magic that can be used to find out what happened to her."

Soolchakan looked sideways at Homproon. "I have magic of my own." He started rubbing his fingers together on his right hand. Electricity started sparking and crackling at his fingertips. He then flicked the electrical energy at one of the rocks surrounding the fire. The rock was split in half by the bolt.

Lomonit was now thinking that Soolchakan was definitely half Kalash. He was not sure what the other half was because his ears were not Kalash but the electrical trick was something that only a Kalash could perform, because they had kept the method a very strict secret among themselves. "Okay, so you can do some magic. Does that mean that you can also do the magic that can divine where she is…was…or went?"

"That…among other things," said Soolchakan.

Tonzozo scoffed. "Is there a place where that magic cannot work? I've heard that there are a few voids like that in existence."

Soolchakan scoffed. "There's only one that I know of… where absolutely no magic works."

Tonzozo cocked his head to the side almost in a mocking

manner. "Did you check that place?"

Soolchakan looked thoughtful for a moment. He sat up straight with his eyes wide in shock as revelation hit him like a sledgehammer. No, he had *not* checked. No one had checked. He had not been there since...when? He stood up. "OH, *H'OOLYACH!*" He started forming the imagery to Jump in his mind.

Lomonit felt that this stranger, from his sudden change in demeanor, had just had a vivid revelatory moment. He just might just do something really stupid and run off into the wild darkness at night chasing after...what? He tried to calm Soolchakan.

Soolchakan finished the imagery and Jumped to that northern sandbar peninsula on the Fortress Island. He had to let his eyes adjust because it had been night where he came from and it was a bright sunny day where he was now. It was also very hot and humid so he had to adjust his breathing as well. After his eyes adjusted he clenched his teeth and started heading for that one-and-only entrance on the west side of the fort on Fortress Isle. He remembered that he had checked every single spacecraft in dimension #45. This was the one place he had not checked when searching for Bonarain and none of the new generations knew about this place. He suddenly stopped in shock as someone screamed behind him.

"WHERE AM I? HOW DID I GET HERE?" Lomonit was spinning around trying to figure out what had happened.

Soolchakan saw who it was and responded. "WHAT'RE YOU DOING HERE?"

"THAT'S WHAT I'D LIKE TO KNOW!   DID YOU TELEPORT US?"

Soolchakan calmed down slightly and slowly walked back to the Kalash. "When I stood up…uh…did you…grab me?"

"Uh…yes. I thought you might do something stupid."

Soolchakan nodded. "Stupid? Like…what?"

"Uh…like run off in the night…and…" Lomonit threw his arms out in exasperation. "I didn't know that…you were capable of…teleportation." He looked around confused. "Especially a teleport…over what seems to be a *very great* distance." He shook his head. "And…pulling an extra load, such as myself, with you."

"Now you do know."

"I…uh…I demand that you take me back!" Lomonit swallowed hard. "I demand it…right now!" He looked rather concerned.

Soolchakan walked up to him and got directly in the face of the slightly taller Kalash. He tried to sound sinister. "*You*…are *not* in any position where you can *demand* anything." He backed off slightly. "I have the capability of sending you back but… everything happens for a reason. You are here. It has been…a very long time since I went to that door to this fort. I may need some assistance opening it. After you assist me…then I'll get you back to that…camp and…that bird you were cooking."

Lomonit cleared his throat. "Do I have your word on that?"

Soolchakan smiled. "No! But again, you don't have any choice."

Lomonit drew his sword and pointed it at Soolchakan. "I demand that you send me back now."

Soolchakan chuckled and folded his arms. "What are you gonna do? Kill me? If you kill me, how will you get back then?" He chuckled again. "Do you even have a clue as to where you are?"

Lomonit had a sour look on his face. His shoulders sagged and now the sword was pointed at the ground. He slowly sheathed his sword. He wiped some perspiration off his forehead, removed his warm cloak and sighed. "Lead on," he muttered quietly.

Soolchakan turned and headed for that door. Lomonit grudgingly followed. Soolchakan had forgotten how far it was to that *only* door. He wondered why they had not come back here with some explosives and blasted a hole in the wall…somewhere near that northern peninsula.

Lomonit was getting very impatient. "Where is this *shnoking* door?"

"It's a long way. We'll get there when we get there."

"Why didn't you teleport a little closer to the door?"

Soolchakan stopped and turned back. "You can't! Magic only works on that northern sand bar of a peninsula. We haven't been able to do any other magic anywhere else on this island."

"You *can't* be serious!"

He chuckled. "Try it! You're Kalash. Do that little magic electrical spark thing with the fingers. Make some electricity with your fingers. See if you can do it."

Lomonit looked rather smug as he held his right hand up and rubbed his fingers together. After several moments he lost his smugness and started looking worried. He raised his left hand and was trying to get the spell working with either hand. He finally gave up, dropped his hands and frowned at Soolchakan. "Okay. I believe you. I've heard that there were places where there was a...magical void...I didn't really believe it...until now. This is weird!"

Soolchakan wiped some perspiration off his forehead. "So now you understand. Let's continue to the door." He spun around and continued on.

They finally finished the long trek to the door. There were several large rocks blocking the door. If you were inside, it would be impossible to push it open - unless there were several very strong people doing the pushing.

Lomonit stood there shaking his head in confusion. "A huge fort like this and..." He scoffed. "...this? This is the one and only entrance?"

"It certainly is," said Soolchakan emphatically. "Once inside...you can check the inner perimeter and see if you can find another entrance but...I never did find another."

Lomonit pulled out his canteen and scoffed. "The only thing in this is wine. Right now, I don't need wine. All that'll do is make you thirstier." He looked at Soolchakan hopefully.

"You...don't have any water...do you?"

Soolchakan smiled. He pulled a canteen out from under his cloak. "I haven't imbibed any *spirits* of any type...in a long, long time." He handed the canteen to Lomonit.

Lomonit took it gratefully. He shook it, pulled the stopper and took a long draw of water. He put the stopper back in and licked his lips. "That is very good, very clean water. Where did you get it? I don't remember any stream in that area that was that clear."

The water was fresh rainwater from the gorge. Soolchakan did not want to give that bit of information away. "You have to know how to filter the crud out." He smiled. "Sometimes you have to use a little magic." He looked at the rocks blocking the door. "Right now, this is all the water we have so...I suggest that we get those boulders moved quickly. There should be more water inside but...we can't get to it until we're inside."

Lomonit nodded. "Yeah! Let's get to it."

Most of the rocks were small enough for one man to move. There were three that they had to work together. There was that last and largest one. It took all of their combined energy to move that one. After they got that last big obstacle rolled away from the door they both sat puffing and panting waiting to replenish their energy. They drank the last of the water in the canteen and now went to the task of opening the door.

Soolchakan was a little suspicious and curious about what had happened. They had left the door chained shut. There was no sign of the chain or the padlock, however, it had been over 4,300 years since he had last been near this door. It was amazing to him that the metal door had not rusted away to nothing. That should have happened centuries ago, especially in this salt air.

The two men now had to use every bit of strength they had in order to pull the door open. The door hinges were not cooperating at all. They finally pulled it open slightly. Lomonit fell backwards as the door creaked open wide enough for Soolchakan to look through.

Standing there askance, with an angry look on her face was…Bonarain. Her rather unkempt sun-bleached hair hung down below her hips. She had a very dark leathery tan – from top to bottom. With the exception of the blue stone on the gold chain and the blue sword strapped to her right leg, she was totally naked. "Well it's about *chokwad* time you got here," she snapped! Her teeth were clenched, revealing that most of them were brown or black, and mainly rotten.

"You're welcome," he responded sarcastically. He wedged his shoulder into the opening to try to push open the door wider. He looked back at Lomonit. "Pull some more. Not enough room to get in."

"I can't pull, I can only push," said Bonarain.

"I'm not talking to you," snapped Soolchakan. "I'm talking to him."

Now Bonarain had a look of concern. "Who…what… who's with you?"

She saw a pair of hands grab the door just above

Soolchakan's head. Soolchakan grimaced as he pushed against the door jam. Lomonit grunted as he pulled on the door. Bonarain decided to find out who else was there later. Right now, she aided in opening the door by pushing on it. The hinges creaked and the bottom of the door scraped against the ground as the opening widened.

The three of them stood there panting and puffing after finally achieving their goal.

Soolchakan finally got enough energy to talk. "Is there any water near here?"

Bonarain nodded. "Of course. There's one of those stone barrels over there. It rained…two days ago and filled the thing." She was pointing off to her right. "Now, who is with you!?"

"Lomonit is with me."

She got in his face. "WHO…is Lomonit?"

Soolchakan grimaced, turned his face away and held his left hand up as a barricade. "Uch…your breath! Aah! Aim your face in a different direction if you're gonna say something. Your breath is a lethal weapon."

Meanwhile Lomonit had been listening to the conversation. "How did you know my name? I never gave it!"

Soolchakan chuckled. "You don't know how long I was listening to you and your friends talking before I went up to your camp." He smiled. He sidled through the slim opening.

Bonarain looked at Soolchakan angrily. "Since you've

brought a friend…give me something to wear."

Soolchakan loosened the tie on his cape. "What happened to your clothing?"

"That stuff rotted away to nothing a long time ago," she said despondently. She accepted his cloak and covered herself.

Lomonit squeezed through the opening.

Bonarain looked at the new man in shock. "He…he's a Kalash!"

"Good guess," said Soolchakan. "Now, where, exactly, is the water?"

Bonarain used a twist of her head and pointed with her chin to indicate the direction as she still had an angry stare for Lomonit. He in turn tried to ease things with a smile and by handing over his cape to her as well. She accepted the cape with a nod (while still staring at him suspiciously) and while the two men went to get a drink of water she used their long capes to cover both front and back.

After a long drink and splashing water on his face Soolchakan filled his canteen. "What possessed you to come here when you did," he said sternly? "As I remember, you were very late in your pregnancy and that is quite a strenuous walk from the peninsula to the door even for someone who is *not* pregnant."

She huffed. "I wanted some *fresh* fruit. I didn't want any of that hydroponics stuff. It tastes more like chemicals than fruit."

Lomonit stood there looking confused. "Hydro…what?"

"Hydroponics," said Soolchakan blandly. He turned back to her. "It was still rather stupid for someone in your condition… uh…" He looked around confused. "Where's the…child?"

Lomonit was still not satisfied. "What is hydroponics?"

Both Owlamites ignored him.

Bonarain hung her head. "Nadiwi was stolen from me." She nearly lost it when she made the statement. She sniffled slightly and looked off to the side as she covered her mouth with her hands.

Soolchakan splashed some more water on his face. "How did that happen?"

"When I…got to the door…coming from the north, I didn't realize that there was someone out there with a boat…coming up from the south," she said sadly. I suddenly felt a certain pain and…I realized that I was in labor." She bit her lip. "I had to go through the whole painful experience in here. By the time Nadiwi was born, some people from that boat were inside the walls." She sniffled. "They were slavers! They grabbed Nadiwi and…I fought them off as best as I could but…I was weakened by giving birth and…I was only able to kill two of them. They left their dead in here…ran off with Nadiwi and…closed the door…locking me inside." She sighed. "I've been stuck in here ever since," she said with another sniffle.

Lomonit was completely confused. "Why didn't you try to get out?"

She huffed. "HOW? There aren't any stairs going up to

the top of the wall inside here. I tried to build a ladder. I didn't have any hammer or nails or wood that was strong enough to make a sturdy ladder. I had nothing to string it together either. I tried building some scaffolding and…that didn't work either…again, because I had no hammer, nails or string…or lumber that was strong enough to stand on. So just HOW was I supposed to be able to get out?"

Lomonit cleared his throat. "Did you, originally, have any kind of shovel?"

She frowned. "Yes, but what are you suggesting? Should I have tried to dig my way under the wall?"

He shook his head slowly. "No. You build a ramp."

"WITH WHAT? I told you I didn't have any hammer or nails."

Lomonit shrugged. "Fifteen or twenty shovel loads, all in the same place at the wall, each day. Eventually you would've built a dirt ramp up the wall. You are now on top of the wall… eventually."

She huffed again. "So now I'm up on top of the wall. What are you suggesting now…that I jump down off of that high wall on the other side?"

He shook his head. "No, you just continue the process. Fifteen or twenty shovel loads dumped outside the wall, every day, in the same place and eventually you have a dirt ramp on the other side. You now *walk* down the other side."

Her strength left her and she dropped to her knees with her

lower jaw sagging.

Soolchakan sighed. "You overthought and overcomplicated the issue. A dirt ramp would've been the simplest method and... while you were trying to build some ladder or scaffolding to escape...you forgot that the simplest method is...often the best."

She was nearly in tears. "A dirt ramp. All this time and...a dirt ramp...would have...gotten me out of here..." She looked up at Soolchakan helplessly. "What year is this?"

Lomonit answered. "This is the year 5474 ATUT."

Her shoulders sagged even more and she was slack-jawed in shock. She looked at Soolchakan who just nodded in agreement.

She covered her face with her hands. "5474...ATUT... and I...could have built a dirt ramp...in just...maybe a year...or less." She dropped her hands and looked up at the sky. "I've been here...since...what...1120 ATUT...at least that's the last year that I remember."

Lomonit scoffed. "1120? It is now 5474. That would mean that you've been here for over 4,350 years. No one lives that long!"

"We do," said Soolchakan with a stern look.

Lomonit looked stern as well. "What kind of half-breed... or any full breed lives that long?"

"We're not half-breeds," said Soolchakan in a disgusted manner. "We are *full* breed Owlamites," he said adamantly!

Lomonit chuckled. "That's impossible. The Owlams have

been extinct for over 2,000 years."

Soolchakan stood up as tall as he could and placed his fists on his hips. "Do I look extinct to you?" He tried to look indignant as he asked the question.

"You can't possibly be Owlams. According to the Teltermak Chronicles, the Owlams were all killed off sometime in the thirty-third century ATUT."

"Guess again!" Soolchakan took another drink of water. "Those cannibalistic Teltermak were our greatest and most persistent enemy. *We* killed *them* in order to keep *them* from *eating* us." He took a deep breath and blew it out. "Whatever this Teltermak Chronicles is it sounds as if it is some kind of historical revisionism. *They* wrote it trying to make *us* sound like the bad guys when *they* were the cannibals."

Lomonit cleared his throat nervously. "Uh…according to the…Chronicles…they said that…uh…you were…totally…uh… evil."

"*Their* version!" Soolchakan walked over to Lomonit slowly. "They tried to make it sound as if we were doing something wrong…in order to make themselves sound benevolent. They wanted to *eat* us! They had a certain insatiable desire for our liver, heart, brain and certain glands under our skin that they used to spice their…other food. We did not want to be food…or spice. We hid ourselves and…we did it so successfully…so totally successfully that you didn't even know we still exist. This way, if there are any more Teltermak out there, they still don't know where we are either. Meanwhile, we killed them whenever and wherever we found them…for *our* survival."

Lomonit just swallowed hard while still looking very concerned.

Bonarain scoffed. "You can worry about all of that stuff later. I've been stuck here for all this time. I want to see my sons…and my friends…and find my daughter."

Soolchakan grimaced. He pursed his lips as he looked off away from Bonarain.

Bonarain frowned and glared at him suspiciously. "What's the matter? What's going on?"

Soolchakan sighed and hung his head. "Yeah…about your sons…uh…the Teltermak kinda…murdered them."

Her jaw dropped in horror. "Shalam and…Monaha… are…*dead*?"

Soolchakan nodded sadly.

"What about…Aya…Zina…Momatak and Amaree?"

He shook his head. "All dead." He looked at her gravely. "Among the dead…are Kiyalee and Chyning."

She sank to her knees and covered her face with her hands.

"The only one left…of the second generation…is Nadiwi… if we can find her."

She dropped her hands and looked up with a tear streaming down her face. "Well you'd better find her. She's all I have left."

He shook his head. "Not quite true." He gave a sideways glance at Lomonit. "I'll tell you more…when he's not around."

Now she was frowning in confusion – so was Lomonit.

Soolchakan sighed again. "I've filled my canteen." He smiled at Lomonit. "Have you filled yours?"

Lomonit reached down at his side with a guilty look on his face. "No. I'll do it right now."

"Good," said Soolchakan somewhat cheerfully. "After you've filled it, we can get out of here and go back to our lives."

Bonarain huffed. "WHAT LIFE? Shalam and Monaha are dead. Kiyalee and Chyning are dead. What's left?"

He shook his head. "First of all a daughter that we need to find! Second of all, there are over 4,600 other Owlamites that *are* still alive and more than ready to welcome you back. The only one that won't welcome you back is the traitor."

Her eyebrows went up with a totally confused look. "Traitor?"

He nodded and sighed. "We have a lot to discuss…once we get home."

She stood up and frowned and cleared her throat. "Uh… how many generations?"

He smiled. "Twenty-one."

Her jaw dropped again. She looked to Lomonit. "Fill that canteen and let's get out of here!"

Lomonit cleared his throat. "One thing – am I going to get out of this…alive?"

Soolchakan shook his head in disgust. "We are *not* what the Teltermak said we are. We have no reason to kill you. You assisted me in opening that door…and I am very grateful for that. You and your colleagues gave me the clue and idea to look here. I…" He pointed at Bonarain. "…and she, we both are *very* grateful for that."

Lomonit looked at some of the trees and other crops inside the walls. "When you snuck up on us, I was waiting for my dinner. I'm rather hungry. I'm even more hungry now, because I didn't get any of that roasted bird. Do you mind if I grab something from here to tide my hunger?"

Soolchakan chuckled. "Go ahead. Take what you want, need or can carry. Just remember that it is a long way back to that northern peninsula."

Lomonit went to a fruit tree and picked several ripe ones. He started eating one of them as he came back to join the two Owlamites.

Bonarain looked around at all of the fruit trees and vegetables that she had been tending for her only source of sustenance during her imprisonment in the fortress. "Did you bring something to lock the door?"

Soolchakan hung his head. He looked up and sniffed hard. "NO ONE ELSE HAS BEEN HERE IN OVER 4,300 YEARS! WHO CARES IF SOMEONE ELSE COMES ALONG?" He shook his head. "They can have the *chogo* thing."

She looked thoughtful for a moment. "You're right." She nodded. "I don't have a thing here that I need to take with me."

He smiled. "Except for the blue stone and sword."

She looked confused. "Are these silly things really that important to *you*…after all this time?"

He scoffed. "You have absolutely *no* idea how important they, or *you* are."

"Well tell me!"

He again looked at Lomonit. "It is none of his business." He looked back at Bonarain. "I'll tell you…once he can't listen in on our conversation."

Lomonit now looked worried. "You *are* going to kill me."

"No, we're *not*," said Soolchakan brusquely! "We're going to take you back to your friends at that campsite. Then my wife and I are going to have a *tremendously* long private conversation."

Lomonit still looked worried.

Soolchakan pointed down. "Is your canteen full?"

Lomonit chuckled nervously. "Yes, it is."

"Do you have enough fruit to tide you over?"

"Yes."

"Then let's get out of here. The sooner we get back to that northern sandbar, the sooner you get back to your friends."

They exited the fort and started the long, long journey back to that sandbar peninsula. Soolchakan led, Bonarain in the middle and a still very worried Lomonit followed. Lomonit also devoured some more of the fruit he had picked from trees inside the walls.

After finally arriving at the peninsula, Soolchakan looked back at the fort. "If I ever do come back here, it'll be in a boat, in the water, just outside of the *chokwad* door."

"I agree," said Bonarain as she wiped some sweat off her forehead. "If I ever do come back here, I will also be heavily armed…just in case any more slavers happen to show up…at a very bad time. I will also *not* be alone here…ever again."

"There's no such thing as a good time for slavers to show up," said Lomonit with a bitterness in his voice.

"Don't make me hate you any more than I already do," said Bonarain.

Lomonit was confused. "Why…uh…should you hate me?"

She scowled at Lomonit. "All that time that I was in there I never figured out a way to get out of there and it took you just a few heartbeats to come up with a solution that I completely missed…" She closed her eyes and shook her fists. "…FOR OVER 4,300 YEARS…on how to get out of there!"

He shrugged and chuckled nervously.

"You just overcomplicated the issue," said Soolchakan. He sighed. He looked directly into the eyes of Bonarain. "**Can you hear me in your mind**?"

She looked a little startled for a moment. **"Yes…I can. OH, that is *so* welcome after all these years**." She had a look of contentment on her face.

"Fine! Let's get that Kalash back to where he was and then I'll tell you a rather long story."

"I need to give him his cloak back. I'll need something to wear before I do that."

Soolchakan sighed. He vanished.

Lomonit looked around shocked. "What happened? Where did he go?"

Bonarain smiled. "He went to get me some clothing."

Lomonit nodded apprehensively. "Clothing."

"Right. Before I can give you back your cape, I have to have *something* to wear."

He smiled weakly and nodded again. He turned away and cleared his throat.

Soolchakan reappeared holding a luxurious looking robe. It was full length, pink, had a rather lavish high collar and looked rather thick. Soolchakan stood between Bonarain and Lomonit and held the robe up like a barrier, hiding Bonarain from Lomonit. She shed both of the capes and ran her arm through the sleeves. She walked away from Soolchakan as she closed the robe and tied the belt. Soolchakan picked the capes up and handed Lomonit his garment.

Soolchakan smiled at Lomonit. "Before we take you back,

I'm going to show you something impressive about our power."

Lomonit had already been highly impressed with the teleport trick. He was curious and terrified over what might happen now. What could possibly be greater than what he had observed already?

Bonarain turned around as Soolchakan approached her. He held his red stone up and her blue stone jumped to meet it. The two stones attached and started glowing a deep purple. Soolchakan grabbed her around the waist in order to hold her from falling. Bonarain threw her head back and moaned. The purple glow completely enveloped her. The glow seemed to run up and down her body with scintillating movements. Just as sudden as it appeared, the purple glow disappeared. She looked a little physically drained as she fell against Soolchakan. He pulled her up to keep her from falling and she grimaced baring her teeth.

Now Lomonit did not know what to think. Yes, he was very impressed. When he had first seen her inside the fortress her mouth was full of rotting and partial brown or black teeth. Her hair was a long unkempt tangled mess. When she grimaced, he saw a mouthful of clean, sparkling white, completely intact teeth. Her hair looked as if it had just been neatly brushed and combed out by some beauty specialist fit for a queen. Her eyes were not bloodshot anymore. She was now the picture of health and cleanliness. Her skin was still tanned, however, the skin did not have that aged leathery look.

The two stones released each other and fell against their chests.

Soolchakan looked back at Lomonit and smiled. "Yes, we are capable of a great many things. Repair of our own bodies is one of them. Killing? Yes, we can do that, but, we only do it to defend ourselves...or defend someone who is helpless and being bullied. Remember, we are not the evil ones. The Teltermak were evil and cannibalistic. That's why we killed them off. As long as you don't try to kill us...or eat us...you're safe."

Lomonit smiled weakly. "I will definitely remember that." 'For the rest of my life,' he thought.

Bonarain looked at Soolchakan. **"Now what?"**

He smiled. **"We send the Kalash back to where he was and we go home."**

"I wasn't there. I don't know where he was."

Soolchakan sighed. **"I'll be right back."** He grabbed Lomonit and Jumped.

Lomonit felt nothing other than a grip on his arm. Suddenly he was back at the campsite and it was close to morning in that area. The grip on his arm was no longer there and he saw no sign of Soolchakan. The sudden change in temperature was a jolt. The Fortress Island area had been extremely humid as well as hot. This place was in the northern area and the nights could be rather chilly. He very quickly threw his cape around him for warmth as he could now see his breath when he exhaled.

Tonzozo and Hihikass walked up to Lomonit looking at him rather suspiciously.

Tonzozo huffed. "I recognize you but...are you still the Lomonit that I know?"

Lomonit sighed. "I am still Lomonit of the Great Garden, the Kalash Elf. The difference now...I have just received an education that has severely knocked a lot of things out of place."

Hihikass smiled. "Such as?"

Lomonit took in a deep breath and blew it out. "What race of Elf do you think that man Soolchakan came from?"

"He is obviously some half-breed," said Tonzozo.

"He is no half-breed," said Lomonit shaking his head.

Hihikass shook her head. "I've never seen any Elf with very tall ears like that...unless they were some kind of half Kalash. How could he possibly a full breed?"

"Because his wife – Bonarain – whom I met - has ears just like his. They're of the same race. They're much like the Roistee in that...they have a way of remaining hidden that...you and I are completely unaware of."

Hihikass looked very skeptical. "How could any race remain so secretive? How could they possibly hide so well?"

"They have." Lomonit smiled. "Do you remember some of the things that you read in the Teltermak Chronicles?"

"Of course," said Tonzozo mockingly. "Why shouldn't I remember?"

"You can forget it," said Lomonit sadly. "That man...and

his wife...they're Owlams."

"That's *impossible*," scoffed Hihikass!

Lomonit shook his head. "I am about to educate you...to what I saw and where I went and the woman I met when we got there. Her ears are just like his. They are husband and wife so...if they are half-breeds then...they're also incestuous." He shook his head. "I don't believe that they're incestuous. I believe that they are what they say they are: Owlams." He reached into a pouch on his side and pulled a piece of fruit out. "Freshly picked off of a tree...on an island...on the other side of the world. He teleported me there and back. Only the most powerful of wizards could do that."

The two Wokig stared in shock at the piece of fruit. It was something that only grew in tropical climates and usually was not shipped out because it would spoil quickly. To see one of these pieces of fruit in North Paselter, freshly picked, at this time of the year, in this area, was impossible. The only way that something like that could be here was through the use of some of the most powerful of magic. This meant that there had to be some kind of good credibility to the story that they were about to hear from Lomonit.

They were all very interested in hearing the rest of his story.

Soolchakan reappeared on the northern sandbar peninsula. "Why haven't you gone home?"

Bonarain bit her lip and sniffled slightly. The sniffle changed to coughing...that was being used to cover the fact that she was crying. "I...forgot how. I'm completely out of practice," she whimpered. "I haven't done any of that for...over 4,300 years." She looked off to the side and sniffled. "I'm going to need to learn it all...again. I didn't even have a way of practicing... how to do any of those things."

He hung his head and took a deep breath. "That's quite all right," he said gently. He pulled her into his arms and hugged her close. He then Jumped to the main room in 12-562 in the gorge. "We have to get you back up to date and...then we have a lot to do."

She looked around at the familiar apartment that she had not seen for over four millennium. Tears filled her eyes. "I want to find Nadiwi," she sniffled.

"That is *absolutely* one of the first things on the list of things that we're going to do." He sighed. "There is also a lot of other things that you need to be informed about." He looked at her blue stone and smiled. "I don't even know where to start with the explanations or...historical events but...I think that the stones may be one of the best places to start...however...let us go introduce you to all of the other living Owlamites."